Praise for the Elysium Chronicles

"Souders' exciting, suspenseful, and action-packed debut novel will be a welcome addition to any library's dystopia collection. Hand this to fans of Suzanne Collins, Veronica Roth, and Scott Westerfeld." —*Booklist* on *Renegade*

"Grim, vicious, riveting. *Renegade* is a haunting, unforgettable debut." —Ann Aguirre, *New York Times* bestselling author of *Enclave*

"A dark and exciting YA novel about how striving for perfection leads to murder and manipulation. A solid recommendation for fans of dystopian fiction." —*School Library Journal* on *Renegade*

"Deliciously creepy and filled with psychological twists, *Renegade* kept me on the edge of my seat until the very last page." —Kristen Simmons, author of *Article 5*

"Debut author Souders addresses antiwar, socioeconomic, and ecological themes in addition to the main issue of adolescent rebellion against crazed authority." —*Publishers Weekly* on *Renegade*

"*Renegade* is a dark tale of deceit, with twists that will keep you turning the pages, and an ending that will have you on the edge of your seat." —Lisa Desrochers, author of *Personal Demons*

"Memory by memory, flashback by flashback, Evelyn's beliefs about her past begin to shatter: her life hasn't always been perfect, and neither has she. Nothing and no one are what they seem, and there is sure to be more to come, thanks to an open-ended conclusion. Fans of Mary E. Pearson's *The Adoration of Jenna Fox* and Teri Terry's *Slated* will find much to like here. Read or reread *Renegade* first for the complete creepy experience." —*Booklist* on *Revelations*

Revelations

J. A. SOUDERS

A TOM DOHERTY ASSOCIATES BOOK

NEW YORK

REVELATIONS

Copyright © 2013 by Jessica Souders

All rights reserved.

A Tor Teen Book
Published by Tom Doherty Associates, LLC
175 Fifth Avenue
New York, NY 10010

www.tor-forge.com

Tor® is a registered trademark of Tom Doherty Associates, LLC.

The Library of Congress has cataloged the hardcover edition as follows:

Souders, J. A.
    Revelations / J.A. Souders. — First edition.
        p. cm.
    "A Tom Doherty Associates book."
    ISBN 978-0-7653-3246-2 (hardcover)
    ISBN 978-1-4668-0096-0 (e-book)
    1. Undersea colonies—Fiction.   2. Secrets—Fiction.
   3. Memory—Fiction.   4. Genetics—Fiction.   5. Science fiction.
   I. Title.
   PZ7.S7246Rev 2013
   [Fic]—dc23

                                2013023853

ISBN 978-0-7653-3249-3 (trade paperback)

Our books may be purchased in bulk for promotional, educational, or business use. Please contact your local bookseller or the Macmillan Corporate and Premium Sales Department at 1-800-221-7945, extension 5442, or by e-mail at MacmillanSpecialMarkets@macmillan.com.

First Edition: November 2013
First Trade Paperback Edition: July 2016

Printed in the United States of America

0 9 8 7 6 5 4 3 2 1

Dedicated to the loving memory of my grandma
Dolores Heiland,
*who was instrumental in making me who I am today
and taught me that anything worth having
is worth fighting for, and that being a lady
isn't synonymous with being weak.*

Revelations

CHAPTER ONE

PATIENT EVELYN WINTERS: Female. Approximately 16 years of age.

Patient still displays signs of amnesia. Evaluation shows worsening fevers, syncope, failure to heal from multiple wounds and infection of said wounds. Patient has failed to respond to standard treatment. Recommended course of action has met with refusal by patient's significant other. No next of kin available. Unsure of patient's ability to consent for herself due to diminished mental faculties.

—MEDICAL RECORD LOG, DR. DANIEL GILLIAN, MD

Evie

My life is just about perfect.

At least I think it is. It's hard to be sure since I can't remember anything from the last sixteen years. My hopes. My dreams. Everything. Gone. As if they never existed. And I will probably never get them back.

It hurts just thinking about it, so I try not to, but the thought festers in my mind as I sit on the beach by the water's edge and push my bare feet into the surf. The waves lap at my ankles as I dig my toes into the sand. It feels good—the chilly water against my heated flesh.

I just *know* I'm running another fever. I'm never not, lately. I scratch at my healing shoulder before remembering myself and shoving my hands into the cool sand. It's only been a few days since my release from the confines of the local medical facility—I'd been there just a few weeks, but it'd felt like forever. Dr. Gillian said, despite the failure of the wound on my shoulder to heal completely, I was healthy enough to leave. I'm not convinced he actually thinks that's true, but he's done so much for me since I got here, he almost feels like family. Or I think so anyway. I don't really remember what family feels like. But, anyway, he's done so much for me, Dr. Gillian, that I could hardly refuse, and even though I wasn't at all sure I was ready to leave the hospital, Gavin was impatient to get me home.

Home. Another pang of something I can't really describe hits me, and tears well in my eyes. I trace my fingers over the etched lines of the silver rose pendant lying between my breasts. I really, really want to go home, I know that. I just don't know exactly where "home" is.

Gavin's dog, Lucy, bumps my shoulder with her head, whining softly. I dig my fingers into her soft fur, staring into the water until the tears that sting my eyes are from the sun sparkling on the surface. Even at sunset, the solar rays are still intense to my eyes, but a bit of my bad mood slips away. It's beautiful today, as it always is, the sky flickering now with the oranges, reds, and pinks of the setting sun.

This is my favorite time of day. When the sun is setting and the last of its fiery fingers caress the water line before relinquishing their hold to the darkness of night. And I can watch as the stars pop out, one by one, to pinprick the sky with their silvery light. The breakers crash against the shore in a steady rhythm. It's lovely. Peaceful. Calming. Like somewhere else I used to know.

Home, I think again, holding the pendant tightly in my fist. Gavin tells me I came from beneath those waves. But I don't know if home is really there. At the bottom of the sea in a place I can't remember and I'm not sure if I want to. Or if it's with Gavin and his wonderful family: His brother, Tristan, and all his chattering and curiosity. His sister, Ann Marie, with her easy happiness, and his mom, whose quiet strength—the same strength Gavin has in spades—resonates from her in waves.

I'll admit, when they're around, it's easy to forget that I haven't always been here. That I haven't always been a part of their family. But still, I know I don't really belong. I'm not sure I belong anywhere.

That thought making my heart squeeze, I push up from the sand, click my tongue so Lucy will follow, and go back into the house I'm supposed to consider my home.

Gavin

The bucket of tallow oil weighs heavy in my hand as I drag it up the two hundred and thirteen steps to the lantern room. I don't suppose we really have to light the lamp anymore, but it's become a custom. My family has kept the lighthouse going since the War. Using the light not to guide ships, but people.

It was one of the few buildings left standing after everything, but our cove was still in better shape than a lot of places. More importantly, it was safe—from raiders and starving animals—due to the coast on three sides and the wall they'd built around the town. My ancestors had hoped to guide those lost in what is now known as the Outlands to the safety of our town. I don't know if my family always lived here or if we took it over when we came across it, but we've been here ever since. No one new has come in ages, not since the mayor was sent from the city to keep an eye on us, but we still make the tallow and light the lantern every night. Just in case.

It's technically Tristan's job—ever since I started spending all my time hunting and providing food for the family—but he has a hard time dragging the bucket all the way to the top, and anyway I don't mind doing it. The mindless repetition of dragging the oil to the top, pouring it into the lamp, winding the clockwork, and lighting it usually gives me some much needed thinking time.

Today, though, I'm just going to enjoy the view. I can see Evie down on the beach, and now that she's with me after being in the hospital for way too long, I just want to bask a little. Even though I've been back on the surface for a little over a month, I can't get over how grateful I am to be home. My mind still reels thinking of what I—we—went through. Genetic mutations. Brainwashing. A beautiful princess needing rescuing. Okay, that part's not true. She rescued me. I just decided I couldn't leave without her.

A smile curves my lips as I glance down over the rail. Far below, the light from behind me shines on her blond head, then continues on its way. She was the only shining light from that hell.

But it's hard to be happy looking at her now. I can tell from how she's holding on to Lucy that she's unhappy, and considering the way she's staring out into the water, I can't pretend I don't know the reason. She's homesick. Even if "home" is the last word I'd use to describe Elysium.

Hell. Living nightmare. Bottomless pit of everlasting tortures. Those descriptions would fit it a lot better, but it's not like she remembers what *really* happened. She didn't even want to leave until she was forced to. By me. No, scratch that. *Because* of me. Because she'd risked her life to rescue me. And it had cost her much more than either of us had anticipated.

I watch, leaning over the rail, as she gets up and walks into the house, Lucy prancing by her side. She never once looks up at me, though I'm sure she knows I'm up here. Not sure if I should feel stung or just let her be; after all, I should know better than anyone how difficult it is to feel lost in a world that's not yours with no one you know or trust. And while I know she cares for me, ever since she left the hospital there's been this awkwardness between us. Like neither of us quite knows what to do with the other now that it's safe for us to touch.

Huffing a sigh, I turn to pick up the now empty bucket, then make my way down the stairs. It's much easier with gravity and an empty bucket on my side.

Taking my time, I put the supplies back into the fuel room, then clean up the already meticulous space. When I finally admit to myself that I can't get it any cleaner than it already is, I wander into the house.

It's quiet, as it usually is after supper, except for the sounds of Tristan playing in his room, making sound effects from whatever toys he's deemed worthy of his time. Mom must have nixed unplugging the water heater for him to play video games for today. Good, because I'm filthy. I glance down at my sooty hands and arms. I need a shower. Besides, I have to pass Evie's room along the way to the bathroom. It'll give me the perfect excuse to check on her.

The floorboards creak and groan as I walk. I used to try and learn which floorboards to use or how to step to avoid them making noises, but it's useless. They're old and they all creak. In fact, I see a loose one poking up near Evie's doorway. I'll have to run to the general store for nails to fix that so she doesn't trip on it. And while I'm at it, I should probably see if I can trade something for some paint. The walls are peeling and Mom's been making noises since Evie came about wanting to fix up the house.

I'm careful to avoid the loose board as I stop at her doorway. But when I peek my head into the room, she's back to staring out her window to the black sea. One hand rests on Lucy's head, which rests in Evie's lap. The other rests on the glass, palm pressing to it, fingers curled slightly, as if she's reaching for something. In the reflection, I can see tears sliding down her cheek. I back away from the door, so she can't see that I saw her, swallow the lump in my throat, and continue on into the bathroom. With a flick of the wrist, I turn on the water. At first it only drizzles out and I glare at the pipe.

"Work, damn you," I mutter. I don't want to have to fumble around in the pump house in the dark. Then it pulses and shoots a stream from the rusty faucet, pouring blackish water into the tub. God, I hate well water. After another half a minute, the water turns clear and steam starts rising from the bottom of the tub. I quickly adjust the temperature and step into the spray.

While I'm scrubbing my skin, I contemplate how to help Evie. I hate seeing her so sad, missing a home she doesn't remember, but going back isn't an option. So the question is, what can I do? I stay in the shower a while longer than I normally would, staring at a crack in the tile, but still no answers come.

Even after I'm finished with my shower and dressed in clean clothes and staring at the ceiling in my room, I don't know. She needs her memories back; that's obvious. But how do we get them back, when we don't know what caused her to lose them in the first place?

Lucy's growl and a movement out of the corner of my eye makes my blood run cold and I jump up, grabbing the bat that is lying next to the bed. My mind flashes back to being in Sector Three, and for a second, silly as I know it is, I'm sure one of those *things* followed us back. Something is creeping around my house—and all I've got to defend myself is a baseball bat.

I grip the bat tightly and tiptoe to the doorway. But what's standing there makes me stop in my tracks. *Not again.*

It's Evie, and she's staring at me with the blankest expression on her face. Her eyes are completely empty. Dead, almost. I've seen those eyes before. In Elysium. On the Enforcers. And, unfortunately, on her.

"Evie? Are you all right?"

She tips her head to the side and I fight back another shudder. *"My life is just about perfect."* Then she slowly turns and walks down the hallway, her white nightgown fluttering behind her.

I'm so in shock, it takes me a minute to realize she's already at the end of the hall and around the corner.

Shit! She must be sleepwalking. I chase after her, but she's already back down to the beach when I catch up to her. She's only walking. How is she moving so fast?

"Evie!" I reach for her hand, pulling it toward me and hoping it'll make her stop. It does. But when she turns, I can only stare at her, while she seems to stare *through* me. She shakes me off and walks forward again. If she keeps going the way she is, she'll end up in the ocean.

I rush forward and make another grab for her hand. She tries shaking me off again, but I ignore it and say, "Where are you going?"

She turns to face me. Blinks once, and says, "Home."

A chill slides over me. "Home?" I ask dumbly.

"Home." She twists back around and yanks away from me, splashing her way into the water.

I lunge forward and pull her back. She spins around and this time, when she looks at me, my instincts yell at me to let her go. I don't.

A wave crashes over us, pulling us apart and knocking me to my knees. Freezing salty water collapses over my head, burning my eyes and nose. I shove up, coughing, and push my hair out of my eyes. She's out of reach already. I don't even think the wave bothered her.

Her nightgown is soaked and her skin glows through it in the moonlight. In normal circumstances, I'd appreciate the view, but I barely give it a passing thought as I wade deeper, trying to reach her before she gets to the drop-off.

"Evie! Stop. Please," I try again, knowing it's useless. Even though the air around me is hot, I'm shaking.

When I'm close enough, I grab for her arm, but we're both slippery from the water and she pulls easily from my hand. The moonlight pours over her and while her eyes are red, they're as empty as they ever were.

I've heard that if you slap someone in shock, it wakes them up from whatever it is that they're doing. I dismiss the thought as soon as I've had it. I can't hit Evie. But another wave crashes on top of her, knocking her over, and when she just stands up and keeps going, I realize I don't have a choice. I don't want to hurt her, but I want her alive. So I grasp her again with one hand and bring the other one up to slap her just hard enough that I hope it'll wake her up . . . but before I can even make contact, she's got my wrist and she's squeezing it, pushing my arm back.

She twists around so she's staring me down. Her eyes are inky bottomless wells. Empty and dangerous. Before I can react, her other arm swings around and I catch a glimpse of her fist as it connects to my jaw. The impact shoves me back and then water is surrounding me and my head spins so much with my ringing ears that I can't figure out which way is up. I panic at first, flopping around, trying to get to the surface so I can breathe. But instinct forces through my panic and reminds me to relax and let my body float. My feet touch bottom and I shove to a standing position. Above the surface, I gasp for breath, shoving my hair from my eyes and searching for Evie, but she's gone. I can't see her.

I turn around in a circle as quickly as I can, but the water slows me down. It doesn't matter, though. *I can't see her.*

"Evie!" I shout, my voice hoarse from seawater and coughing. I push forward toward the drop-off. "Evie! . . . *Evie!*" Nothing. No answer, except the waves as they push toward shore.

My eyes are blurry from the salt water and the panic tears burning them. "Evie. Please! Answer me."

Then, by some miracle, the moonlight reflects off of something white and I know it's her. "Evie!" I shout again, pushing toward her, forgetting about the drop-off in my hurry to get to her.

I go under mid-yell, swallowing seawater, but push up and spit out what I can. I just keep saying her name as I swim closer, because I can't seem to say anything else. She's not moving and her hair is all over. I can't even tell which way she's facing.

My heart stops when I get to her and see she's facedown. I roll her over and drag her out as fast I can, using the waves to my advantage, but when I get her onto the beach and kneel over her, she's not breathing.

"Oh God. Oh God," I whisper, shoving her hair from her face. I breathe into her mouth, but her chest doesn't even rise. There must be water in her lungs. I have to get it out.

"Come on, Evie." I push on her chest, shoving on it harder and harder, screaming her name. "Evie. Please. Come on. Please." I kneel closer to her mouth and push more air into her lungs, hoping to displace some of the water. Nothing happens. I shakily feel for a pulse, moaning when I don't feel one.

"Wake up, damn it," I say, pumping even harder on her chest. I refuse to give up. I'm not going to let her die. Not now. Not like this.

CHAPTER TWO

Notice: You are now entering the Outlands. Safety cannot be guaranteed past this point. Proceed at your own risk.

—SIGN POSTED AT EXIT GATES TO THE OUTLANDS

Gavin

I pace the hallway in front of Evie's room. The old worn hardwood floors creak with each footstep and I feel exactly how I felt six weeks ago when I carried her into the hospital. Except at least she was breathing then.

My legs shake as I remember how pale she was this time. Her lips turning blue no matter how often I tried pushing air into her lungs. Her body was as limp as the sacks of flour I used to cart around for Mr. McGreely, and just as hard to run with. I tripped twice in that short run and cut a long deep gash into my arm trying to protect her when I fell. If Asher hadn't heard my yells and come running, then rushed to get Dr. Gillian . . . I don't even want to think about that.

I stop pacing and glance over, scowling at the dark-haired

boy leaning against the wall by the corner, talking quietly with my mother. Asher. Former best friend, current asshole. But there's no doubt that I owe him a huge debt after tonight.

The door I've been pacing in front of squeaks open. Dr. Gillian looks exhausted and I know I don't want to hear what he's going to tell me, but still, I have to ask.

"Is she all right?"

"She'll be fine."

I don't really hear what else he says—something about a dry drowning and her being extremely lucky—because my whole body sags in relief. She'll be fine. That's all I hear. Over and over in my head. *She'll be fine.*

"Gavin," he asks, pulling my attention back to him. "Did you hear me?"

I nod quickly. "Yes. Of course. Whatever you want."

It's obvious from the look he gives me that he knows I hadn't heard a word. With a sigh, he takes off his glasses and polishes them on his shirt. "I'm concerned, Gavin."

I don't say anything. I don't want to hear what he has to say.

"This . . ." He pauses. "This episode she had, where she walked into the ocean, she says she doesn't remember any of what you said happened."

I nod. I expected that. She didn't remember anything the other times, either.

"She also told me this is the third time she's blacked out in almost as many days."

"Um . . . well, technically it's only twice. The first time

I'm pretty sure she only freaked out because Lucy was running straight at her."

He lifts an eyebrow. "Gavin, we need to be serious here. You have to realize how grave this is. What she's having, these blackouts—they're what's called a "fugue state." It's concerning because I'm not sure if this is a psychiatric issue or a physical one. I can't even run any of the basic tests like a CT scan to make sure there isn't some sort of brain damage. I simply don't have the equipment." He screws his face up in frustration, before straightening his features. "She needs to go to Rushlake. This is just . . . beyond what I can do here." He spreads his hands out in front of him in a helpless gesture.

"You know I can't go to the city. Not after . . ." I trail off, my gaze drifting over to Asher. I allow myself a second to glare at him before focusing on the doctor again.

He pats my shoulder. "This *will* happen again. Will you be around next time? More importantly, can you afford to watch her every hour of every day to make sure that when it does, she won't walk back into that ocean?"

I open my mouth, but no words come out. He's right. There is absolutely no way I can be around her 24/7. Even if I could give up hunting and everything else to be around her, I have to sleep sometime.

He nods at me, then at someone behind me before turning back around and disappearing through the door.

"I'll take her."

I slowly turn to face Asher. "Absolutely not. *If* she goes,

I'll take her. This is none of your business and we don't need your help." It burns that I already owe him for helping with Evie. I'll be damned if I'll owe him another favor.

He touches my arm. "Gavin, come on. Let me help."

"No." I cross my arms over my chest. "The last time I let you 'help,' I ended up losing everything. I'm not letting you do that to me again."

My former best friend's face pales and then reddens almost instantly. "Oh, come off it, Gavin. They're never going to let you into the city." He glances at my clothes. "Even if you do manage to clean up enough."

"We'll get a visa from the mayor."

"My father?" Asher barks out a laugh. "Good luck with that. He won't give you one."

"He'll have to," I say.

Asher laughs again, but this time there's no humor in it. "That's where you're wrong. He doesn't have to do anything he doesn't want to." Then he shrugs. "Go ahead and ask him though. Good luck." He starts to walk away. "You know where to find me when you change your mind."

Evie

The air is heavy with heat and humidity. Between that and the exhaustion from almost drowning, my whole body feels leaden. So I just lie here and stare at the spiderwebs of cracks spreading across the ceiling and walls. I imagine them as thin fingers reaching for me, coming to steal me away from this world where I don't belong. I almost wish they would, so I'll stop endangering Gavin and his family.

This makes three. Three incidents since I left the medical facility. Three times I've hurt Gavin or almost hurt someone dear to him. The first was the day they brought me to live with them. The dog, Lucy, came out to greet me—well, everyone really, but she ran straight for me with her tongue lolling out and her teeth showing. The next thing I know she's on the ground underneath me and Gavin is prying my hands from around her neck.

Luckily, everyone agreed that they'd have reacted the same way, given the fact that I'd never seen a dog before and it did (kind of, sort of, probably not but maybe) look like she might be attacking. No one, including the dog, seems to resent me for it. Now Lucy follows me everywhere, like a little yellow dog-shaped shadow.

The second time, I don't even know what started it. I was sleeping. When I woke up, I had broken into the room where Gavin stores all of his hunting gear. I was standing in the middle with an assortment of weapons around me, and one in each hand. When Gavin had called my name, I'd spun around with both weapons drawn, my head screaming at me to *kill the Surface Dweller.*

Now I've almost drowned myself—and Gavin—trying to get "home." I don't even know where that is!

I can't stay here. I can't stay where I'm going to harm someone because my brain decides to shut off and my body just does whatever the hell it pleases.

With a sigh, I lie back against the pillows and close my eyes against the hominess of the room. I don't want to see how they've made this room nice for me, with soft, sweet-smelling bed linens and the beautiful furniture. They're a little scratched and damaged, but it's easy to tell they're the best in the house. And so is this room. With the beautiful flowers which are changed every few days—by Gavin's mother no doubt—and the white lacy curtains at the windows that look like they're almost brand new. Ann Marie's wedding stuff filling up her side of the room. I don't want to see any of it, because I've done nothing but cause them problems and they've done nothing but try and make me feel comfortable and at home.

For a while there'd been the soft murmur of voices and I'd hoped Gavin would come to visit me, but the murmur died down a while ago and Gavin never came. Maybe that's for the best. I don't know what to do. It's happened three times. It's sure to happen again. And next time we may not be so lucky.

Eventually the door creaks open and Gavin pokes his head in. My heart soars when I see him. I open my mouth to say his name, but he places his finger over his mouth and scoots in, shutting the door quietly behind him. He strides across the room, his long legs eating up the floor in two steps, and when he pulls me gently into his arms, my heart skips a beat.

He lifts my chin with his finger so I'm looking into his beautiful silvery gray eyes, and for what feels like forever and no time at all we stare at each other. Then, finally, his mouth is on mine. My eyes close and my stomach flutters as my head spins. For a moment, as our lips touch, I feel right. Like maybe I *am* home.

Then he pulls away and reality crashes in again, like the waves crashing against the shore. This isn't my home, and I'm going to end up killing someone if I stay here. I have to talk to him.

But before I can, he says, "We have to be quiet. I snuck in. The good doctor thought it would be better if you rested without me bothering you." He rolls his eyes. "Mom's got the door guarded, but she had to use the bathroom, and everyone else is asleep, so I took advantage." He smiles, then kisses my nose before nudging me over with his hip and lying down beside me.

"And when she comes in to check on me?"

He shrugs and crosses his arms behind his head.

With a shake of my head, I pull the arm he has closest to me down and then wiggle around until I find a comfortable spot, and lean my head against his shoulder. It feels so nice to have him next to me like this. I don't want to ruin it by talking about how broken I am.

When I wake he's still there, standing next to the one window in the room and gazing out through the salt-stained glass and leaning against the peeling windowsill. Hearing me shift, he turns. He looks exhausted and I can tell he didn't get a smidgen of sleep last night. Guilt licks at me. I know it's because of me. Once again I'm causing problems just by existing.

I run my fingers over the grooves of my necklace. His eyes follow the movement of my fingers before moving back up to meet my own. We stare at each other, and I'm sure we're both doing our own survey of the other. The tension in the air is palpable, but then, as if someone flicked on a light switch, the tension disappears. Gavin's lips quirk into a small smile and he moves toward me. Before either of us can say anything, the door to my room squeaks open and we both turn toward it as the doctor bustles in. He lifts an eyebrow when he sees Gavin, but doesn't say anything to him. He just asks how I'm feeling.

The words slip out without conscious thought. *"I'm just about perfect."*

Gavin's head whips around and he blanches. He exchanges a look with the doctor, who says, "Well, let's just take a look and make sure of that, shall we?" After a series of noises I can't interpret, Dr. Gillian finally says, "Everything seems fine. And I don't believe there's anything else I can do here." He stares at Gavin when he says it and I have a feeling he's saying more than what I hear.

Gavin won't meet my eyes, proving my suspicions. I don't like it. What aren't they telling me?

I open my mouth to ask, but Dr. Gillian continues quickly. "I'm going to release you, but you're to take it as easy as you can in the next few days. If you feel something out of the ordinary, you need to let me know immediately."

I want to know how I'm supposed to tell what's not normal when everything is strange, but I don't ask. He's not going to know either.

CHAPTER THREE

Memory is a fickle creature. As easy as it is to lock something into your memory, it is as simple to unlock it. For a memory system to function properly it is essential not only to activate the relevant information, but also to inhibit irrelevant information. There are many memory phenomena that seem to involve inhibition, although there is often debate about the distinction between interference and inhibition.

—EXCERPT FROM DR. FRIAR'S ESSAY ON MANUAL
MANIPULATION OF MEMORY RECALL

Gavin

I walk Doc out of the house. He takes a moment to reiterate, "She really should go to Rushlake."

I know!, I want to shout. Instead, I hand him the package of cookies my mom baked last night, the fresh fish I caught this morning while Evie was sleeping, and some of the venison jerky he loves so much. "Thanks for everything, Doc."

He stares for a moment, then sighs. "It might be a good idea to focus on discovering what the trigger is. Sometimes it's just a matter of preventing it." Then he says, "My favorite part of making house calls to you all is still the payment. And calls in the winter are always the best. Ginger cookies are my favorite." He lifts the package of cookies and winks before turning around and making his way down the path that leads to the rest of the village.

I swipe my hands over my face. How the hell am I supposed to find her trigger? There doesn't seem to be one. The first time she attacked my dog. The second, she was sleeping. The third? Who the hell knows? Where's the correlation?

A hand lands gently on my shoulder and I can tell by the way my nerves tingle that it's Evie. Fixing a smile on my face, I turn to face her and give her a once-over. She doesn't look near as tired as she did this morning. Not even close to how tired I feel.

She gives me a small, puzzled smile. "Why did you give him fish?"

"Payment for making a house call."

"Payment? Fish are money?" She looks even more confused, and I bark out a laugh.

"No. We don't really have a lot of money, but I fish and hunt, so generally we trade him for his services. He needs food and we need medical care." I shrug. "It works well for both of us."

She frowns. "So you gave away your food because I needed medical care?"

I have a bad feeling about this conversation. "We pay for

all medical services with food or Mom's sewing—even people from the city love the clothes she makes. That's how it works here. Mr. Steris trades his services—he's a metalsmith. And Mr. Pok barters his best ale."

"But you gave up *your* food for *me*."

I kick at the dirt with the toe of my shoe and shove my hands in my pockets. "Yes, but that's how we always pay for things. Not just medical care. We buy grains from the farmers, or from Mr. Pok, or Mr. Steris, or anyone in this town really, by trading meat or whatever Mom makes. Some pay us, like the mayor's wife. But mostly the barter system works well for us."

"That's not what I mean!" she yells, startling me. "You gave your food up for me! Food that could be used for feeding your family or trading for things that are much more important than me."

Her eyes are all bright and shiny, and panic makes my nerves tingle. I hate when girls cry. I never know what to say, how to help. Unsure what to do, I pull her to my chest and hug her tightly.

"It's not a big deal, okay? It's just some fish and cookies. And my mom loves to bake."

"But I'm causing you problems by just being here." She plays with the necklace at her throat.

Finally I get it. I lift her chin up with my finger so I can look at her face. "Look, Evie, it's not a hardship to have you. I love having you here. And I *like* that I'm able to do something to help you. I've felt so useless lately. You saved my life, Evie. And all I could do was wait for the doctor to help you when you needed me. So, if all I can do is give a few hours of my time catching some fish and giving them to Doc, then that's what I'm going to do."

"Still, I can't impose on you like this. It's not right. I need to do something to ease the burden on you."

"No, you don't." Her immune system is just barely beginning to tolerate the surface. What does she think she's capable of doing to help?

She purses her lips, and a determined look comes into her eyes. "You have to lock me into my room at night. Starting tonight. At least I won't walk into the ocean."

I almost want to laugh, but then I realize how serious she is. "No, Evie, that's crazy. I'm not going to lock you up like a criminal."

Her gaze is hard like a diamond. "You will. I refuse to endanger you and cost you any more fish."

I can't help the laughter that bubbles up in my throat. She's serious. Dead serious, but the way she said fish was just so ridiculous. I have to press my lips together to keep from laughing out loud.

"Gavin, please . . ." The hard edge is gone from her voice. Now she sounds desperate. It tears at me. But so does the thought of locking her up.

"What if you have to go to the bathroom?"

"I'll hold it. I'm not a child. Now promise me, or I'm not going another step with you." She crosses her arms.

Maybe it would be for the best, I tell myself. It's to protect *her*, not me, after all. I sigh. "All right. We'll try it."

She blinks, then sighs and hugs me tightly. "Thank you."

"Anything for you." I kiss the top of her head and hold her for a few minutes, enjoying the feeling that she's all mine.

After a long time, she pushes away. "What was Doc talking about? About having to go to a city. And something about a trigger?"

Damn it. She heard. I clear my throat to give me time to come up with something. I can't take her to the city. They'll chew her up and spit her out. I can't let her go through that. Not after everything she's already been through. "He thinks you should go into the village. Meet some more people so you're not always cooped up here and wallowing." I grin at her even as my stomach turns from the lie. "Who knows? Maybe something there will trigger some of your memories."

The way she watches me, I know she doesn't believe me. She's going to call me out on it. I know she is . . . but then she nods. "Well, I do feel a little shut in." She smiles and slides her hand into mine. "I'd love to see your village and meet some of these people you've talked about."

She looks so happy with the idea, guilt weighs on me like an anchor. For a minute I want to tell her the truth, but then she pulls me in the direction Doc took.

"It's this way, right?" Her voice is light and bubbly. I don't think I've heard that sound from her. Ever.

I let her pull me down the path.

Evie

Nerves threaten to strangle me, but I'm excited. My heart is beating so fast I'm out of breath after only a few steps. I've heard and seen it from a distance, but I've never been to the town proper. I should have. Maybe I don't feel like I belong because I've never tried to be a part of life here.

I lick my lips. The town's buildings loom in front of me, and even though my nerves make me queasy, my curiosity is overwhelming. I try to imagine what these people will be like. Gavin has shared some stories about them. And I met a few of the women when they came to visit me in the medical center. I hope the others will be like them.

I take a few hesitant steps toward the town, passing the hospital—a run-down building that looks a lot like Gavin's house, inside and out—and take it all in. One pristine white building towers above all the rest, with a tall spire that juts up into the sky, and it has a large clock on the side of it.

Gavin follows my gaze. "That's the mayor's house. They built it right after I was born, when the city sent the mayor to . . . uh . . . help us."

I glance over at him only to see him scowling at the ground, but then he points to another building slightly closer to us. "And that's where Ann Marie and Josh are going to move. It's the newest building. My mom and Ann Marie say it's beautiful inside. And they say the building is strong enough to withstand the hurricanes even though it's so tall."

I frown. "Hurricane?"

Gavin's younger brother, Tristan, jumps in front of me, startling me. I almost scream before gaining control of myself. I had no idea he was even following us.

"Oh, it's a really bad storm and it's so cool!" he says. "The winds are so strong they can rip trees right from the ground and toss them miles away. Once, a few years ago, one totally tore our neighbor's house apart while they were in it! And another time . . ."

"Tristan! That's enough," Gavin says, giving him a look.

"Sorry," he mutters, looking anything but. If I wasn't horrified about the hurricane, I'd laugh at his expression.

I turn back to Gavin, my heart in my throat. "What's a storm?"

He glares at Tristan. "It's just something where there's a lot of wind and rain. No big deal, usually."

That sounds terrible. "When is the next . . . hurricane?"

"Don't worry about it. They only come during the summer and it's been years. We'll be fine." He shoots Tristan another look.

I nod, but swallow, my stomach feeling hollow.

Gavin clears his throat. "Er . . . as I was saying, the mayor's house is the largest, and they've been adding new buildings around it since then with the help from the city. We should go so you can meet some more people." He sees my expression and adds, "Everyone is really friendly. Don't worry. They're going to love you."

Tristan grabs my hand and starts pulling me farther into town. It doesn't escape my notice how Gavin doesn't so much as protest Tristan tagging along. He must do it a lot. It makes my heart flutter a little knowing how much Gavin cares for his family. How close they are. How close they *want* to be. It's odd how the village changes the farther inland we go. The buildings closest to the shoreline—the two or three of them that aren't completely fallen down—are small, squat, wood structures that have seen their fair share of wind, rain, and sunshine. They were probably pretty once, but now they sit in various stages of disrepair. The windows are coated in thick scales of salt water, and the wood is grayed and cracked in places.

The buildings on the other side of those are sort of strange. Gavin tells me people live in them, so they must be housing of some sort, but they don't look anything like Gavin's three-story house with its red bricks, faded black shutters, and wraparound porch. They're barely taller than me. All four walls and the roof are made with ridged metal sheets that are stained red with rust. There are so many holes in the metal, the walls are practically none existent. A strong wind could probably blow them all right over. As we pass, I glance in the open doorway of one and see a chair and table that look like they've seen better days. From my position, it's hard to see if there's anything else in there, but as I'm looking, a woman steps out, wiping her hands on her jeans.

When she sees Gavin, she lifts a hand in an absent wave. Her gaze moves to me and although she looks curious now, she extends the wave in my direction. I flutter my fingers back and she smiles in return before walking around the side of the house. I follow her movements with my eyes and watch as she climbs into a knee-high fenced-in area. I recognize a group of chickens. Gavin has some behind his house and every morning Tristan goes out and gathers eggs for breakfast. I wrinkle my nose when I think about how dirty and gross-looking they are before he washes them. I don't even want to *think* about where Gavin told me they come from. I shudder and Gavin glances over.

"Are you all right?"

"Yes. Of course." My stomach still tumbles like driftwood in a wave, but I press my hands to it.

He gives me a strange look, then shrugs and continues forward. We pass some more of those strange little metal houses, which are placed randomly on the sand until we get to a set of buildings that seem to be laid out with more thought. They're all an equal distance apart and the same distance from the dirt path. While they're in various stages of completion, it's easy to see they're all going to look exactly the same as the one finished one. Two floors high, if the windows are any indication, with white walls and light blue roofs. It strikes me then, how dirty everything is here. Even the new buildings and the ones that are still skeletons of what they will be have a thick layer of dirt and grime. I don't know why, but it bothers me. *Dirt leads to disease. And disease to death.*

We follow a large path, passing another row of those apartment-type buildings before getting to other buildings in various states of repair. Some look brand new, like the general store. Tristan disappears into the building without saying a word and Gavin only shakes his head.

Next to that is something called Sheriff's Office and it, too, looks new, but not quite as . . . shiny as the general store, whose windows glisten in the bright sun and blind me even through the dark sunglasses I'm forced to wear to protect my eyes.

Across the street, other buildings look old and worn out. Tired, almost. Like the building called Bar. There are even metal poles on the dusty windows. Next to that is a dusty building housing the Metal Smith, with a hole in its brick wall. The roaring and banging sounds coming from the large opening make me nervous, and, for some reason, it's hotter standing outside of it than it is anywhere else. The air is all wavy in front of me.

A man—at least I think it's a man—wearing a striped shirt and jeans with some kind of black apron pokes his hat-covered head out the opening. When he sees Gavin, he waves. "Gavin! Do ya have a minute? I finished the repairs on the shotgun. Thought you'd want a peek."

Gavin grins and pulls me over to the opening while the man disappears inside again. When he returns, he's holding a gun. He hands it to Gavin, then does the funniest thing. His eyes move over to me. He blinks. Then blinks again. Then his eyes grow round and he whisks his hat from his head and balls it in his hands. "Pardon me, miss. Didn't see ya there." His dirt-streaked face turns bright red.

Gavin glances over, but quickly goes back to studying the gun. "Oh, Frank, this is my girlfriend, Evie. Evie, this is Frank. He's the metalsmith. He's a genius. If it's made from metal he can work magic."

Magic?

Frank blushes even more, wringing his poor cap in his hands so tightly I'm afraid he's going to tear it.

I do a little curtsy. "It's a pleasure to meet you."

Frank looks slightly confused, but nods. Then he turns his attention back to Gavin. "What'cha think?"

Gavin looks up and nods. "Another great job, Frank. Thanks!" He holds his hand out and I watch with interest as Frank takes it and shakes it. I've seen Gavin do that with Dr. Gillian, too. "I'll have Tristan drop by with the rest of that boar I owe you later. Okay?"

Frank nods. "Or whenever." He focuses back on me. "He's good folk." He jerks his head toward Gavin. "You won't find a better person than Gavin, miss. He oughtta be mayor, instead of that yahoo they got in the mansion now." He spits on the ground as if just saying "mayor" leaves a bad taste in his mouth. I jump away and try not to show how disgusted I am by it, but I must not hide it well, because he says, "I beg pardon, miss."

I force a smile and try not to look at the ground where he spat. "Think nothing of it."

He gives me that strange look again, but smiles back before winking. "I charge the mayor up front and double."

Gavin laughs. "Next time charge him triple." He pulls the shotgun's strap over his shoulder and takes my hand, waving with the other as we leave.

When we get back to the street, I turn back around in time to see Frank shove his hat back on his head and disappear behind the wall again.

Gavin takes me on a tour of the town, stopping at almost every building to introduce me to the people inside. There are so many people, considering how small the township really is, that I can't keep them straight. Only two stick in my head. Mr. Pok, who runs the feed and grain store, and Mrs. Little, who runs the general store with her three adorable daughters.

After asking about his mother, Mrs. Little hands Gavin a bolt of fabric. "Here's the rest of the payment for that pheasant your ma brought me the other day. Sure was a pretty thing. Tasty, too." She winks at him. Then she hugs me. My whole body tenses. Gavin's mom and sister are big on hugs, too, and it always makes me feel peculiar. But, as I do with them, I force myself to relax and then, unsure what else to do, decide to hug her back.

"Welcome!" she tells me. "I'm so glad to see you're well enough that you can visit!" While she's talking, another customer comes in behind her. A boy that looks to be about Gavin's age.

Everyone in the town has been a bit strange to me, but this one is the most bizarre one yet. His dark hair has a blue streak in the front, and his button-down shirt is loose over his slacks. Instantly there's tension in the air. I glance over at Gavin, who is scowling again. The new boy, on the other hand, stops in his tracks when he sees us. They watch each other carefully, reminding me of the way Lucy behaved when a different dog came over and wanted me to pet it. They circled and growled at each other for a long time, while I sat petrified—I still don't know if I was scared of them or of myself—until Gavin's mother came out and chased the other one off with a broom.

Mrs. Little clears her throat and we all turn to her. "It was wonderful finally meeting you, Evie. You come back here anytime, ya hear? Gavin, you get on back to your mom now. She'll be waiting for that fabric and I don't have time to be cleaning up after the two of you."

Gavin looks like he's going to argue, but Mrs. Little places her hands on her hips and Gavin ducks his head. "Yes, ma'am." He walks past the boy, who nods his head and smiles at me as we pass. I smile cautiously back and the boy's grin grows.

As soon as we slip out the door, I grab Gavin's arm. "Who was that?" I ask.

He shrugs and keeps going. "No one."

"Didn't seem like no one." I have to rush to keep up with him. He seems in a hurry to get away from the store.

"Just an old friend."

I stop and turn, calling over my shoulder, "Well, if he's an old friend, then I should meet him. Maybe we should be friends, too." I only take one step before Gavin's in front of me, his hands on my shoulders.

"He's *not* your friend. He's not *anyone's* friend. You can't trust him. Ever." His eyes are cold and hard. It's scary, but kind of sexy too. Heat spreads from my stomach outward. I've never seen him like this. I glance over his shoulder and see the boy walk out of the store. He pauses when he sees Gavin, then turns and walks in the opposite direction.

"Why not?" I ask, moving my eyes back to Gavin's.

He's quiet for so long, I think he's not going to answer, but finally he says, "He— His father is the mayor. And the mayor is sent from Rushlake City. People from Rushlake *never* do anything without expecting payment in return, and you *do not* want to owe what they want to be paid." His eyes are haunted, and though I know he's not telling me the entire truth, I can't push him. It's obvious the real reason isn't something he wants to talk about.

Instead, I peer over at the building next to us. It's brick, like the rest of the buildings, but like the general store almost the entire front is a shiny glass window. The words "Butcher" are painted across in black and gold paint. "So . . . what's this place? Are you friends with the owner, too?"

He glances over. "Sal works here. I generally bring my game here after I field dress it. They turn it into steaks or sausages or whatever it is we want. It's also where we bring the chickens when they stop laying. The farmers bring their cows and pigs." He grins at me. "So, yeah, he's a friend of mine."

"Great." I push through the door. "Then introduce me."

Like at the general store, a bell tinkles whenever the door moves. "Be out in a sec!" a man calls out from a door behind a counter filled with various meat products. My stomach twists seeing them all laid out behind the glass, glistening red in their icy beds.

Swallowing hard, I turn away from the counter, which runs almost the entire length of the wall farthest from the door, leaving only a small space behind it for whoever runs the shop. Above that space are large pieces of meat—as large as me at least—hanging from giant hooks on the ceiling. The rest of the shop is empty, all the way to its clean white walls. That's where I keep my eyes.

Just then a man's voice booms through the room. "Gavin! I was hoping you'd stop by soon. Doc stopped by with those blue gill you'd caught . . ."

I turn as he talks, but what he's saying is lost when I see him. He's a large man, barely fitting behind his counter in either height or girth. His hair—what's left of it—is dark. His skin tone is somewhere between Gavin's golden hue and Doc's dark color. But it's his apron that I'm staring at. That I can't tear my eyes from. It was probably white, once upon a time, but now it's completely covered in blood.

The rusty scent of blood is thick in the air, getting thicker the longer I stand here. It makes me nauseated and not a little scared. A horrible chill enters my bones and I shudder.

As if from a distance, Gavin asks, "Evie, are you okay?"

I nod, digging my fingernails into my palm and trying to force a smile. I will not be an inconvenience. Not again. It's just a little blood. From the animals. It's part of life.

My head spins, and I glance around trying to find something, anything to look at besides the blood on this man's apron. I see the counter with all the meat in it, but instead of steaks and chops, it's littered in body parts.

Human body parts.

Arms with their hands pressing against the glass as if trying to break out. Legs split open with their bones showing. Even severed fingers.

It's not real. It's not real. It's not real. But when I turn away from the counter, looking at the butcher again, he smiles at me and I fight back a scream. His face is streaked with blood, his teeth painted in it and bits of gore. His whole body is blanketed in blood. From head to foot. Gleaming, shining brightly in the sun. Blood.

When we get to the end of the trail, there's a body lying on the floor, surrounded by the light of my flashlight, just as I expected. But what's there is far worse than anything I was anticipating.

There's a man leaning over the body of a woman, who is most certainly dead. Or at least I hope so, because the man is ripping her apart . . .

. . . He slowly turns, so he's facing us, then tilts his head to the side, watching us.

A shiver runs down my spine, and Gavin's breath catches. I tighten the grip on the pistol, preparing to raise and fire if need be.

"It is my privilege to follow Mother's orders. We don't question Mother." *Then he leaps toward us. . . .*

I run. I don't stop to think. I couldn't if I tried. I don't know where I'm running to. I don't care. As long as it's far away from the butcher and his display of severed body parts.

The world spins uncontrollably. Black spots swim in front of my eyes. I can't catch my breath and my heart is pounding as if trying to escape the confines of my chest. I hear Gavin calling my name, but it's as if he's kilometers away. I'm vaguely aware of falling before I completely succumb to darkness.

CHAPTER FOUR

Attention Outlanders: Only preapproved individuals are allowed entrance into Rushlake City. To obtain approval, please visit your local mayor for a visa.*

*Approval is not guaranteed. All outlanders approved for entrance are subject to the Rushlake City Community Standards. Any violation of these standards may result in the forfeiture of the visa and formal ban from readmittance.

—NOTICE ON VILLAGE BULLETIN BOARD

Evie

When I wake, I just stay where I am—from the softness under me I assume it's my bed—while visions of what happened flit in and out of my memory. My body is stiff and sore. My arms feel like lead and it hurts to breathe—like I'm inhaling glass slivers. When I open my eyes, I find myself staring directly into Gavin's silver-gray eyes.

"Gavin!" I exclaim, my voice hoarse, forgetting everything that happened to grab him in a hug. I don't know why, but absolutely every time I see him, it doesn't matter what I've been through. He makes me feel better.

He clings to me, his arms shaking a little. He just holds me like that for the longest time, and I enjoy every second of it, even though the pressure he exerts on my still-healing shoulder makes my chest ache.

He pulls back and looks into my eyes. "It happened again."

I don't know what to say to that. It's not like I can deny it. It did happen again. Obviously.

I nod anyway.

"Damn it!" He pushes away from me to pace the small room.

Shivering from the sudden coolness that fills the space his warmth vacated, I hug myself and follow him with my eyes. There isn't much room for him to pace, though. Not with all of the paraphernalia for his sister's wedding packed onto her side of the room. He curses when his foot becomes entangled in something white and lacy.

"Gavin," I whisper, my throat raw and burning and guilt eating a hole in my heart.

He spins back around and crushes me to his body again, causing me to squeak when I try to breathe. He buries his face in my neck.

"You scared me," he whispers into my skin.

"I'm sorry." I smooth his hair. "I didn't mean to upset you."

Before he can say anything, there's a knock at the door.

The boy from the general store, the one with the blue hair, pushes his head through the opening.

Gavin jumps up and blocks his way. "What the fuck are you doing here, Asher?"

"Nice way to talk around a lady, *Mr.* Hunter." Asher lifts a brow and crosses his arms over his chest. "You kiss your girl with that mouth?"

"Kiss my ass."

"Nah. You're not my type. I prefer them slightly less hairy." He grins at Gavin and I see the corners of Gavin's mouth twitch before he firms them back into a straight line. Asher sighs. "Just thought you'd like to know my dad is on his way here."

Gavin blanches. "What the hell did you do?" Then, before Asher can respond, anger flushes his face. "What is wrong with you? Destroying my life wasn't enough the first time?"

Asher glares at him. "*I* had nothing to do with this. He heard his newest resident went tearing through town screaming her head off, then passed out twenty feet from the ocean. He thought he'd 'check in on her and offer assistance if it's needed.' I, on the other hand, thought I'd actually be helpful and give you a heads-up. Especially since this might be a good way to get her the help Doc thinks she needs."

Gavin pauses his glowering long enough to shoot me a worried look.

Just then there's another knock on the door, and Gavin's

mother peeks around the corner. She focuses on me, but I have the distinct feeling she's talking to Gavin. "Evie has another guest. And he brought flowers!" Her smile is forced when she says it. Her eyes flicker to Gavin and Asher and then back to me. "Are you up to seeing him, dear?"

"Uh . . ." I look at Gavin for help.

"Of course she's up to seeing me," a male voice says from behind Gavin's mother. "I won't stay long." He pushes past her and stands just inside the door while I stare. His hair is blond streaked with silver, but otherwise he is an almost exact duplicate of Asher, only older. Wait. No. I look briefly at Asher, then back to his father. The mayor's eyes are completely different. They're a sea-foam green, and cold. Hard. They remind me of someone else's, but, of course, I can't pull up the memory. As always, my mind keeps the pieces of my former life just out of reach.

His eyes flick over Gavin and his nose crinkles—only for a second, as if something smells bad—before he studies me. His eyebrows raise a fraction, and there's something in his expression I don't quite understand. But the way his eyes roam over my body makes me want to pull the blankets up further. I grip tighter to Gavin's hand.

Gavin squeezes back, but steps forward, holding out his other hand to the mayor, who ignores it. Gavin clears his throat and lets his hand drop.

The mayor smiles, but it's neither kind nor happy. "So, Evelyn, is it?" He looks to Asher for confirmation, but Asher doesn't so much as nod. The mayor narrows his eyes at his son and turns back to me.

"Yes . . . sir," Gavin answers, and although it's only an instant, I hear the hesitance before the "sir."

"I'm Kristofer St. James. I'm the mayor of this fair town. I see you've met my son."

I nod and take the flowers he offers me. I don't like him. I don't need Gavin's warning not to trust him. Everything in me is warning me away from him.

"How are you feeling, young lady?"

"Fine," Gavin interjects quickly before I can. "She's just fine. She doesn't need anything. *We* don't need anything."

"Gavin," Asher says under his breath.

Gavin glances over to him, then me, then seems to make up his mind about something. The mayor watches us all with this knowing look on his face. For some reason this makes me angry. What is he so smug about?

"I'd like to request a visa to get into the city," Gavin says, completely confusing me. The city is where Doc wanted me to go, but Gavin had said that going into the town proper *was* the city. So why he'd need permission from the mayor, I have no idea.

The mayor's eyebrows lift and he looks to me as if asking if he misunderstood before turning back to Gavin. "Why?"

Gavin tells him, but only of how I don't remember anything from before I came and that Doc is at a loss to what it could be. I'm grateful he doesn't mention the blackouts and freakouts, but then he goes on to explain that Doc had suggested that someone from the city with more training and experience would be able to help me, and I realize he lied to me. The city isn't the town. It's somewhere else altogether. And Doc thinks they can help! I can't understand why Gavin would keep this from me.

My blood boiling, I skewer him with a look, promising myself we *will* talk about this when the mayor leaves.

The mayor taps his finger against his lips. "So . . . you want to take Evelyn to Rushlake in the hopes of finding a doctor who will overlook your Outlander status and treat her. Do I have that right?"

"Yes . . . sir."

"And how do you propose to pay for her care? Do you have any money?"

Gavin looks at me, then at the mayor. "Um . . . no."

"I see." The mayor moves to look out the window. Gavin and I glance at each other, then look back at the mayor when he says, "You do realize that is out of the question, don't you, Gavin?"

"Sir?"

"There is no reason for me to allow you to travel to the city so you can beg for help. Which is essentially what you'd be doing: begging for someone to help you. Do you have any idea how badly that would reflect on me?"

Gavin only shakes his head, but his frustration is practically palpable.

"Besides, where would you stay?" the mayor continues.

"No one needs your wild game there. They have stores full of anything *money* can buy. Would you sit on the street with an empty cup? Or, maybe play some kind of instrument and let people throw coins at you? Find some kind of tent city where the other beggers live?"

Gavin doesn't say anything, but his teeth clench. I'm not sure why, but this is the final straw that sets me off. This is Asher's *father*?

I shove myself to my feet and the room spins for a second, but my voice is cold and calm when I say, "Mr. Mayor, I can't imagine anything Gavin Hunter would do that would reflect as badly on you as your own behavior. I consider our business complete. Good day, sir."

"I beg your pardon?"

The silence in the room is thick with tension and fear, though I can't remember feeling less afraid since I woke up in the hospital.

I focus my gaze directly into his eyes, unblinking, as an invisible string seems to pull my posture straighter than my injured shoulder has allowed in weeks. "I will not be treated like a commoner."

"Evie . . ." Gavin whispers, but I silence him with a flick of my wrist.

At first, the mayor meets my stare with red spots of anger on his cheeks, but after a moment he pales and looks away. A wave of dizziness threatens to overwhelm me as the adrenaline of my anger fades, and I turn. Gavin gets to his feet, his eyes wide with concern, and reaches hesitantly toward me. I shake my head slightly. I will not let the mayor see even a moment of weakness.

The mayor clears his throat, and says, "Perhaps you misunderstood me. I didn't say I wouldn't help *you*, Evelyn."

I glance at the mayor over my shoulder. He smiles and watches me for a minute before gesturing for us to sit again.

I wait for him to take a seat first before lowering myself to the edge of the bed.

He continues, "I said *his* going would be out of the question. Not yours."

I look to Gavin, only to see a tic in his jaw. The mayor goes on, either unaware of Gavin's increasing annoyance, or not caring. "Gavin is an Outlander; he would never make it in Rushlake. But you, Evelyn . . . you're different. You were obviously raised with a certain . . . quality, shall we say, that is lacking in the average Outlander. Even if you can't remember any of it."

"Say what you mean, Mr. Mayor."

He smiles and nods graciously, like he's indulging me. Obviously trying to take the power back. It sets my teeth on edge, but I let him speak. "I would be willing to sponsor your treatment. Set you up with the best doctors and the best places to stay while you're there. You wouldn't have to beg, or borrow. Steal." He glances at Gavin. "To get the help you need. You'd only get the *best* care."

Remembering what Gavin said about people from the city, I say, "And what do you suppose I would I owe you in return?"

The mayor waves a hand in front of his face, the diamond on his pinky ring sparkling. "There's no need to worry about that now. We're both reasonable people. We can come up with something at a later date. But Gavin stays here. You'll have to go alone."

I look down at Gavin and he shakes his head. "No," he says softly.

The mayor smiles, as if confused. "Beg pardon?"

Gavin stands, drawing himself to his considerable full height as he sets his shoulders. "I said, no. She's not going alone." His voice is strong, but I can tell from the way his throat is working that he's not comfortable standing up to this man.

The mayor only continues to smile and looks at me. The ultimate decision is in my hands. If we don't go, it'll be my choice. My choice to continue putting myself, and Gavin's family, in danger. I can't let that happen.

Still, I shake my head. "That's unacceptable. I won't go without Gavin."

The mayor shrugs. "Suit yourself. Request denied, then."

"Mr. Mayor, I have been led to understand that you're unable to guarantee the safety of your citizens outside the gates. Do you honestly expect me to go unescorted into a territory you yourself cannot control?"

"I have offered you my terms." For whatever reason, he's decided he's back in control.

"Very well. I can see there's no point in any further discussion. When you are prepared to grant my very reasonable request, we can continue. Until then, I'll ask you to leave." I stand, walk straight past the mayor, and open the door, waiting for him to go.

The angry red spots are back in his cheeks. I've pushed him too far, I can see that, but something in me won't back down. I don't even know where these words are coming from.

"Will you let them both go, if I go?" a voice says from behind me. I whirl around to see Asher staring at his father.

I turn just enough so I can see both the mayor and Asher. The mayor purses his lips and this time I can't control the shudder. It's so familiar; it makes the blood in my veins freeze. I just wish I could place where I've seen it before.

"You want to go to the city?" the mayor asks him.

Asher shakes his head. "No. Not really. But Evelyn needs to go and the only way that's going to happen is if they get visas."

"Why are you offering?" his father asks with narrowed eyes. Then he pauses. "Who is this girl to you?" Gavin lifts a brow as if he is wondering the same thing.

Asher only smiles. "You've been wanting me to go to the city for months now and I've refused." He shrugs. "So, *Pops*, what's it going to be? I'll go to the city like *you* want, only I take Evie and Gavin, like I want. We'll call it a gentleman's agreement."

The mayor narrows his eyes and it's so quiet I can hear the *splash* of each wave as they pummel the shore even through the closed window.

Finally the mayor nods. His eyes sparkle and I'm reminded

of a cat I saw the other day toying with a mouse it had caught. I have to wonder what he's got up his sleeve. "Fine. But there are things I need you to do in the city when you get there. Do you understand?"

Asher makes a face, but nods. "Fine."

"I'll have Greta draw up the papers." The mayor walks away, his dismissal obvious, but his easy approval unnerves me. He was so set on denying Gavin passage. Why would he be comfortable sending his son with us—an Outlander he obviously detests and the crazy newcomer? It doesn't make any sense.

I keep these thoughts to myself. I'll talk with Gavin about them later when Asher isn't around to be offended.

But Gavin is obviously less concerned than I am about offending Asher. He turns to him and says, "We don't need your help. We can figure out how to get into the city on our own."

Asher steps right into Gavin's face. "You don't understand. The city is *not* going to let you in, even with your visa. No matter what you think. You're an Outlander and without a sponsor you don't get in. *So get over it.* You *need* me."

To his credit, Gavin doesn't even flinch, let alone back down. "I don't want you doing me any favors." His voice is infused with anger. He's practically vibrating with it. I can feel the hum of his emotions from here.

Asher takes a step back, but I don't think it's because Gavin intimidates him. "I'm not doing it for you." His eyes meet mine and I tilt my head in confusion. "I'm doing it for her. And it's not a favor." With that he turns around and starts to walk away. "We should leave first thing in the morning. Meet me outside the village gates at sunrise."

Gavin's soft snores beside me are oddly soothing. At least he's sleeping. I have to admit, I'm a little jealous, but he didn't sleep the night before, so I doubt he'd have been able to pull off another night without somehow figuring out a way to secure his eyes open.

But I'm restless. The more I lay awake staring at the ceiling, the more I want to jump up and pace the room like Gavin does. My heart feels like it's going to pound out of my chest and even though I'm breathing, I feel like I'm suffocating. I keep wringing my hands to relieve the ache that isn't there. My body needs to move, and move now. Or I'll explode. I'm sure of it.

Carefully, so I don't wake Gavin, I slide out from underneath the sheets and out of bed. He stirs and instantly I freeze. He only rubs a hand across his nose and rolls over so his back is to me. The T-shirt he fell asleep in pulls tight across his back, showcasing the muscles in his back and shoulders.

I stare. Who wouldn't? But even though my whole body protests, I turn away and make my way to the door instead of crawling back in beside him and making him help me forget all my worries about tomorrow. He deserves to sleep.

Even so, I'm disappointed when the cool doorknob turns easily in my hand and the door opens without so much as a whisper. And not just because Gavin promised to keep me locked in, but because it means nothing is stopping me from continuing on my path to get out of the ever-shrinking room and get some fresh air down by the shoreline.

With the floor cool and smooth under my bare feet, I shuffle as quietly as I can down the hallway and out the back door, which I've learned doesn't squeak like the front.

The sand is still warm from the day, but is soft, crunching softly as I walk. The water laps at the shore, making soft whooshing sounds. The instant I hear it, the tension in my body starts to ease. And when I see the ocean, the rest of it fades away.

Pulling my skirt tight against my body, I sit close enough to the waterline to let the water lap at my feet, but not enough to soak me if an errant wave decides to go a little further than normal. I lay down, crossing my arms underneath my head and staring at the stars. They're almost the best part here. They're just so beautiful and free. I feel wistful just looking at them.

My mind wanders as I lay there, and before long I feel myself drowsing. I know I should get up and walk back into the house before I do manage to fall asleep—Gavin could wake up and if I'm not there, who knows what he'd do?— but I can't summon the energy.

Without warning the hair on the back of my neck tingles and I know I'm not alone. But I don't get up. I know who it is. There's only one person who can make my nerves jangle like a whole fistful of bells.

Gavin.

When I feel him stare down at me, I open my eyes, finding myself peering into the most gorgeous gray ones. They're worried at the moment, as they are most of the time, but I give him a shy smile and the relief in his eyes is almost instantaneous.

"Hey," he says.

"Hi."

"Scared me. I didn't know where you'd gone. Why didn't you wake me up?"

I reach up and press a hand to his cheek, enjoying the scratchy feeling of his stubble against the sensitive part of my wrist. I stare into his eyes. The beautiful gray shines in the moonlight like polished silver. A delicious thrill courses through me as his gaze travels down my face to my throat and comes to rest on the little v-shaped patch of skin on my chest. It's almost like he's taken his fingers along that path instead of just his eyes.

And when those same eyes flash up to meet mine again, my heart skips a beat, then pounds so fast it's like it's in a race against itself. The want—no, need—is burning so brightly in his eyes I can feel its echo within me.

I move my fingers to the back of his head, tangling my fingers lightly in his hair, then pull him down so his lips are a hair's breadth from mine. He continues to stare down into my eyes as if they're not the only things that he's seeing. It's like he's seeing into my soul and seeing me, really seeing me. As terrifying as it is, it's also thrilling.

"I love you," I whisper, unable to stop myself. But instead of the sad look that's come into his eyes every other time I've said it, his lips slowly curve into a smile. One that swells my still racing heart to the point it almost hurts.

"I love you, too. Always," he whispers back, and I have only a moment to think how much I've wanted to hear those words without his usual hesitancy, before his lips breach the short distance between us and I can't think anymore at all.

His lips are soft and hard at the same time, like he's holding back. I pull him closer, savoring his taste. He pulls back almost instantly, his eyes roaming over my face, that familiar worry gleaming in them for only a second before it disappears and he kisses me again. This time he's not holding back. I kiss him back, desperately craving his taste. His scent. His feel. Him.

His hands are rough over my body, but I don't care. He's making me feel more alive than I've felt in a long time with each touch of his fingers on my skin. The stubble on his chin is scratching my skin and I crave every delicious scratch.

He only pulls away for air, but every time, I feel like I'm drowning and hyperventilating all at the same time. It's too much, yet not enough, and I never want it to stop.

CHAPTER FIVE

During the War it seemed that even Mother Nature was taking sides. While massive rains of almost biblical proportions were only one of her weapons, flooding destroyed many cities and left others cut off completely from the "mainland." The rains were followed by drought, which left many previously inhabited lands barren.

—EXCERPT FROM *A BRIEF HISTORY OF THE 21ST CENTURY*

Evie

Gavin and I stand outside the gates, our packs resting on the ground by our feet. The moon has set and the sun hasn't risen yet, so it's practically pitch dark. I shiver in the chilly air. While I love the cold, I'm not used to it.

I wonder, though, if it's really the weather that's making me shiver or if it's my nerves. One of the first things Gavin taught me when I was released from the hospital was that I should never leave the gates of the village when it's dark. There are too many hungry animals that hunt at night. He wasn't very specific about *what* animals, but I didn't really expect I'd stray too far from him and never asked.

Even Gavin appears nervous as we wait. I know he is thinking of all the things that could, and probably will, go wrong. He's already got his shotgun in one hand and his body is tight as he surveys his surroundings. After a minute, though, he relaxes and picks up his pack with his free hand. He slings it over his shoulder and stares out over the coast.

That nervous energy of his is still humming, and he looks so sad looking out over the water that my heart clenches.

I want to tell him it doesn't matter. That I'm okay not remembering anything of my past. But I can't. It wouldn't be true and he'd know it. Besides, it's not the only reason we're going. It's not even the reason he's going with me. It's just *my* most important reason, so I keep my mouth shut and reach for my bag instead.

The movement causes Gavin to turn toward me. "You ready?"

His voice is still thick with sleep and his drawl even more pronounced than usual. He stifles a yawn and crosses to me. The dark circles under his eyes, barely visible in the pre-dawn light, make me remember he hasn't been sleeping again. And it's my fault. We'd done nothing more than kiss, even after I'd let him pull me back to bed, but I'm sure he stayed up all night to watch me, even after I'd fallen asleep. He's going to make himself sick if he doesn't get some sleep soon.

I nod in answer to his question, but keep a stranglehold

on my pack, twisting the strap in my fingers. Gavin glances down and eyes my bone white fingers, made even whiter by the pressure I'm exerting on the strap. He places one of his bronzed hands over mine. The contrast is striking, but that's not what causes me to shiver. It's the warmth of his hand on mine.

He doesn't say anything, and I look up from our hands to see him watching me carefully. It's not the look he gives me when he's trying to see if I'm all right. It's different this time, and it makes my breath catch.

The sun is just rising behind him and while the sky is slowly starting to lighten, his gray eyes are still in shadow. A lock of his hair has fallen over one of his eyes. I reach up to brush it away, but he grabs my hand and just presses it to his cheek.

My stomach flutters and my heart trips in my chest. I can't tear my eyes from his, not that I want to, even when the sun comes up behind his head and threatens to blind me. I could stare into them forever and never have another care in the world.

But before anything can happen, Asher tosses his bag at our feet and says, "Mornin'! A great day to destroy our lives, don't you think? The birds are singing, the sun is shining . . ."

Immediately I step back, the pack dropping from my loose fingers, while Gavin makes a disgusted sound. He roots around in his bag and says, "If you didn't want to go, why'd you volunteer to take us?"

Asher shrugs. "Well, it certainly wasn't for you."

Gavin gives him a tight smile. "Anything you do for Evie, you're doing for me. Or did you forget that?"

Asher's mouth thins into a line.

Gavin shrugs. "But if you want to stay here, stay. I'm sure I can figure out some way to get into the city on my own."

Asher snorts. "They wouldn't let you within a hundred feet of the gates without me and *my* paper." He pulls a paper from his bag and waves it back and forth.

Gavin tries to grab for it, but Asher only folds it up and shoves it into his pocket, then smiles at me, nodding his head. "And a fine morning to you, Princess." He wiggles his eyebrows at me and I have to fight a chuckle. It's obvious he's only doing it to upset Gavin, and from the way Gavin is fuming, I would say it's working.

Shaking my head, I say, "Good morning, Asher."

Gavin glares at him. " 'Swear, if I didn't need you—"

"Well, you do. Get over it." Asher reaches down for my bag at the same time I do and our hands bump. He gives me another of his cocky grins. "A gentleman always assists a lady with her luggage. Hunter can handle the rest."

Gavin makes a grab for the bag, but I say, "I can take it," and lift it before he can. It's heavy for me, but there's no need for the two of them to start a quarrel now, especially over something so petty. I refuse to be a bone they fight over. And if they've started this stuff now, it's going to be a *long* trip.

Asher, however, keeps his hand on the bag so I'm not able to flip it onto my back. His tone changes, losing that air he had before. "Are you sure? It's at least a week's walk from here. You'll need all the strength you have to get there. And after yesterday . . ."

"I'm sure. I feel just fine today," I lie, giving him my most winning smile. I'm freezing and I ache everywhere, not to mention the bag feels like it weighs a hundred kilos. My arms threaten to shake as I struggle to keep the bag in front of me.

It's obvious neither of them believe me. Asher continues to frown and even Gavin is watching me with a strange expression. Guess I'm not as convincing as I hoped. After a minute, Asher turns on his heel, dropping my bag, and runs back into the village.

"*Now* where is he going?" Gavin tosses his hands into the air.

I let the bag drop back to the ground and try to decide whether I should sit while Gavin starts his pacing. I've just about made up my mind to when I hear the strangest thumping sound. It even vibrates the ground. Nervous, I look to Gavin, who frowns in the direction Asher went. He doesn't seem scared, only confused.

When I turn back around, I see Asher riding what looks like a cloud of dust, but is actually a giant animal with long legs and an even longer neck. Clamping down on the squeal that wants to erupt from my mouth, I step back into Gavin, who rubs a hand up and down my arm.

Asher drops down off the leather seat and stands next to me. The beast lifts its head and shakes it back and forth, causing the straps on its head to jingle.

Pure panic makes my heart race and I gasp and jump away, bumping into Asher, who chuckles. The beast blows out a breath and I have to fight the urge to flee. The beast is tall, looming above me. Maybe even taller than Asher. It's silvery, but glows pink in the sunrise. Its eyes watch me with every move and, if I didn't know better, I'd say they were laughing at me.

"Relax. She's a good horse. She won't hurt you," Asher says, his tone soft and gentle.

I don't relax, but I do stop trying to run away from it. "A horse?" I've heard of horses. I think. The term is familiar to me, at least. I glance at its sides. I thought they had wings, though. There don't appear to be any. That's disappointing. I've been wondering what it would be like to fly.

"There are no cars outside Rushlake. You want transportation—it's the horse or nothing."

"Transportation?"

He gives me a smile. "You really are a princess, aren't you? Trans-por-ta-tion?" He pronounces each syllable slowly.

I know the word, but it doesn't fit. I don't see how this animal could be used for travel. How would you control it?

Gavin fills me in. He always seems to know exactly what I'm thinking. "We ride her." He pats the large thing sitting on its back. "And she'll carry us to where we need to go. The city's a long way from here, you'll want her to do the walking for you. Trust me."

He's always matter-of-fact when he has to explain the

obvious to me, but I can't help feeling stupid every time. It's always worse in front of other people.

"Plus the best part is she works for hay and sugar cubes." Asher chuckles to himself and gives the animal a pat on the neck. It makes a soft sound and I catch a glimpse of large teeth under its loose lips.

I swallow hard.

Asher pats something on the back of the animal. "See that seat? That's how we ride her. She's also used by the farmers to do . . . whatever it is they do." Gavin snorts, but Asher ignores him and continues, "She's a good girl. Aren't you, Starshine?" She raises and lowers her head in what I can only call a nod. He pats her neck again and she leans her large head down and nibbles on his hair.

Afraid she's going to eat him, I gasp, but she pulls away and huffs out a breath as if to tell me to stop being ridiculous.

Curiosity outweighs terror, and I reach out a hand to touch her neck . . . but curl my fingers into a fist and drop my arm at the last second.

Asher takes my hand. "It's okay. She won't hurt you." He smiles down at me, then turns to the horse. "Evie, this is Starshine. Starshine, this is Evie."

He places my fist on her neck and my heart pounds. After a minute, though, when the beast does nothing more than stand there, my heart settles and I uncurl my fingers to rub my hand down her neck.

It feels different from anything I've ever felt before. The skin is warm, and firm. The hair is soft and thick, coarse. I have to admit I like the feeling. And that she's very pretty. Tentatively, I step closer. Starshine moves her head and stares at me, the straps over her head jingling.

I'm startled, but I don't move. Her eyes are the prettiest blue I've ever seen. I swear I can see kindness in them. And intelligence.

"See? She's a good girl. So?" Asher's eyes sparkle with mischief. "May I offer the lady assistance in mounting her noble steed?"

Before I can say no, Asher bends and nudges my foot into his hand. He murmurs a few instructions to me, but it's all I can do to hear him, much less understand before I find myself in the seat on the horse's back, one leg on either side of her wide chest. My skirt hikes up my thighs and I fight the urge to tug it back down. It won't do any good anyway.

He winks at me. "Probably should have worn jeans instead of that skirt, Princess."

I ignore that, although Gavin said the same thing to me this morning. But the hand-me-down pants from Ann Marie make me uncomfortable. I can't really explain why, but I feel out of place in them. Not to mention, they're a bit large in the hip area, making me jealous of Ann Marie and her figure. Even though my skirt is just as borrowed, it's somehow more familiar.

"Uh, Asher, I . . . I don't know how to ride a horse." I try to not look as terrified as I feel. It's a long way back down to the ground and I clutch tightly to the saddle in hopes of keeping myself firmly in place.

He only grins and swings into the saddle behind me, causing me to grab wildly for purchase and shriek when the whole thing tips slightly.

"Not a problem. I'll be right behind you. I promise I won't let you fall."

Before I can even think of what to say, Gavin grabs Asher's arm and tugs—sending Asher crashing to the ground with a thump—before taking the leather straps attached to the horse's head and walking forward with her. The horse starts walking and I cling to the knobby thing again, trying not to scream when the saddle shifts with each step.

Gavin looks up at me from where he walks next to the horse's neck. "You're doing great, Evie. Just keep holding on to the horn"—he taps the thing sticking up from the seat— "and holler if you want me to stop." Then he leans back and kisses my leg just below the knee.

My stomach flutters and I smile down at him, wanting to run my fingers through his hair. Actually, I want to do much more than that. But I'm too afraid to let go of the horn.

Instead, I glance behind me to where Asher is just now pulling himself into a sitting position. He glares at Gavin for a second before pushing himself to his feet and limp/running to join us again. This time he stays on the ground.

No one really talks. We're all probably just too nervous, but as the tortuous sun drags itself across the sky and nothing happens, I begin to relax. The horse's steady gait rocks me until, between that and the heat of the sun, I start to drift.

I try to fight it, but after a while I give up and let myself float, staying awake only enough to not fall off the horse. It's not like it matters if I'm alert. There's nothing worth paying attention to anyway. Nothing to see, except kilometers and kilometers of sand and pale blue sky. There aren't even any clouds to stare at. Which makes me a little sad. Gavin had taught me, when I was first allowed to go outside, how to pick out shapes in the clouds. We'd spent hours that first day, nuzzled up next to each other, pointing out different shapes between kissing. The kissing was my favorite part. Even now my stomach flips thinking about his lips against mine. Or on the side of my neck. How he held my face between his palms. Or ran his fingers through my hair, just staring at me, my heart beating so hard in my chest, I was breathless just from looking at him.

And now, the last few days. Nothing. Like we're just really good friends.

A sigh escapes my lips and I blink back to the present to find I'm staring at him. He turns around with a frown.

"All right up there?"

I smile at him. "Perfect."

He grins at me and the sun shines on him, highlighting his golden hair and making his bronze skin glow. My heart starts hammering as fast as it had in the memory and, for a second, I feel dizzy as we beam at each other.

Then Asher clears his throat and I realize with a start we've stopped walking.

"Are we going to stand here all day and stare at each other

or are we going to try to get to the city sometime before the next war?" Asher grins at both of us.

For the very first time I can remember, Gavin actually blushes. He quickly turns around, makes a clicking sound, and starts forward again. Starshine continues on while I drift back into hazy, sleepy boredom.

It isn't until the sun is high in the sky that Asher forces my attention back on the trip. "Forest dead ahead!"

Gavin scowls. "Can we not say 'dead' in conjunction with forest? I've had quite enough of dead forests, thank you very much."

This confuses me, but I'm completely focused on the forest. It doesn't look at all how I pictured. "Forest" may be a bit of an overstatement, actually. It's just a collection of sad-looking trees.

Asher taps my knee and I glance down at him. "Not much of a forest, huh? It's really just a bunch of scrub oak clumped together and some pine trees with palmettos tossed in for good measure." He rubs a hand over the back of his neck. "But it'll feel great to get out of the sun for a while. And the shade will cut some of this awful heat."

He's right. It feels about twenty degrees cooler the minute we step into the shade. Shortly after entering, we find a clearing and stop for a rest and some lunch. Which, to my dismay, consists of jerky. And even though my nose wrinkles at the sight of the shriveled meat, I eat it anyway.

I just want a solid hour or two to nap, but entirely too soon, Gavin is telling us we need to start going again. And I find myself back on the horse and traveling down that worn path again, trying to ignore how bored and sore I am. Asher is mumbling to me about something, but I'm so hot and tired, his voice is more a droning sound than anything else. I'm finding it harder and harder to stay awake. Suddenly, the entire saddle jerks to the side and I let out a short scream when I feel myself tilting sideways as someone jumps up behind me.

Before I can fall, a strong arm snakes around my waist and pulls me close to a toned chest and stomach. I relax almost instantly. I know who it is even before I look behind to smile at Gavin.

"It's okay," he says in my ear. "I won't let you fall."

His voice is husky and I shiver, relishing the feel of him being so close. "Okay."

Asher heaves a world-heavy sigh beside us and we turn to frown down at him. "I see how it is. Completely ignore me. I'll be just fine being the only one on foot."

Gavin smirks at him. "It'll get some muscles in those skinny little bird legs of yours." He leans against me again and gently pushes my shoulder until I'm facing front, then traces his fingers down my arms, whisper light, until his hands are over mine.

"Grab the reins," he whispers. And I do, because when he talks like that, it's hard to resist anything he asks me to do.

His hands tighten around mine, causing my hands to tighten around the reins. For the next little while I amuse myself by letting Gavin teach me how to control Starshine. It's fascinating, how just a slight pressure from my fingers or my heel tells her exactly what to do. I have to admit I'm quite enjoying myself, but I'm enjoying the feel of Gavin's body against mine more. Wicked thoughts—thoughts I have no business thinking ever, let alone with Asher less than an arm's length away—fill my head and I bite my lip, hard, to try and force them away.

Unfortunately, or maybe it's fortunately, Gavin seems to be thinking the same thoughts. He kisses down my neck, starting just below my ear and moving toward my collarbone. My breath catches in my throat and I let my eyes drift closed.

Now this is more like it, I think.

His hands move from mine to rest on my hips, his fingers trailing along the edge of my waistband, inciting little fires along every single one of my nerve endings. My fingers slip from the reins and I start to twist around to face Gavin, but he only breathes, "Don't," in his gloriously husky voice, then goes back to brushing his lips along my neck. The stubble on his jaw prickles my skin.

A throat clears and I blink heavy lids. I try to focus on Asher, who's grinning up at us. He hands me the reins. "You might want to hang on to these, Princess. Horses have a way of knowing when their riders aren't paying attention."

Blushing, I take them from him. "Thank you."

Gavin only continues his onslaught to my nerves and hormones by nuzzling my neck and running his rough fingers across my stomach. I have to force myself to concentrate on breathing and paying attention to the path ahead of us.

"Stop!" My voice is hoarse and I have to clear my throat. "Stop."

Gavin chuckles but does as I ask. He crosses his arms across my waist and rests his forehead against the back of my head. It isn't long before his breathing evens out and his body sags against me. I'm fairly certain he's fallen asleep. It's slightly uncomfortable, but I don't dare wake him up. He needs the rest.

By the time we finally stop to make camp for the night, my back hurts from leaning over the horse. When Gavin helps me down, my legs are stiff and patches of my skin feel raw from the leather saddle, so it's hard to walk at first. I stumble my way over to where Asher is setting up camp.

"All right, Evie?" Gavin asks. He sounds more rested than I've heard in days, especially considering he'd been sleeping on a moving horse in what had to be the most uncomfortable position ever.

"Just tired . . . and sore." I rub at the tightness in my arms.

Asher smiles over, knowingly. "You'll get used to that. Couple more days riding and you won't be sore at all."

"Wonderful." Just what I wanted, more pain.

To take my mind off all that, I help Asher set up the tents—one for each of us. But still my back aches to the point that when we're finished, I'm grateful the only thing left to do is wait for Gavin to come back from hunting for some fresh meat.

I settle myself next to the campfire Asher is setting up. Asher keeps sneaking glances at me, and when he sits next to me, he asks, "How are you feeling?"

"Still a little sore." My stomach growls and I press a hand to it in an attempt to make it stop. "And hungry, I guess."

Asher laughs and scoots closer. "Me, too. Wonder what our famous hunter will bring back."

"Famous?" I give him a sidelong glance.

"He's the best in the village, Princess. Why do you think they always send him to go?"

"I'd never thought of it before." I trace patterns into the dirt. It's true. Gavin *is* always off hunting.

"That boy can catch anything." Asher shakes his head. "But it's not a job I'd want. Never being home . . . Only getting to see my family between trips . . ." He glances over at me as if he's going to say more, but then turns back to look at the crackling fire.

I can't pretend that I don't understand what he's telling me. That life with Gavin is going to be difficult. When I'm not having issues anymore, Gavin is going to have to go back to a normal hunting regimen. Which means he could be gone for days at a time, and I'm going to spend a lot of time alone. And worried.

But he's the only thing I've got in this world. Or any world, really. I can't remember what life is like without him.

I miss being able to remember.

Gavin's given up so much of his life for me, and it doesn't seem like that's going to end any time soon. I know he can't afford to sit around babysitting me forever, but I'm lost without him. It's like I've lost *myself* somewhere along the way, and I don't know what's important to me, or what I want out of my life.

Asher and I stare into the fire in silence while worry twists my stomach into knots.

When Gavin finally comes back, he's got some kind of fluffy, bloody thing in his hands, and he's wearing a huge smile.

"Caught a rabbit!" he says so excitedly that even though my stomach turns, I give him a smile back. Then bite my lip against the burning in my stomach and force myself to look away until Gavin's got it cleaned and strung up on the spit he placed over the fire.

He comes to sit next to me, the rabbit skin in his hands. "I'll save this and take it back to Mom. She'll have this whipped into a hat for you in no time." He looks so proud of himself that I have to smile back at him and try to look as excited as he is about it.

However, I don't miss the look of amusement Asher gives Gavin. He catches my eye and shakes his head, then goes back to poking the fire with a stick.

Before too long Gavin is dishing out the meat, and despite the fact that I really don't want to eat it, I dig in. Gavin sits next to me, his hip pressed tightly against mine. No one talks during our meal. It isn't uncomfortable like before, but I'm not stupid—I can still feel the tension between the two boys. Although I'm curious, I don't ask. Gavin will talk to me about it when he's ready.

When we finish eating, Gavin gathers all the bones. Without saying a word to either Asher or myself, he walks into the woods. He's gone for so long, I begin to get worried and start wondering if maybe I should go look for him. Just when I've made my mind up, he reappears.

"I want to show you something," he says, ignoring Asher. "Come on." He smiles at me and holds out his hand. Without hesitation, I take it and let him lead me to the tree line.

"Hey!" Asher calls. "Where are you two off to?"

Gavin gives him a look. "If it was any of your business, I'd be taking you too."

Asher glares at him. "You better not be ditching me."

Gavin scowls. "Don't tempt me." Then he tugs on my hand and pulls me into the darkness of the woods.

Even though it's pitch dark in the trees now, Gavin navigates expertly through them. The woods are filled with strange sounds—a kind of chirping. The rustling of leaves in the trees. Closer to us on the ground, a strange sound that sounds like someone asking, "Who?"

I'm sure I feel something slither over my shoe, but when I tell Gavin and ask him what it might be he just says, "Don't worry about it. You don't want to know." Taking him at his word, I cling to his hand and follow, trying my best not to think of what could be around us.

Eventually, we reach a break in the trees. He steps out into it, but I'm more hesitant. There's something about this place. It's solemn. Peaceful. I'm not sure I should disturb it.

But Gavin pulls me out of the trees. Moonlight streams over him, giving him a ghostly appearance, and I shudder.

"Come on. You don't want to miss this." He tugs me into the center of the circle, then drops down in the grass to lie on his back and look up into the sky, like we're going to look at clouds again. Unsure, I lower to the ground next to him and look up. In this circle, for as far as the eye can see, there's nothing but the blue-black of the sky and the silver of the stars.

"Oh . . . wow," I finally say when I can get my breath back. "That's even prettier than the stars over the water."

"That's because the light from the village mutes them. Here, there's nothing to dim the sparkle. And each of them has a story," he says. He points to some stars. "Like there, that's Orion. He—"

"Was a hunter. He was turned into a constellation when he died," I finish for him, excitedly, almost giddy with the awareness that I actually know something.

"Yep." He sounds a little disappointed.

I give him a sidelong glance and point up. "What's that one?"

Gavin

I don't know how long we lie there, staring at stars, me pointing out constellations I'm sure she already knows, but too soon, I push to my feet, then lean over and help Evie to hers.

"Time to head back to camp. Asher is probably freaking

out." Under my breath, I mutter, "If we're lucky, maybe a coyote ate him."

"Gavin," Evie says, but there's laughter in her voice.

Sighing, I push through the underbrush, following the path we made earlier. Halfway there, I see a really pretty flower. It actually looks like two flowers attached to one another. The bottom part has orange, spiky petals and the top part is white and looks almost like a rose. It seems to almost glow in the moonlight. Remembering back to the gardens Evie had in Elysium, I don't think she's ever seen one like this.

I glance behind me, but she's not paying attention to me. She's watching the ground with a nervous expression. I'm sure she's hoping to avoid whatever slithered across her foot earlier. Probably just a snake looking for his burrow. But her distraction is enough, and I pluck the flower from the ground and carefully keep it from her sight.

It doesn't take long before the sounds of a crackling fire and Asher's grumbling find us and I push through into the little clearing with our tents.

Asher jumps up quickly, panic on his face. When he sees it's just us, the panic turns to relief, then anger. "Where the hell have you been? I was worried you got eaten by a bear or something."

I wave him away. "Bears haven't been seen here in years."

While Asher glowers at me, Evie slips past and weaves her way sleepily toward her tent. I stop her by placing my hand on my shoulder. "Wait. Evie. I found this for you."

She turns back around, confusion written on her face. I shove my hand forward, opening it, and show her the flower sitting in the palm of my hand.

She smiles and reaches out to take it, but I ignore her hand, pushing her hair aside, then sliding the flower in behind her ear to hold her hair back. She touches the flower and beams up at me, and for a second I see the girl I met in Elysium instead of the shadow of her she's become. Then the smile slides off her face and it's almost like a veil lowers over her eyes. They go from sparkling with joy to dull and lifeless.

She tilts her head, still looking at the flower, then plucks it from behind her ear. She pegs me with her eyes and I fight a shudder. "My flowers are *not* to be removed without my permission. Mother *will* be informed of this."

She skirts around me while all the hair on my body stands on end.

Not again.

She walks straight toward the woods, and I have to force my shaky legs to move forward. Just hearing her say "Mother" with that expression has made my muscles weak. But I have to stop her from wandering into the woods. Bears may not be an actual problem, but coyotes are. Along with snakes, bobcats, and panthers.

As if to prove my point, the telltale scream of the panther punctuates the air. It sets my teeth on edge how eerily it sounds like a woman.

"Uh . . . Evie?" Asher says, following me, following her.

To my—albeit short-lived— relief, she drops to her knees

just on this side of the woods. She's muttering to herself, but it's so quiet, I can't make out more than a few words.

". . . Unbelievable . . . poor thing . . . never have I . . ."

The entire time she's mumbling, her hands are moving—she's clenching one of her hands. Her other hand travels from in front of her, to beside her.

"Sara," she says without looking up. "These need to go to the Science Sector. Macie is expecting them."

Macie? My stomach sinks when she turns to look at us. What makes my chest even heavier is that I know when she looks at me, she isn't seeing me. Her eyes are still dead and dull.

She tilts her head to the side, looking around. "Where's that foolish girl now?" she mutters. She focuses on me and for a second I think she actually sees me, but she only says, "Locate Sara Penderson. Tell her she is to report to me right away. These herbs need immediate transportation." Then she turns back to the ground.

It hits me then, what she's doing, and it breaks my heart because I'm powerless to help her understand it's not real.

Asher meets my eyes over her head. "What is she doing?"

"She's tending her garden," I say, my voice cracking.

CHAPTER SIX

Of all the creatures found in the Outlands, the vulture-hawks are the most dangerous. Created by scientists during the War to help clean up the massive quantities of carcasses left behind by war and natural disaster, their hawk-like traits quickly proved to be useful as an almost perfect weapon.

—EXCERPT FROM *HUNTER'S FIELD GUIDE TO THE DANGEROUS ANIMALS OF THE OUTLANDS*

Gavin

I don't know what to do. I feel as lost and terrified as I did when she ran into the ocean. She's just sitting there, thinking she's cutting flowers. I'm afraid to touch her. Afraid that'll be the thing that breaks her completely.

Asher kneels next to me. "What should we do?"

"I don't know," I whisper.

For almost ten minutes we sit next to her, both of us unsure what to do. The more we sit here, the more I'm worried she's never going to come out of it.

But all of a sudden she blinks, her eyes focusing on mine.

"Gavin? Where . . . ?" She looks around, confusion written plainly on her face. She peers down at her hands, covered in dirt, then back up at me. Her chin trembles and she lets out a long, low sigh and closes her eyes. "It happened again?"

I touch her shoulder, but she jerks away, so I drop my hands and say, "Yes."

Her hands curl into the dirt. "I see." She swallows. "I, uh, I don't feel so well. I think I shall try to sleep now." Her voice is hollow as she slowly pushes herself up from the ground, dirt and dead leaves clinging to her skin. I jump up to help her, but she pushes me away. I'm sure I see tears sparkling on her lashes. I watch, helpless, as she walks toward her tent and into it.

She's always reminded me of the dolls Ann Marie used to play with when we were younger. But now, like this, Evie reminds me more of my grandmother's china dolls—the ones for show, not play. Fragile. Delicate. Where one wrong move—or a rogue baseball—would shatter them into a million pieces. I want to cradle her in my arms and hold her as close to me as I can. But I know better than to think she'll let me.

When I turn, Asher is staring at her with wide eyes and he's almost as pale as she is.

"Is she okay?" There's a slight tremor to his voice and when he looks at me, I see fear that mirrors mine. I don't want to see it. It only reminds me how powerless I am.

The answer is obviously no, and I want to shout that at him, but I bite down on the anger. Instead, I shake my head.

"I don't know. I just don't know," I say, letting fear turn into anger. "Why don't you go do something useful and get more wood for the fire?" I probably shouldn't be angry with him right now. He really has done us a favor by convincing his father to let us go. Except now I owe him a favor. Again. And I'd promised myself I'd never owe him for anything again.

Asher glares at me for a minute and I stare right back. Then he takes off into the trees. It isn't hard to hear him crashing around. It's a good thing we've already eaten; any game that was nearby is definitely gone now.

After a few minutes, I go in to check on Evie. She's asleep, so I sit on the ground by her head. When she calls my name out in her sleep, I lean down and whisper, "I'm here, Evie. I'm never going to leave you." I touch a hand to her freezing cheek. "We're going to find a solution to this. I promise."

I'm not sure if she hears me, but she seems soothed. My hand shakes when I pull it away. I don't know what to do. We're still days away from the city and I'm afraid she's not going to make it that long. That she'll have another episode and there'll be nothing I can do to stop it.

What started this, this time? I slip back out of the tent to sit next to the fire, thinking. She seemed like she was fine, a little tired, obviously, but she'd been laughing and joking with Asher while she helped him set up camp. She'd been just fine when we'd watched the stars. It could have been anything.

Asher startles me when he tosses an armful of wood in a

pile next to the fire. He doesn't say anything to me, only glances at Evie's tent, then heads back into the trees for more wood. After one more trip, he hunkers across from me. Silent, he pokes the fire with a stick, every once in a while tossing more wood onto it.

Afraid to fall asleep, I sit and fight to stay awake, but my eyes start to droop as I watch the dance of flames.

"How long has she been like this?" Asher asks, startling me. He, too, is staring into the fire.

I don't know how much I should say, so I don't say anything.

He looks up and meets my eyes over the flames. "Come on, Gavin. What do you think I'm going to do to her? What do you think that information is going to do?"

"I don't know, but I'm not taking any chances. You've hurt the ones I love enough."

Asher throws his hands in the air. "Christ! You still haven't let that go? That was years ago. We were kids! I didn't even know what I was doing!"

I look away from him. "It's not about that."

"The hell it isn't. Don't think I don't know why you didn't want me to help you get to the city. Don't think I don't know you warned Evie away from me."

My head jerks back in his direction. "What did you expect, Asher? You betrayed me! My family! To please your daddy you betrayed mine. And for what? To prove that you weren't one of us. Weren't an Outlander like me."

"I didn't know that was going to happen!" Asher shoves

the stick into the fire. A log falls and splits in two with a loud *crack*, sending a shower of sparks flying into the air.

Suddenly, Evie screams. It sounds like a name, but I can't make it out. Asher and I run to her tent, and I crawl into it with her. There's barely enough room for us; my head brushes the ceiling of the tent even sitting. Her eyes are open, but they're glazed, and it's obvious she isn't awake. She claws at the bag, trying to force herself out.

It's gut-wrenching seeing her like this. I lean down and whisper in her ear like I've done so many nights before. "It's okay. You're fine, Evie. I'm right here and Mother's long gone. Just rest now." I pet her arm, trying to soothe her. After a few more minutes of coaxing, she finally sinks into another fitful sleep. The only comfort I have is she won't remember anything in the morning.

I look up again and see Asher watching me with horrified eyes. "What *happened* down there, Gavin? And don't you *dare* bullshit me. I don't care what you think of me. I just want to help."

Glancing back down at Evie, I brush a strand of hair from her face and then sigh when she murmurs something about Timothy. "More than you could ever believe," I say. "Much more than you could ever believe."

Even though I wasn't going to tell Asher the whole messy story, when I sit back down by the fire it all slips out. I don't know why, but once I start I can't stop. It's like reliving it all over again, but seeing it from someone else's perspective.

My whole body feels separated from itself. I don't feel any of the terror I experienced the first time. I tell him about finding the tunnel in the cave, and the long trip down that ended with my hunting partner and I stumbling into Elysium, and the turret, which detected unregistered DNA, that claimed his life. Evie finding me, protecting me from Mother's wrath, and how she gave up everything to help me escape. How, because of me, she found out she'd been brainwashed to be an assassin for Mother, then later turned into breeding stock because of Mother's whims. The whole story of her being an Enforcer, and what it does to her.

When I finish, Asher is just staring at me, his eyes wide. He glances down at Evie and shakes his head. "Maybe it's better that she doesn't remember any of it."

"I thought that at first, too, but now she's got these damn nightmares every night. And flashes of memories when she least expects it. Sometimes, I barely recognize her anymore. Not to mention these strange episodes. I'm not sure if that's any better."

Asher goes back to staring into the fire. After a minute, he looks up at me again. "Why didn't you ever tell anyone?"

I frown. "Tell anyone what?"

"About me? You're so set that I ruined your life. Yet you know something about me that could destroy me, yet you haven't ever told anyone."

I blink. It takes me a minute to realize what he's talking about. I shake my head and roll my eyes. "One, because it's not any of my business, or anyone else's for that matter. And two, I'm not like you. When someone tells me something in secret, I don't share it with anyone for *any* reason."

He narrows his eyes at the fire, as if he's trying to puzzle that out. I decide that I'd rather be lying next to Evie than sitting out here with him. To make sure she can't sneak out of the tent without me knowing, I slide into the sleeping bag with her. Before long I find myself falling in and out of sleep, waking several times throughout the night to soothe Evie back to sleep when she has another of her fits.

When she wakes me for what feels like the thousandth time with a sharp kick in the shin and screaming incoherently again, I know I'll need to talk to Asher first thing in the morning and go over the map with him to come up with a better, faster route to the city. Evie needs help and she needs it quickly.

The birds singing in the trees wake me. I groan as I sit up. The little bit of sleep I've been getting is only a giant tease that makes my muscles sore. My joints pop when I stand and stretch.

To my surprise, Asher is already awake and poring over the map.

Trying to rub the sleep away, I run a hand over my face. "What'cha doin'?"

He startles, but moves over so I can sit next to him. "Trying to come up with a faster route."

I don't know why it annoys me that he had the same thought as me. I would have had to ask for his help anyway, since he's gone back and forth from the city much more than I have. At least this way it isn't a favor. So I nod and glance down at the map. "What do you think?"

"The fastest route is this way, through this town." He slides his finger over a black dot. "If we go that way, it will shave off at least three days from our trip. With any luck we could be in that town tonight and then another day, maybe two, and we'd be in Rushlake."

"Why didn't we go this way in the first place?"

"No one does." He won't look at me.

"Why?"

He hesitates, before finally saying, "I don't know. But my father was adamant that we never go that way."

Well, that's ominous. I think about it, weighing the risks. It's not smart to ignore that kind of warning in the Outlands. But with Evie getting worse and worse . . .

"Let's do it," I say.

We don't waste any more time; we both head back to camp and start tearing it down.

"We'd move faster if we don't carry anything that isn't necessary." Asher folds up his tent.

I lift an eyebrow. "You want to dump it?"

He shakes his head. "Starshine can carry it. This will be nothing for her. And then we'll have both hands free if we need them."

I nod. "Yeah, okay, let's get it all together."

We spend the next few minutes packing everything up and only when I have to, do I wake Evie. She's groggy and her eyes are still glazed with sleep, but she's lucid and able to walk and talk.

It worries me how flushed her skin is, but I can't think about it right now. There's nothing I can do about it. The only way to help her is to hurry our asses up and get her to the city.

Asher helps Evie onto the horse, while I break down our tent and then start securing our supplies to Starshine. I've just about tied the last supply, when I realize it's gotten really quiet. Too quiet. I look around, trying to figure out what has my instincts humming. The only sounds are Asher and Evie talking quietly. He's got her laughing again, with that stupid fake Southern gentleman charm he likes to use. Reluctantly, I have to admit I'm grateful. He's taking her mind off what happened last night. And considering how far it is to the city, and my increasing fears she won't make it all the way there without having another issue, making her happy needs to be a priority. Even though she's smiling and laughing, I can't help but hear how tired she sounds.

I glance around again, reassured that Evie is safe.

All of a sudden a scream tears through the silence. The three of us share a startled look and fear makes my nerves vibrate. I don't know what's screaming, but whatever it is, that's a sound of terror and pain. I've heard it before in the Outlands and it never leads to good things. The worst part is, it doesn't sound very far, and it's growing closer.

"What is that?" Evie's voice is shaky, and she's watching me with equal parts fear and trust and that scares me to death because I have no idea what to tell her. But I know we have to get out of here.

"You don't want to know," I finally say. "But we have to move. Now!" I fumble trying to tie the last item to Starshine, because the screaming is now so close I know whatever it is, is going to break into the clearing any second. My heart is beating so fast, it practically hurts and I can feel it pound in my head.

Then my worst fears come true: the animal—a deer, I think—bursts into the clearing. It's hard to tell exactly what it is because chunks of its skin are shredded off, claw marks mar the parts that aren't torn off, and blood covers the rest of it. One ear is completely gone and its mouth is open in its scream. And surrounding it, trailing behind it, is a whole flock of birds.

They're huge. At least three times larger than any bird I've ever seen. I curse under my breath. I've never heard of them being this close to the village. And I've never personally seen one, even considering I've been hunting in these woods since I was a kid. It makes me nervous that they're here. Not just for us, but for what it means for the village.

I can only stare in shocked horror as two of the birds grab the deer on each end of its body, lifting it into the air. I want to close my eyes. I know what's going to happen. I want to run to Evie and block her from seeing this, but I can't move. I'm petrified, stuck exactly as I am, forced to watch the deer's grizzly end as the rest of the flock latches on to it.

Horrible ripping and shredding sounds mix with the flapping racket. The deer's screams get louder and tear into my heart for only a second before it's abruptly cut off. And in just another second I see why. The flock breaks into three, flying into the trees with three different parts of the deer.

My stomach lurches as I glance at Evie and Asher. If it were just me, I probably wouldn't even be worried. I can protect myself, but I can't protect all of them and Evie has to be my top priority. I have to get out of here. I have to get Evie out of here.

"What are those things?" Evie asks. She doesn't look as nervous as I know she should be.

"Vulture-hawks," I say, trying to keep the fear from my voice. "They usually don't bother humans, but they're mean."

"I can see that," Asher says, staring up into the trees.

"We should get out of here. Now." I glance around for my gun so we can get going and my heart sinks when I see it. Oh God. It's still lying where I left it when I went to help load up Starshine. Just a few feet from where the birds disappeared into the trees.

I'm not willing to leave it behind. We'll need it. I'm sure of it.

I race toward it, hoping the birds will ignore me for their kill.

Something heavy falls to the ground just inches from my outstretched fingers. I'm certain it's the deer, but it's hard to tell after the work of the birds.

I don't want to, but it's like I have to. I look up into the branches and see them staring down at the deer—at me—with their red beady eyes. One of the birds makes its telltale caw, which sounds more like the screech of a hawk than a vulture, but has a way of making your skin crawl. Suddenly they're all making the same screeching sound. I slam my hands against my ears in an attempt to block out the sound. They start dropping from the tree to resume their attack on the dropped carcass. Their movements would be fascinating if they weren't so violent. I can hear the crunch of bones between their beaks.

We have to get out of here.

Then, without warning, one of the birds swoops down off its branch and flies straight toward me.

I duck and it misses, but there's an unmistakable look in its red eyes. It's out for blood.

"What the hell?" Asher yells at me. "I thought you said they don't bother humans!"

"I said they *usually* don't bother humans." Without sparing Asher a glance, I grab the shotgun.

Before he can react to that, the rest of the birds descend. Evie screams out when one claws at her wounded shoulder. Her eyes turn dark blue, the haze fading from them as if someone flipped a switch. I recognize that look. That's the one she got in Elysium whenever her "Conditioning" kicked in.

In a lightning-fast move, she snatches one of the birds from the air in front of her, but it pecks at her face, going for her eyes, and only misses because she tosses it aside. It squawks when it lands on the ground and struggles to get back up.

She immediately grabs another, but this time grabs its head and the muscles in her skinny arms bulge. A second later, the bird's head is no longer attached to its body.

Blood sprays into her face, but she only bares her teeth in a snarl and lunges for another.

Holy hell.

I grab Asher, who's trying his best to beat away the birds attacking her, but only getting his clothes and skin shredded in the process. There's already a long gash across his left eyebrow.

"Get on the horse!" I yell, hissing when a claw pierces the skin on my shoulder.

"What?" he yells back. The air around us is a frenzy of beating wings and piercing screeches.

I swing the gun like a bat at another bird. "I said, get on the horse. Get Evie out of here! I'll catch up." It gets around my swing, but I swing again and manage to knock it away.

If he doesn't hurry, I don't know how much longer I can keep them back. Starshine whinnies and starts to rear, but startles back to her feet when Evie plants a foot on her neck.

She's trying to stand, I realize, despite the horse's restless movements.

"What about you?" Asher swings his arms around again, causing the birds to scatter for a minute.

I force a smile. "I've got this. No big deal." He doesn't

look convinced and I raise my voice. "Get her the hell out of here. If you want to make up for what you did to me years ago, you'll get on the fucking horse and get her out of here."

He glances over at Evie, who is batting away more birds. One is tugging on her hair and she's screaming as it threatens to pull her off the horse. Another keeps swooping at her, but missing. She can't seem to get ahold of them anymore, and as I watch, her foot slips off Starshine's neck, dropping her hard onto the saddle. Asher takes a step closer to her.

"Don't you dare let anything happen to her," I yell to Asher, dodging another bird, and rearranging my grip on the shotgun. It's time to put this thing to use as more than a club. "Get her to the city. No matter what."

At first he doesn't say anything, but then he nods.

"Thank you," I say.

"I'm not doing this for you." He vaults onto the horse, taking the reins. A bird screeches as he knocks it away with a closed fist. The rest scatter when Starshine shakes her head violently.

Good enough. I nod and he nods back.

"She'll be safe. I promise," he yells back.

That gets Evie's attention and she looks over, her eyes clearing as they meet mine. The Enforcer is gone. For now.

She shakes her head, and struggles to get down, but I only smile at her.

"I love you, Evie." I press my fingers to my lips, then hold them out for a second, before I slap the horse on her back flank. She rears, then takes off away from the camp with a thunder of hooves.

Although I'm worried as hell to leave her in Asher's hands, I'm also relieved that I know she's getting away and safe. For now, at least.

That leaves me standing in the thick of all the birds, as they dive bomb and swirl around me, trying to grab pieces of flesh.

I pump my shotgun. "Bring it on!" I yell, and shoot.

CHAPTER SEVEN

Danger! Nuclear Materials. High Levels of Radiation Present.
—Rusted sign attached to one lone section of
chain-link fence in the Outlands

Evie

No!" I yell. "Gavin!" I struggle to get away from Asher, but
it's no use. My muscles are weak and I don't even so much as
budge him. "Gavin!" But he's gone now. I can't see him. The
birds have completely covered him.

My heart is in my throat, my stomach on the ground. I
want to scream. I want to cry. I want to kick something
until my toes are bloody. But none of those are going to do
Gavin any good.

And as much as I want to get away from Asher and run
back to Gavin, there are two birds who did not stay with
Gavin. One tears at me, while the other tries to rip chunks
from Asher. I bat at them with my arms, but my coordina-
tion is off and I miss every time.

My arms are more like limp noodles than muscle and bone. I don't understand where all the strength I had just seconds ago went.

One of the birds reaches out with its claws and grabs a hunk of hair, trying to lift me from the seat. Screaming, I flail around trying to dislodge it. If it weren't for Asher still holding me tightly around the waist, I would already be up in the air.

Holding me has left him open to the second bird, which slashes at him repeatedly. With each swipe of its talons it opens up another gash on Asher's body. He winces every time, but doesn't let go of me, or the reins. He just continues to press Starshine to run faster. I'm still no use. I'm just too slow. My arms don't want to cooperate. It's as if I'm trying to swing out underwater.

But then the bird slices across Asher's neck with its talon and, when I see the blood run down Asher's throat, there's this click inside of me. Just like before.

Everything seems to disappear except that gash. My blurry vision clears. My hearing is better, and even though I can still hear the slash of wings against air, the thunder of the horse's hoofbeats, and the birds' screeching caws, I'm able to differentiate one from the other. They're no longer just a mess of noises. But the most important change is the strength I feel in my arms and legs. I don't feel ill anymore and my muscles are no longer spaghetti.

As if on instinct, I grab the horn in front of me and push myself up on my arms. Asher removes his arm from around my waist and I kick my legs around so I'm completely turned around in the saddle and facing Asher, who stares at me wide-eyed for the shortest of seconds before turning his attention back to the trail in front of us and hooking his arm around my waist again.

I reach out to snatch the bird that's yanking on my hair. It wrenches out a good amount of hair and my vision swims for a minute as each strand disconnects from my head, but I don't let go. Instead, I adjust my grip on it like I had with the bird earlier, so I'm holding it with one hand on its head and the other around its body. Then I twist and yank.

There's a loud cracking, snapping sound and soon the bird is in two pieces. Without so much as a wince, I toss it to the ground and go for the second bird. Unfortunately, it saw what I did to the first and won't be as easy to grab. The good part is, it's got its full attention on me now. It dives at me instead of Asher this time.

I miss, but not because I couldn't get my body to cooperate—it flies just close enough to strike out at me, but never close enough for me to grab it. Then, after the fifth dive, I see my opening. Right before it tries to claw at me again, I twist my body to the side and lunge forward, practically falling onto the ground, but I've got the bird and Asher has me.

Again I rip its head off and toss the halves over Asher's head. Even through the horse's hoofbeats, I can hear the parts thump onto the ground.

Satisfied, I search the air to make sure there's no other, but it doesn't appear that any more have followed us. That only relieves me for a minute as I glance at Asher. For an instant I have the strongest, strangest urge to . . . kill him. To take his head between my hands and twist so I can watch his lifeless body hit the ground with a thud.

Just as quickly as I think it, I force the thought away, shaking off the shock. That's disgusting. Why would I possibly want to hurt Asher, let alone kill him? The hate and anger I feel toward him completely fades as I glance at his neck and the slashes over the rest of his body, then mine. We're both entirely lucky that we survived that. And if two were this hard to beat, I can't imagine what Gavin was—*is* going through.

There's so much adrenaline pouring through my veins, but my whole body is tense with anger. Is this something normal for me? Am I usually this angry? If . . . *when* I get my memories back, will I even like myself?

It's no use, though. As clear as my mind feels right now, I still can't recall anything. And the worst part is I don't know who I'm most angry with: Gavin for forcing me to leave, me for not fighting harder to stay, or Asher for taking me away.

However, anger is as useful as tears, which is to say not at all. So, I force my mind away from Gavin and focus instead on what I did to the birds. I have no idea how I was able to do what I did, but it didn't feel wrong. It felt right. Like that was how I was supposed to be, and I've just been living in a fog all this time. It's the first time I've felt right since I got here. I sneak glances at Asher trying to determine how he feels about what I did.

Asher only looks at me a few times, but I don't see disgust or any of the other things I imagined would be in his eyes after what I just did. Things *I* feel about what I just did. In fact, he seems impressed—the wonderment in his eyes speaks volumes—and not at all surprised that I did it. Or even that I *could* do it. It's as if he knew, which is odd, since *I* didn't even know I could do that.

Without warning, because I can't see where we're going, we burst out past the trees and into the full sunlight—and heat—of morning. I wince and shadow my eyes with my hand, but even then we don't stop. In fact, Asher pushes Starshine to run even faster.

I glare at Asher, but he won't look at me. Won't even let me turn around to sit properly. Instead, I'm stuck facing him, facing where Gavin got left behind.

"We have to go back!" I yell.

"No."

"But Gavin needs us!" Needs me. I can't leave him.

"He's smart. He'll figure out how to get out of that and find us. If we go back, we'll just get hurt." His eyes meet mine for a moment before focusing back on the path. "*You'll* get hurt. I'm not taking that chance."

"But look what I did to those birds! I could help him!" Even though what I did to the birds disgusts me, I wouldn't hesitate to do it again to save Gavin.

He shakes his head. "That was only two birds, Evie. Not a whole flock."

"But—"

"I'm not going back, Evie!"

His jaw is tight as he clenches his teeth and I know beyond a doubt that no matter what I say or do at this point, I'm not going to get him to change his mind. He thinks Gavin is dead. That much is obvious, but *I* refuse to believe it.

Gavin's not gone. He can't be.

If he doesn't want to go back to find Gavin, I'll force him. I sit up as straight as I can, and then in one quick movement I bring my arms and legs up to my chest and wedge them between Asher and me. Then, as hard and as quick as I can, I push. Asher's mouth forms a little "o" of surprise as he flips over the back of Starshine to land on his butt on the ground.

Starshine starts to slow, but before Asher can get back up, I spin around so I'm facing forward, grip the reins as I settle my feet into the stirrups, and tug on the reins as Gavin taught me. Starshine circles around, stomping her hooves, so we're both facing Asher. He's back on his feet now, brushing at the dirt on his pants and wincing.

I dig my heels into Starshine's sides and she bolts forward again, this time back in the direction we came from. Asher jumps out of the way just in time as we thunder past, but before we get more than a few meters—just inside the tree line—I hear a shrill whistle.

Starshine stops so quickly that she ends up standing straight up on her back legs and I find myself dangling from my fingertips. She leans a little to the left and I'm horrified to see she's going to fall directly onto me. I let go of the reins and fall to the ground with a thump. Somehow, Starshine manages to stay upright before dropping her hooves to the ground again with a thud that shakes the ground.

I scramble to my feet and climb onto her back again, but before I can kick her into action, Asher jumps onto her back behind me. He grabs hold of me, pressing my arms tightly against my sides. Even though I'm struggling, I can't seem to call up the strength I had earlier. He manages to twist me around, so I'm facing him again, somehow keeping my arms by my side and wrapping his own tightly around me, so I can't manage to get even a finger between us. But I continue to fight, struggling as much as I can.

"Stop it! Just stop. This is ridiculous. Don't make me hog-tie you, then hitch you to the horse like a blanket." He lifts an eyebrow. "I'll do it. Gavin asked me to protect you. And that's what I'm going to do. You're not going back that way. *Now stop trying to fight me!*" He shouts the last part, startling me, but that's not what makes me stop. It's what he said about Gavin.

I open and shut my mouth a few times, before I finally force out in a whisper, "Gavin put you up to this?"

He rubs a hand over the back of his neck. "Er . . . yes. But he'll catch up with us. Now come *on* before more of those things follow us." He glances around at the trees as if expecting the flock to appear at any minute, which I've no doubt is completely possible.

With no choice left, I try and get more comfortable. It's not an easy task. My thighs ache, not only from straddling the horse, but because of the way I'm turned and pressed tightly against Asher.

After wiggling and shimmying for a few moments, I finally let go of embarrassment and propriety and just hitch closer to Asher. I wrap one leg around his hip, letting the other lie over his thigh.

The adrenaline I had just moments ago rushes out of my veins as fast as it poured in. The horrid heat feels like I've ridden straight into a volcano. My head spins and my thoughts are all fuzzy and mushy.

I curse myself for it. I'm so sick of being sick. My eyes slowly close, and I fight to keep them open, but I'm losing the battle. I don't want to fall asleep now. I want to go back for Gavin. But my body doesn't care what I want and, despite all the sticky blood on his shirt, I slump over into Asher's chest.

His arm tightens around me, pulling me even closer. "It's okay. I've got you," he says.

I can't fight it anymore, so I stop trying, letting the exhaustion and sleep take over.

The slowing of the horse wakes me and I blink my eyes against the bright sun. I'm still tucked up tight against Asher, which makes me feel guilty and uncomfortable. I push away gently and clear my throat when we stop.

As if someone throws a switch, everything floods back and rage wells up inside me. My hands curl into fists, my nails biting into the flesh of my palm. I open my mouth again to demand we go back for Gavin. I don't care that Gavin told

Asher to leave, or that he'll meet us. We need to go back. But Asher looks down at me and the rage rushes out of me just as quickly as it came. He looks as miserable as I feel. Exhaustion is pouring off of him in waves.

Unsure of what to say, I close my mouth. Instead, I look down and notice the bleeding from the wound on his neck has slowed. And while it's still trickling blood, he's already lost a lot. His throat and shirt collar are covered in it. And so am I.

When he slides down off the horse, he stumbles a few steps before falling to his knees. I quickly slide down, ignoring the deep ache in my own joints and limp over to him, but he pushes me away.

"I'm fine," he says, his voice rusty. "Just tired."

I reach out to his bloody gash. "This needs attention. It's bad."

"It's fine. I'm fine," he says again, but when I go to get some water from the canteens and some cloth to clean his wounds anyway, he doesn't stop me.

Trying to locate Gavin's pack, I search through the supplies quickly. I'm sure he has some kind of first-aid kit. He's a hunter. Accidents happen. He'd need something to handle them. Of course, that makes me think about how he's all alone out there with *nothing* to help him.

If he made it out at all. My breath hitches at the thought, and I press a hand to my mouth before I quickly push the thought away, refusing to even think about it. If I do, then I'll fall apart, and I don't have time for that right now.

I find the little white box with the red cross on it and open it. There are only a few packets of sterile bandages and some gauze left. Since it's better than nothing, I sit next to Asher and pull out a few of the packets, pouring water on the gauze. I gently dab it on his neck, trying to get enough of the dirt and blood from the wound to see how bad it is.

He hisses, but doesn't stop me. The wound is deep. Thank Mother it missed any major blood vessels or muscles, although it still has to hurt like crazy.

"I'm sorry I kicked you," I say, not looking at him.

Asher rubs a hand over his chest. "Not gonna lie. It hurt like hell. But I get it. Let's just forget it. Consider it water under the bridge."

I nod. Using some gauze and the smaller adhesive bandages as a tape, I carefully bandage it. It's not pretty, but it's functional. Finished, I start to pour some more water onto the spare gauze to clean his throat, but he stops me.

"We may need those in the future. Here." Asher takes off his shirt and hands it to me. "Use this."

I wash the rest of his neck, trying to get the remainder of the dirt and blood off him. Probably not strictly necessary, but it gives me something to do and makes me feel useful.

After not being able to go back and help Gavin, I feel I need to do this one thing. My chest feels heavy when I think about him. Did he make it? Is he coming for us? Was he hurt? Does he need us? Does he need *me*?

Even though it's completely clean, I continue to scrub at Asher's neck. He grabs my wrist and stops me.

"Evie." His voice is soft. He waits for me to look up and, when I do, I see something in his eyes. But I refuse to acknowledge it. Not now. Not ever.

His eyes search my face, but I tug my hand from his grasp and turn away, meticulously placing each bandage into the box one by one and making sure they're placed perfectly before I stand and put the box back in the packs.

"You should rest," I say. "You've lost a lot of blood. And we should wait for Gavin to catch up." He doesn't say anything, and I can't stop myself from continuing. "It shouldn't be too much longer before he does, but I'll pull the stuff off Starshine. She should be able to rest, too."

At first he doesn't do anything, but I don't turn around. I just continue to uselessly pull at the ropes. When I can't get my fingers to cooperate enough to undo the knots, I move to the saddle straps and unbuckle them. I'm just about to try and lift the saddle when Asher's hands fall on top of mine.

He doesn't say anything. We just stand there, my hands on each side of the saddle, his over the top of mine. It's almost suffocating, him being that close, but I need it. I want to lean against him and soak up the comfort I know he'd offer. And Mother knows I need all the comfort I can get right now.

But then he sighs, and the moment passes. "I've got this," he says. "You shouldn't be lifting anything this heavy."

More exhausted than I care to admit, I nod, slipping my hands out from under his before ducking underneath his arms. I sit back down on the sandy ground a few meters away, as just those simple tasks have already exhausted me. With my whole achy body elated at being able to sit, I begin tracing designs with my finger in the dust.

I'm working so hard to keep from thinking of Gavin that I don't notice anything until I feel a burning in my shoulder. I hiss and yank away, twisting to see what's trying to take a chunk out of me now.

Asher sits behind me, holding a wet cloth in his hand. "You got clawed, too," he says quietly.

Moving my gaze to my shoulder, I see long gash marks next to the old ragged, infected wound that never seems to get better. I nod, gesturing for him to continue before turning away again.

He carefully cleans all the gashes on my upper chest and arms, and even tries to tend to the wound in my shoulder. Then he washes the blood from my face. When he finishes, I hug my legs to my chest and rest my cheek on my knees, closing my eyes against the bright sunlight. My head pounds from the intensity of its glare.

Asher sits next to me, and then taps my leg. I glance over to see he has a pair of sunglasses in his hand. *His* glasses. I take them with a grateful smile. "Thank you."

He shrugs. "You looked like you needed them."

For the next several hours we wait, Asher occasionally getting up to rustle through the pack or check on Starshine before sitting down a distance away from me. We stay lost in our own thoughts until the sun starts to disappear behind the horizon.

A strange sound comes from the direction of the woods

and I jump to my feet, straining to see what made it. However, all I see in every direction is more sand and dirt.

The sound comes again and Asher stands and mutters under his breath, "That's not good."

What did he say? I ask myself, but before I can ask aloud he's kneeling in front of me.

"I'm sorry, Evie. I—I don't think he's coming."

"We don't know that yet. He'll come. Any minute now."

He glances over when the strange sound splits the air again. "We can't wait any longer. That sound? It's coyotes. And they're going to be hunting soon. We need to get somewhere safe."

The name makes my blood run cold. Gavin said something about them last night. If he was afraid of them, then I know I should be, too.

"What about Gavin?" I demand. "He needs somewhere safe, too. He's going to be looking for us. We can't just leave!"

"*If* he's alive, he'll survive. He's a hunter. He knows how to survive out here way better than we do. He'll be fine."

He touches my leg when I don't move. "He'd want you to go, Evie. He made me promise to keep you safe. He's going to look for us someplace safe, right? He sent you away to protect you, not get eaten by coyotes because you're too damn stubborn to listen to reason."

I open my mouth to refuse again, but then shake my head, the logic of that finally entering my heat-addled brain. I don't know what coyotes are, but that sound makes my stomach twist with fear, and Gavin hadn't wanted to run into them either. He knows what they are and how to get away from them. I'm sure. And Asher's right; Gavin would want me somewhere safe. That's where he'll look for me.

"No. Of course, you're right." I hold out my hand to him. "Let's find somewhere safe."

Chapter Eight

Caution! Restricted territory. Nanite-affected area. Unauthorized entry banned.

—Sign bolted to Outland city gates

Evie

We don't push Starshine as fast this time, but Asher isn't exactly taking his time either. The sun is setting quickly and before long the entire area will be dark as pitch with nothing but the moon for our light. It's not even a full moon. I hope he slows down once the sun sets—I worry we will push Starshine too fast and something we can't see will cause her to trip and fall. I voice my concerns, but Asher brushes it off.

"The sooner we get to shelter, the safer we'll be," he tells me, not even glancing over his shoulder at me.

Left with no choice but to agree, I shut my mouth. I have to trust him to get me to where we need to go. Gavin obviously did. At least enough to send me away with him. And I trust Gavin.

As the sun disappears, so does the heat, and while the cool was a relief at first, now it has gone almost too far. Goose pimples prick my exposed flesh. I keep my arms wrapped around Asher's chest and press myself closer to him for warmth. It doesn't help all that much.

Another howl echoes in the air. It's a sad, lonely sound, but it chills me just the same. I realize that they're getting louder and more frequent. They sound like they're just behind us. I look around to see if the animals are close, but there's nothing but darkness.

Asher pats my calf. "It's all right. We're a moving target and, unless they're starving, they won't come after us."

"And if they *are* starving?"

He pauses, then says, "Then we'll have to hope Starshine's faster than they are."

I swallow. I don't like the sound of it, yet we don't have much choice.

"How far until we find shelter?" There is a small quaver in my voice. I hope he doesn't hear how afraid I am.

"Not much. A couple hours. Probably."

I fight back a groan. Hours. Of riding a horse. In the dark. With carnivorous animals at our heels. Lovely.

I immediately feel guilty. Gavin's probably having much worse problems. He doesn't even have a horse, or any gear, or food. Medical care. My chest aches for him.

For what feels like forever, we ride. Starshine is moving fast, blowing wind into my eyes so I squeeze them shut. My whole body aches with the effort of staying on her back and holding Asher. If I weren't gritting my teeth, they'd be chattering in the cold.

My shivering isn't helping my fatigue. My head throbs with each of the horse's footsteps. I suspect I'm dehydrated—my tongue keeps sticking to the roof of my mouth, and my lips are chapped and sore—but I don't dare ask Asher to stop for a drink of water. Who knows how far back the coyotes are. I imagine them pursuing us with pointed teeth, foaming mouths, and red eyes, their bodies as tall, if not taller than, Starshine's. I don't know what came over me earlier, but it's obviously not dependable. I can't rely on those instincts to appear again and help us out if we need it. So, I cling. I shiver. And I pray we get wherever we're going just a little faster and that Gavin isn't too far behind us.

When I tremble for what feels like the thousandth time, Asher rubs his hand up and down my leg, quickly.

"I'm sorry," he calls over his shoulder. "It shouldn't be long now."

Afraid to speak in case I bite off my tongue, I nod.

When I shudder again, he says, "Maybe you should sit in front of me. Like before. You'll stay warmer."

It's tempting, but I'm not sure I should. "No," I say.

"Are you sure? I don't mind. You'll be a lot warmer."

I can't even respond because I'm shaking so hard, so when I can finally say something, I murmur "Yes" into his ear.

He slows immediately, but then, without warning, I hear another howl, practically right next to us. I start, then glance over in the direction of the howl. This time I see something. A set of yellow, glowing eyes.

Then I hear it—just under the sound of the horse's hoofbeats is the sound of other animals running and panting for breath.

"Asher?" I say.

"I see 'em," he responds back between clenched teeth. He digs his heel further into Starshine's sides and she jumps forward, running as fast as she had before.

One of the dog-like creatures makes a leap at us, just barely missing my leg. I bite back a scream and cling to Asher.

"Don't panic. They'll sense your fear."

I try not to, but when another one lunges at me, its claws scraping over the exposed skin of my leg, I can't help but scream. My leg is on fire and I can feel and smell the blood dripping down it.

"Evie!" Asher yells back. "Did they get you?"

Before I can answer, another dog jumps at us and I kick out with everything I have. I feel my foot connect with something fleshy and the dog yelps.

"Evie! What happened? Are you hurt?"

I can't speak over the pain so I just nod, but then I realize he can't see it, so I force out a "Yes" through gritted teeth.

"How bad?"

Before I can answer, yet another dog leaps at us, this time grabbing onto Starshine's backend.

She rears with a high-pitched whinny that sounds disturbingly like a scream, and it's everything I can do to hang on to Asher. The dog is shaken loose and falls with a yelp to the ground. Starshine lands with a bone-jarring thump, and if it's possible, she runs even faster.

Burying my face into Asher's back, I hang on to him as tightly as I can. Through his back I can hear him murmuring. "Come on. Just a little more. Almost there."

The dog-beasts are still behind us—I can hear them—but they're falling back by the second. I turn and watch as their yellow eyes grow smaller and smaller until they disappear completely in the dark.

Relieved and perilously close to sobbing, I press my lips together and my body even closer to Asher. He doesn't slow down for several minutes, only letting Starshine drop to a fast walk when the horse's breath is chugging like an engine ready to fail.

He turns to me and his eyes are wide in the moonlight.

"Are you okay?"

"I—I don't know. They clawed my leg."

He glances down, but I doubt there's enough light for him to see anything.

"We're almost there," he says after a minute. "Just a few more minutes. I think. Can you make it that long?"

"Of course," I say, although I don't know for certain. But I know now why he wanted us to get away from where we were so badly. There is absolutely no way I'm letting him stop to take a look at my leg. I'd rather lose it completely than give those . . . things time to catch up.

Gavin flits into my mind again. I seriously hope he found

a safe place before we did. Those things were not playing around. I don't even want to think what they'd do to him if they found him.

True to Asher's word, it's only a few minutes before I see what looks like the shadow of buildings rising up out of the dark. Asher lets out a relieved sigh and pushes Starshine to put on an extra burst of speed, racing toward them.

He stops short when he sees a tall wall surrounding the town, like the one surrounding our village. He follows it around until we find a large gate. It's closed, as it should be after dark, but unlike in our village there is no sign of a guard.

Asher pulls Starshine to a halt and then jumps off. "Stay here," he says, and I nod, trying to rub warmth into my arms and looking around to see if I can see any of those dog-beasts again. It terrifies me, standing out in the open like this, but I don't see that I have a choice. There is a protocol we have to follow, I'm sure. There always is.

"Hello?" Asher calls. "Anyone here?"

There's no response but the echo of his voice. I tremble again and curl into myself, trying to make myself as small as possible. It's entirely too quiet for my tastes. The only sounds are the echoes of Asher's voice.

"We're from Black Star Cove. A village a few days' travel east of here. We just want some shelter for the night as we pass through to Rushlake City."

Nothing. Not even the sound of wind.

Asher turns back to me and shrugs before turning back to the gate. He presses on one of the gate doors and with a loud squeal it swings open. It's worse than the proverbial nails on a chalkboard. I slap my hands to my ears, then wince when the movement causes my head to feel like I've split it open.

He freezes, waiting for an alarm to go up, but when it doesn't, he pushes the gate wider. It squeals again, but nothing else happens. He then comes back to me, and takes the reins, guiding Starshine through the gates before shutting them again.

"Guess no one's home," he says.

I don't say anything. Even though I should feel better that we're not just standing outside the gates waiting to be those animals' next meal, the whole place has my nerve endings tickling. I worry my pendant between my fingers. The village is dark, made darker in some spots because of the buildings that block out the moonlight. Almost all of the buildings reach for the stars, jutting out of the sand like fingers. I cannot believe how tall they are. They are at least three or four times taller than the mayor's house in the village. Not to mention intimidating, with their yawning doorways and hundreds of dusty windows that show us nothing but inky darkness. The shadows are so thick it's almost like I could reach out and feel a solid wall.

"What is this place?" I shudder as I stare into yet another pitch-black opening.

"It's a city."

"Not the one we're going to, right?" Please tell me this isn't the city that was supposed to cure me.

"No. This one is smaller. And probably abandoned, from the looks of it."

Asher jumps back into the saddle and continues farther into the city, slowly. It's still too quiet. Disturbingly so. The only sound is Starshine's hooves making clacking sounds on the hard ground. I shiver, but this time it has nothing to do with the cold.

"Asphalt," Asher murmurs. "Interesting."

I glance around, and that's when I see them. People. A bunch of them, standing in strange poses—as if time stopped and they were stuck in whatever move they were making at the time—just outside the doors of one of the tall buildings. I straighten and my hand tightens on Asher's shoulder.

"What's wrong?" He turns to look at me when I don't respond. He follows my gaze and pulls Starshine to a halt. "Is that a person?"

"People. I think." I keep my shaking voice quiet. I don't know why, only that I'm almost scared to talk. As if the people are only sleeping and I'll disturb them if I speak at a normal volume.

"Hello?" he calls to them, making me jump. "Can you help us?"

They don't so much as budge and we exchange a look before he dismounts and cautiously proceeds toward them. When he's within touching distance, he pauses, then starts laughing.

"What?" I demand. What could possibly be funny about any of this?

"They're just statues!" he says.

"Statues?" I rub a hand over my forehead and look again. The placement is odd. And why in Mother's name would they make them in such odd poses? It makes me wonder who lives here.

"That's weird," Asher says, tilting his head sideways as he studies the statues.

"What?" What I really want to ask is *What now?*, but I don't.

"They're all wearing real clothes. They're a bit torn and dirty, but they're real clothes." He tugs on one of the sleeves of the closest statue. I try to come up with an explanation, but can't. The whole thing is sort of creepy.

Asher comes back and vaults onto Starshine, prodding her forward with his heel. It isn't long before we see more of the eerie statues. They're placed so haphazardly, I start to wonder if they were positioned to make it appear as if people are living here. Like, maybe this town was meant to be some strange museum of what the world was like before the War. Some are clustered around doors leading into buildings, others at the cross streets we pass. The closer we get to the city center, the more there are.

"Whoa!" Asher exclaims as we get to a large, squat structure made of metal and glass, standing in the middle of the path.

"What is that?" I ask.

"It's a car. Like they have in Rushlake. But it's all rusted and falling apart."

Peering over his shoulder, I see more of them. They line up in an almost straight line behind the first one, reaching as far as I can see. All in various stages of falling apart. I try to get a good look as we pass; then I gasp.

"Asher!" I say, pointing excitedly. "Look. Inside the cars. More statues."

Even in the dark, I can see his eyes widen. "What the hell?"

But there's no ready explanation and we continue forward, ogling at the strangeness of it all. As we continue, we see more dispersed between the cars. Some are posed as if running from something. Running in the *opposite* direction we're moving. Others are holding smaller, child-sized statues in their stone arms. Some are huddled close to their cars, their arms over their heads. I can't understand why anyone would build something like this. It's creepy.

I shudder and wrap my arms around my body. "What *is* this place?"

"I don't know," Asher responds, and even he has a slight waver in his voice. When he squeezes my knee in comfort, there is nothing comforting about the tremor in his hand.

And while I can't help but think we should turn around, curiosity has me gripped tight. We push forward. The closer to the center we get, the more haphazard the placement of the cars and statues. It is as if the child playing with his toys got tired of setting them straight and just tossed them about and left them however they fell.

I stare at yet another statue as we pass by so closely I can see the expression on its face. Its mouth is wide open as if screaming and terror is etched all over its face.

When we finally get to what appears to be the center of town, the building that stood there is completely gone. The only thing left is a huge crater where it stood. Bits of metal, concrete, and glass litter the circle.

Asher leaps from the horse and strides toward the crater. Curious and unwilling to be left alone in this morbid city, I follow at his heels. When I make it next to him, he reaches out and grips my hand tightly in his. And this time I don't pull away. In fact I squeeze harder, clamping both my hands around his. In this dead city of fake people, it's nice to have a connection to someone alive.

Together we walk to the center of the crater, then stop. He releases my hand and kneels down in the dirt to sift through the wreckage. After a minute or two he lifts something up and studies it, then sighs, and hands it to me.

I take it and look it over. It appears to be a human hand, carved in stone and cut off at the wrist.

"What is this? A piece of one of those statues?" I scrutinize the piece. It feels like stone, but it's different. More porous. It makes my skin crawl just holding it.

"Yes. And no," he says, studying more of the debris. "They're not statues."

"Then what are they?"

"They're . . . they *were* people."

I drop the hand, a sour taste filling my mouth. When he

looks up at me, his eyes are filled with horror. I almost wonder if it isn't just a mirror reflecting back what I'm feeling.

"This town was destroyed with a nanobomb."

"Nanobomb?" For some reason the term sounds familiar to me, but I can't place where I heard the term.

He stands, brushing the dirt from his hands. "They were used during the War when they wanted to overtake an entire city, but didn't want to completely destroy it, or wanted to keep it useable. It was the quickest way."

"How?" I wheeze out. My chest feels like there's a band around it compressing until I'm breathless.

He meets my eyes and I know what he's going to say before he does. "When the bomb explodes, it disperses nanobots—tiny robots so small that they're invisible to the human eye—into the air like an aerosol. When a person breathes the aerosol in, they breathe in the nanobots, and they start attacking the body from the inside out. Sort of like a virus. In this case, it caused the body to calcify at an accelerated rate. Virtually turning them into stone statues."

CHAPTER NINE

Toward the end of the twenty-first century, nuclear weapons were almost completely abandoned in favor of the more effective bioweapons. These weapons could easily clear out entire cities, without making them uninhabitable for invading soldiers.

—EXCERPT FROM *A BRIEF HISTORY OF THE 21ST CENTURY*, "BIOWARFARE"

Evie

Oh, Mother," I gasp, but a band of fear must be compressing my chest, because when I suck in a breath it catches in my throat and I start coughing. Coughing so hard that blackness creeps in the sides of my vision until all I can see is a pinprick of the scene in front of me.

Asher slaps my back as if I'm choking, but it doesn't help. It only makes it worse, a metallic taste coating the back of my tongue. But finally I stop and, while I'm catching my breath, I look around at the statues that stand outside the circle. It's all so hard to believe, but explains a lot of things. The way they're dressed in real clothes, the poses, the looks of terror.

"But . . . why are they still here? Why did they just leave them like that?" Tears sting my eyes and my voice shakes, but disgust is almost as prominent as the sadness ripping through me that anyone could be so callous.

Asher won't meet my eyes when he says, "I don't really know, but considering how much damage there is to the surrounding buildings, I have to think this was one of the sites where they tested the prototypes. They probably realized that this city was too far gone to do anything with it and left it."

Now the disgust is definitely more prominent than the sadness. It makes me speechless. The lack of respect is just mind-blowing.

Asher is watching me with a strange look. "Did you ask for your mother a minute ago?"

At first I have no idea what he's talking about and the change of subject is a little jolting; then I realize he means what I said before I started choking.

I wince and slump my shoulders, ducking my head so I don't have to look at him when I say, "It's just something I say . . . sometimes. When things surprise me."

"Why?"

It doesn't sound anything other than curious, so I relax a little. "I don't know. Gavin says it's something from . . . before. One of the things that stuck in my head even after I lost everything else. I don't know why I do it, and Gavin doesn't tell me . . ." I trail off when I realize how silly that sounds. My saying something and expecting someone else to tell me what it means. It's ludicrous. I hate it. Feeling helpless like this.

Asher stares at me with this strange look on his face, before he shakes his head. I think I hear him mutter, "Despicable," but before I can question him, he smiles at me and says, "You're a strange one, Princess. Come on. We need to find somewhere warm to sleep before you shiver yourself into pieces."

It's then that I notice I'm a bundle of tremors. Every muscle in my body aches, especially my heart, which is beating furiously in my chest. My lungs feel like they're being compressed against my ribs. I rub the heel of my hand against my rib cage.

My teeth are chattering again, but I can't tell if it's from fear or the cold. Either way, I just want to leave this city. There's no way I'm staying here. Not with these statues watching over us.

When I say as much to Asher, he says, "We don't have much choice. This is the safest place until sunrise." As if to punctuate his claim, a howl disturbs the quiet of the town. I rub absently at the scratches on my legs. "Besides," he continues, "this is where I told Gavin we were heading. *If* he's coming, he'll try to meet us here."

I can tell he doesn't really believe Gavin is coming, but I'm not willing to take the chance. If waiting in some creepy town is what I need to do, then that's what I'll do. "Where do we start?"

"Let's try to find a spot inside one of these buildings."

That, of course, proves easier said than done. Almost all of the structures are so badly damaged they'd either provide us no protection from the elements, or are in danger of falling over. It isn't until we get to the other side of the town, as far from the bomb blast as possible, that we find one relatively intact. It's the smallest of them. Just a squat block building with a flat roof.

Asher kicks open the door, and peers inside, like he has at least a hundred times in the last hour. But this time, when he emerges, he has a smile in his voice.

"Found one." His voice is scratchy from exhaustion.

While I get down from Starshine, he pulls a flashlight from one of the packs. "Come on, we'll check the rest of this building out together. I don't want to leave you out here all alone."

I don't want to be alone either, but . . . "What about Gavin?"

He frowns. "What about him?"

I make a disgusted sound in my throat. "What if he comes while we're inside? How will he know where we are?"

He rolls his head on his shoulders and rubs his eyes. "Evie . . ."

I know what he's going to say, but I don't care. I cross my arms over my chest. "Look, I don't care what you think. He got away from the birds. All right? He got away and you're not going to convince me any different. Now how is he going to know we're inside?" Even I can hear the desperation in my voice, but I ignore it.

His eyebrows have winged up under his hair and he just stares at me. Finally, he sighs. "Starshine. She'll wait here until we get back."

"Wait." I glance over at her and see her staring at us with sad eyes. "We just can't leave her out here."

He mutters something under his breath, but says aloud, "We won't. We're just going to check this place out and make sure it's safe. We'll come back out for her in a few minutes. I'm sure no one's around here to care whether we bring her in the building to stay warm. And by that time," he continues when I open my mouth, "I'll have figured out a way to mark that we're here."

Uncomfortable with leaving her out here and still doubtful Gavin will find us, I don't immediately follow when Asher disappears through the open door.

Only when he pokes his head back out and asks "Coming?" do I make up my mind and follow him in. It's only for a few minutes. We'll be right back out.

Inside, our flashlight reveals glimpses of the place. It's a strange mishmash of a house and some type of military out-post. As if someone lived here until the very moment the army took over. I wonder if that happened before or after the bomb drop. If it was before, that would explain a lot—the calcified statue people, and how they were just left. They were probably used as a deterrent to keep people away from this area. The statues certainly gave the abandoned city a creepy feeling and if I could have avoided it, I would have.

I follow Asher as he wanders around the tiny building

until we locate a steel door set into the wall of a long hallway.

He hands me the flashlight and forces the door open. Surprisingly it opens without so much as a squeak or squeal. I hand him back the flashlight, then follow closely behind him as he walks through the door.

It's nothing but a pitch-black corridor. No light reaches in here, and my nerve endings go into overdrive. I try to focus on the area illuminated by the flashlight, but a memory is tugging at my mind.

Without warning, the lights flicker and go out throughout the complex. The red emergency lights stay lit, but ahead the hallway is dark. I reach into my pack and pull out my flashlight pin.

When I click it on, the light cuts through the darkness. It's actually brighter than the lights that would have lit the hallway, but it isn't big enough to dispel all of the gloom.

We keep our guard up, sticking close together. Our arms brush together, and at first I have to fight the urge to jerk my arm away. I bite my tongue, hoping the pain will be enough to distract me from my homicidal thoughts, but it isn't until he squeezes my hand—a simple gesture of his promise to protect me—that I'm able to push the thoughts to the side.

I can't fight this much longer. I hope we reach the submersibles soon.

After a few minutes, he releases my hand and I have to resist the urge to grab out for him again. It's the only thing grounding me from going crazy, but we can't take the chance of holding hands. We don't know what's ahead.

Suddenly my foot slides in something wet and I almost fall to the ground. I throw my hands out to the side to catch myself with the walls.

When I lift my foot, my shoe makes a sucking sound. I tap Gavin on the shoulder, then point to the floor. "There's something here," I say.

He nods and stands watch over me, while I kneel to shine the small light onto the floor, careful not to let my knee dip into whatever the sticky mess is. It's a puddle of something dark red, almost purple. I tilt my head, then stick my finger in it and bring it nearer to me to study. It's slightly tacky, like wet glue or drying paint.

Bringing it to my nose, I sniff at it. It has a metallic scent, like rust. Then it hits me. I know exactly what this is. It bothers me that it took me that long to figure it out.

When I turn to show Gavin, he's already staring at the puddle with a look of horror on his face. "Blood?" he asks.

"Oh, Mother," I whisper, staring at my hands. They're covered in blood. "No. No. It's not real. Not again."

"Evie?" Asher asks, turning toward me. When he does, he illuminates the walls, revealing a patchwork of gory handprints.

I shake my head. "No. No."

I stare, unable to blink while a rivulet of blood escapes and trickles down from the tip of one print's thumb. They're fresh. Whoever made these isn't far away.

A sound comes from behind me and I spin around, finding more prints. Some of these are near the floor and aimed upward, as if someone had crawled up from the ground. I press my hands to my eyes. This can't be real. Not again. My hands are wet—tacky—and I remember the blood on them. I yank them away with a whimper.

"Evie?" Someone touches my arm. It must be Asher, but the voice warps like a record slowing down. "What's wrong?"

It isn't Asher. It's Gavin, and he's smiling at me. His chin is already red, and more blood oozes from the space between his teeth. It's not a smile. Not at all.

"Gavin!" I can only whisper because fear has robbed me of my voice. I can't breathe. My chest feels like a horse is sitting on it.

His jaw drops, almost as if he means to speak, but instead blood spills out to patter wetly into the congealing puddles at my feet. He raises one hand to me, stretching his fingers like he can't decide if he wants to caress my cheek or grab my face. The action splits white cracks into the blood coating his palm. I want to run, but all I can do is lean away from him, my muscles tight and protesting.

"You must be starving," he says with that same strange smile. When he lifts his other hand into view, he's holding a severed arm.

Finally, my body frees me from its paralysis. I spin around and try to race away, but I find myself looking into the face of a girl about my age. Her blond hair is stained pink and red, matted to her head. There's something gray clinging to her temple that for some reason I'm certain came from inside her head. Her scalp is split open there, showing a glint of bone, but she doesn't seem to care. She stares at me, unaware of the trickle of blood running into her right eye. I have the strange thought that her eyes are a lovely sapphire color, but it's obscured by the hate in them as they bore into mine.

Macie! my mind whispers. And for a second, I'm overjoyed, but— "You're dead," I say.

"You left me," she says. "You left me to die. You didn't even try to help me. You're selfish, Evie. How could you?"

"I tried. I wanted to. But . . . you—you were already gone," I say, fighting the urge to cough. I can't seem to catch my breath and every time I inhale I hear a high-pitched wheezing sound. "I—I avenged you."

"You took my life, then you took my love." Her eyes roll back up into her head so only the white shows, yet she still walks toward me. "I trusted you. I *helped* you. And you left me to die, then killed the only man I ever really cared about. You're a murderer, Evelyn. A cold-blooded murderer."

"No, no," I whisper and back up, right into someone. I whirl and see Gavin again.

Up close, I see deep gouges in his cheeks and forehead. *The birds.* Blood runs freely from his injuries, making his face a mask of blood.

"You left me, too. You said you loved me, but it was a lie. You've done nothing but want to go back home since you got here. Then you ran away with Asher when I needed you the most."

"No, no! That's not true. I—I wanted to help you, Gavin,

but I couldn't get down. It's Asher's fault! He wouldn't let me down. I tried! Really I did."

"Liar," he and Macie yell, both of them stepping forward and trying to pin me between them. "You didn't care. You never cared."

Shaking my head, I try to slip out from between them. Their voices grow louder and louder, until it's just one horrifying scream. I slap my hands to my ears and run as fast as I can away from them. The walls are just a blur of black and red.

I run as fast and as far as I can, but they're chasing me, the sound of their footsteps echoing behind me.

"Evie!" they call after me. "Wait!"

But I don't stop. I can't stop. No matter what, I can't stop.

I can't breathe. My lungs are on fire and my legs are shaking from exhaustion. I don't know how much longer I can run. I don't even know where I'm going.

"Evie! Stop! Please!" a familiar voice calls after me.

White lights bob ahead of me. The ghosts of the people I killed. I'm a murderer. A killer. I turn down a corridor, and for a minute they're gone, but that relief is short-lived. They spring back up in front of me. Taunting me.

"There's a poor wee little lamby . . ."

They want me to follow them to my own grave.

"The bees and the butterflies pickin' at its eyes . . ."

Screaming, I take another turn, desperate to get away, but the voices echo off the rusting walls. *"The poor wee thing cried for her mammy."*

"No!" Without warning, my legs give out on me and I crash onto the ground. The skin on the palms of my hands and knees tear, causing tears to prick at my eyes. The floor is wet, sticky, and the stink of iron clogs my nose. My lungs heave, pulling the metallic smell—fresh and old mingled—deep into my body. I can smell it, taste it, feel it inside me like a sickness.

I try to push myself up, but I can't. My legs and arms are shaking too much. So I just lie there, coughing and wheezing, tears pouring from my eyes.

A hand touches my back and I jerk up, trying to force it away. Again, it's no use—I don't even budge it. "Evie. It's okay. I'm here," the voice says. "It's not real. Whatever it is you're seeing, it isn't real, but I am. And I'm going to help you. I just need you to trust me."

The voice is familiar, so I turn slowly to see who it is. The person is kneeling over me, the light in his hand facing down into the pool of water I'm lying in and reflecting up enough that I can see his face clearly.

"Asher?" I ask, feeling a huge amount of relief. There's no blood on him. His eyes are clear, if a little worried, but he's normal. *Normal!* And I can't hear the voices anymore.

He nods. "I'm right here. Don't worry."

Forcing myself to muster all the energy I have, I throw myself at him, burying my face into his shoulder. He falls back onto his butt, but holds me to him, his arms tight around my back. "It's okay. You're okay. Nothing is going to hurt you," he repeats over and over again, patting my back as if I were a fussy baby.

I can only sob and gasp into his shirt as the terror fades away and I remember where I am.

After a long while, I pull away and wipe my face on my sleeve, embarrassed by my behavior. *Tears are a weakness.*

He watches me for a moment, then says, "Are you okay?"

I nod and refuse to look at him. "Yes. I am. Now. I'm sorry. I don't know what happened. I saw . . . Gavin and a girl—Macie, I think . . ." I trail off when I realize he will have no idea what I'm talking about. *I* don't even really know what I'm talking about; how can I expect him to?

"It's okay. It's my fault. I shouldn't have brought you in here."

We sit quietly for a few minutes before he stands. "Can you walk?"

"I think so." Despite the fact that my legs still shake and burn as if they're on fire, I push myself up. No more tears. No more weakness, I promise myself.

"Don't worry. We'll figure a way out of here."

We try to retrace our steps, but I don't remember how I got to where I was, and Asher was too busy trying to keep up with me to pay attention. So we find ourselves exhausted, in pain, and thoroughly lost.

We eventually find a large supply room and Asher shines his light around it. One of the walls is stacked to the ceiling with boxes, but is otherwise empty. He shuts the door and shoves some of the bigger boxes in front of it, preventing anyone from entering without our knowledge.

"We should try to get some sleep," he says, and I nod. I'm absolutely exhausted. My head is foggy with it.

He goes through a couple of the easily reachable boxes, and dumps their contents onto the floor. It's nothing useful, of course. I don't even know what any of it is. However, he takes the now empty box and starts tearing it apart.

When he's finished doing whatever it is he's doing to it, he lays it down on the dusty floor, and gestures for me to lie on it. Exhausted, I curl up in the middle of it, surprised by how comfortable it actually is. It isn't exactly a feather bed, but it's a hundred times better than the cold, hard floor. However, even though it's not as cold in here as it was outside, I continue to shiver—huge shudders that wrack my body. It's in that moment that I really, really miss Gavin. My throat is thick with unshed tears.

He's never going to find us. When he finds the city, he's not going to find us and he'll think we left him and it's my fault again. A tiny voice in my head whispers that it doesn't matter because he's dead anyway, and *that* is my fault, too.

I curl tighter into a ball. No. He's not dead. I refuse to believe it.

Asher shuffles closer, looks down at me for a moment, then seems to make up his mind about something and crawls next to me, lying on his back and obviously taking care not to touch me. Instantly, I feel warmer with his body heat licking at my skin and I crave more of it. And even though a voice yells at me in my head not to, that skin-to-skin contact is punishable by death, I roll over and curl into his side, resting my head on his chest. He tenses immediately, but doesn't push me away. After some hesitation, his arms come around me, holding me to him.

Soon, our combined body heat makes sleeping bearable and I fall asleep, soothed by the sound of his heartbeat.

CHAPTER TEN

Due to possible biohazard or nanobot contamination, all personnel must exit through the decontamination stations and submit to a full body scan.

—SIGN BOLTED TO WALL IN UNDERGROUND FACILITY

Evie

I wake when Asher gets up. Although it's still as dark as before, my eyes are already adjusted and I can see fairly clearly now. It's obvious he's trying to be as quiet as possible, and if I hadn't noticed the drop in temperature between us, I probably wouldn't have awakened.

"Where are you going?" I sit up and rub at my scratchy eyes.

He starts, then turns around. "Sorry to wake you, Princess. I was going to try and find a way out of here."

"Without me?" That stings. That he'd just leave me all alone here. Especially after what I went through last night. I draw my knees up to my chest and hug them to me.

"Only temporarily. As soon as I found the exit, I would have come back for you."

I can't help but glare at him. "And if you ended up more lost? Then what?"

From the way his face twists up I can tell that wasn't something he'd considered. He confirms it when he doesn't say anything. It worries—terrifies—me that he'd leave me like that, but then again, I guess I can't really blame him either. I suppose after what happened last night, if I'd been in his position, the thought of trying to find the exit alone would have crossed my mind as well.

I push myself shakily to my feet and sway for a second when my head spins. It's not long, but obviously long enough to scare Asher as he rushes to me and slips an arm around my waist. I push him away.

"I'm not helpless. I can walk by myself. I just got up too fast. And I'm tired."

He removes his arm, but narrows his eyes at me, then turns back to the door. He moves the boxes out of the way, then flicks the flashlight back on. We try retracing the steps we took the night before, but it's hard. All of the corridors look the same, especially in the dark, and with all its corners and twists and turns it feels like a gigantic maze. I almost expect to wind up face to face with a sphinx, with a riddle to figure out.

We take our time, trying to remember each hallway we go through and create a map inside our heads. Asher keeps mumbling "Left, right, left, left" under his breath every time we turn a corridor or go down a set of stairs, and I'm tempted to be perverse and ask him which way to go. Left? Or right? Just to see him get flustered when he forgets the pattern. But I don't because I've lost track of the pattern myself and if he remembers it, it may be the only way we get out.

There's still a chill in the air, and it causes goose pimples to rise on my skin. The scent of mildew and something worse—something that I can't place—is thick and causes my already sore lungs to fight each and every breath. The light from Asher's flashlight is dim, and only reveals meters and meters of gray walls. The lack of color makes me feel like my eyes aren't focusing, and I find myself blinking too often. Sound travels strangely as we walk, sometimes echoing, sometimes seeming to swallow even the soft sounds of Asher's mumbles, my wheezing, and our shoes scraping against the debris on the floor. It has me on edge, but I don't say anything to Asher, just stay close to him. The only other sound is the occasional plop of water as it drips onto the floor, startling me every time.

In the back of my mind, I hear the echoes of memories trying to force their way up to the front, but I shove them back every time.

I won't have another attack. Not if I can help it.

As we walk, curiosity causes us to push open some of the doors. We use the flashlight to illuminate as much of the rooms as it can, which isn't much. Each one shows us something new. Some look like some sort of lab. Others are obviously sleeping quarters. And others are like nothing I've ever seen before. Even Asher has no clue what they could be. One of these rooms has odd machines set in a half circle around a strange bed. The machines look to be made of plastic and are really tall. At least as tall as Asher. All sorts of tubes and wires are hanging off each one and there's an accordioned attachment on the side of the machine. Silver metal boxes rest on top with the words "Halothane," "Isoflurane," and "Desflurane" on the side of them.

I frown and enter the room, trying to get a closer look.

"Evie! Get back here," Asher whisper-yells.

I ignore him and continue toward the machine. To the right and slightly above the strange metal boxes, there's a thing that looks like Gavin's television screen. Below the boxes there are four or so dials. Each dial has numbers and letters below it that look like some kind of chemical compound. And I have *no* idea how I know *that*.

There's a thick layer of dust on the contraptions, so obviously this place has been abandoned for a while. I open the top drawer of the machine and find syringes, medicine vials, and tubes. With a shudder, I quickly shut the drawer and turn toward the bed. Straps crisscross over the top and, like the machine, it's covered in dust.

"What is this?" I ask, trailing a finger over the strange machine.

"Anesthesia. It's used to put people to sleep for medical procedures and . . . experiments . . ."

How odd, I think and go back to join Asher, who takes my arm, firmly leading me out of the room.

Looking up at him, I ask, "Do you suppose that room was used for sexual experiments? Like a study in sexual response, perhaps?"

He stops in his tracks and looks down at me, his eyes wide. "What? No. Why would you think that?"

I shrug. "There was a bed, and the straps . . ." I trail off, blushing at the smile crawling over Asher's face.

"And what, pray tell, do you know about sexual practices that involve straps?" There's laughter in his voice.

I straighten my shoulders and lift my chin. *"I am well-versed in the ways of mating."* I frown. Where did that come from?

"You are, are you?" he says, still laughing. He threads my arm through his. "Well, then, do tell. I'm obviously not as 'well-versed' as you."

I have to laugh and lightly punch his arm. "You wish."

He laughs back. "Yes. Yes I do." But he drops it and we continue on our way.

Finally I spot a pinprick of light, growing brighter and brighter the closer we get.

Asher and I grin at each other, then rush to what looks like it could be the outdoors, but when we get to where the light is coming from, it's not an exit. It's a large wall-sized window. Curtains cover it, so it's impossible to see what the window shows, but we frown at each other. The confusion in his eyes mirrors my own. If we're underground, how is there a window?

We creep to it, and when Asher pulls the curtain away, I gasp. It's a window that looks directly into water. From the murkiness of it, it's easy to tell it's some kind of lake, though the glow of the surface isn't too far overhead. Asher looks over at me, then places a hand on my shoulder. "You okay?"

"Of course." But I swallow at the lump in my throat. This view reminds me of something, and it has my nerves tingling. I can't recall what it is, and that has me even more nervous. I'm grateful for Asher's presence. He studies me a bit longer, then shrugs and goes back to peering out into the water.

"I wonder why this is here," he says.

I don't have an answer, but I don't think he was looking for one anyway. My legs feel weak and it takes almost all of my strength to continue forward, but I step closer to get a better look. The water is a really light green and if I look up high enough, I can see through it to the surface. It's too dark to see the bottom.

The blood rushes out of my head and I feel a bit dizzy. I press a hand to the glass to steady myself.

I shift so I can see Asher. "I've never seen water this color before. Have you?"

He shakes his head—the way he does it makes me think he didn't really hear me—and goes back to staring at a metal nameplate on the side of the door. Just as I turn back to the water I hear him say, "Oh, Jesus."

Before I can ask him what's wrong, something slides across the glass. I jump, but figure it's probably just a fish. It *is* a lake after all. Maybe it's even a mermaid. I saw an old water stained and torn picture of one in Ann Marie's room and I've wanted to see a real one ever since. But when I eagerly lean closer, I scream.

And scream. And scream. I can't seem to stop myself from screaming.

The dark object sliding across the glass is a body. Well, what's left of the body anyway. The bottom half of it is missing and a lot of the skin appears to have melted away.

Asher spins me around so I'm facing away from the glass and forced to stare at him instead.

"Don't look, Evie. Just . . . don't look."

I stare into his eyes, trying to focus on them, but I can't. I can't think. Everything in me is telling me to run. I try to fight it; I know the thing on the other side can't hurt me. But despite that, I can't help but think—know—the body is going to break the glass, trying to get to us, and we'll either drown, or end up being eaten by it.

Asher rubs his hands up and down my arms, his voice soothing, even though I can't understand what he's saying, yet my mind still screams at me to run.

So that's what I do. I run. Back into the dark, and as far away from the window as I can get. Asher's behind me; I can hear his feet pounding behind me and I *want* to stop. But my body won't let me. It's like I'm on a runaway train with no way to get to the controls and stop myself from hurtling through the Tube at Mach 10.

"Evie!" Asher calls, and while I can hear the desperation, I can't even slow.

I just keep running, placing one foot in front of the other, as I try to locate the exit. Even when my lungs burn and spots flare into my eyes, I keep turning corners and pounding up stairs and banging through doors, hoping each one will bring me closer to the one that will set me outside.

Then, without warning, I burst out into the sunlight. My feet stumble when they hit the different texture of the sand after the concrete of the hallways, but surprisingly I don't fall. I just continue to run.

The light blinds me, but even then I don't stop. I can't. If I stop, even for a second, the monsters will get me.

"Evie! Stop! Don't go any further!" Asher yells from behind me. From the echo of his voice, I can tell that he's outside like me. There's even more desperation to his voice now and the pounding of his feet speed up.

Suddenly the ground underneath me slopes and I lose my footing just as something hits me in the back—hard. I land chest-first on the ground, all the air rushing from my body.

Whoever landed on me stays on my back and we're rolling down a hill, our limbs flailing wildly and getting caught on each other.

"Shit. Shit. Shit," Asher grunts in my ear and suddenly there's a jarring motion and we stop rolling, but we continue to slide for a few more meters before we're able to stop completely.

I immediately roll over onto my stomach and try to push up on my hands and knees, but I can't breathe, and can only manage a few strangled gasps.

Asher is yelling at me again, but I can't respond and the sunlight is still blinding me so I can't see him.

Finally, just as I feel I'm going to pass out, I manage to pull in a shaky breath, and collapse onto the ground, squeezing my eyes tightly shut as sweet, sweet oxygen fills my lungs.

Asher speaks directly into my ear. "Are you okay? Did you get hurt? Do you have any burns?"

I shake my head, and just continue to lie there, sucking in all the air I can get. It doesn't stop the burning in my lungs, or my pounding heart, but the spots in front of my eyes are slowly fading.

"Okay. That's good. That's very good." There's a thump next to me and he says, "I'm just going to lay here for a minute and catch my breath. Okay?"

I nod again.

For several minutes we lie next to each other, our breaths panting out before they slow and even out. I just want to lie here forever, but unfortunately, the foulest stench is assaulting my nose. I can't even describe it, but considering what I just saw, I'm sure it's dead bodies.

When I can breathe normally again, I slowly open my eyes, blinking against the bright sun, and even though it's bright and the sunlight stings my eyes, I can see. Frantically

I look around for the bodies to make sure they're nowhere near me.

But I don't see a single one. I frown. The smell is getting stronger and now it reeks exactly like the rotten eggs Gavin's mother found in the hen coop.

"Oh, Mother, what is that *smell*?" I sit up and cover my nose with my hand.

"Sulfur," Asher gasps, pushing himself up to a sitting position. "The lake. It's not a lake."

I look at him, wondering if he hit his head on a rock or something on the roll down. "I don't understand."

"There's no water in it. There must be a lava vent under it or something because it's all sulfuric acid now." He gestures to the lake, mere centimeters from our feet. "And if I hadn't tackled you, you would have run right into it."

Chapter Eleven

No admittance into Rushlake City will be authorized without this visa. Please safeguard this document as a replacement will not be issued if lost or stolen. Use of this visa constitutes acceptance of Rushlake City Community Standards. Only those individuals listed on visa will be accepted into the city.

—Instructions on visa

Evie

To say the thought that I would have run blindly into a poisonous lake doesn't terrify me would be a lie, so I decide it's better not to think about it at all.

"Thank you." My voice is so soft I almost can't hear myself.

Asher continues to look out over the acid water, before pushing to his feet. "We've got a long road ahead of us without Starshine and our supplies."

"Where's Starshine?"

"Probably waiting for us back at the town." He holds his hand out at me.

I take it and let him pull me up. "Aren't we in the town?"

He helps me up the slope, then gives me this lopsided smile. "See for yourself."

When I look at where I presume we came from, I only see a tiny little metal shack not much bigger than the door itself. It's the only thing for kilometers in every direction. All I see is brown dirt and blue sky. It looks just like when we stopped yesterday and waited for Gavin. The only difference is the gross-smelling not-water lake and the metal shack a few meters from it.

"Where did it go?" As soon as I say it, I realize how stupid a question it is. Between last night and this morning we could have walked kilometers underground. It's not the town that moved, but us. I did it again. With a groan, I sit back on the ground. "I'm so sorry."

Asher pulls me back to my feet. "It's as much my fault as yours. I'm the one who pulled you into that space. I should've thought that through a little better. If I'd known . . ." He trails off and I want to tell him there was no way he could have known I would do that. *I* didn't even know I would do that. But he continues. "We'd better get going. We've already missed most of the morning."

He starts in a fast walk and I have to rush to keep up.

"How do you know which way to go?" I ask.

He gestures to the sun. "Sun always rises in the east. Rushlake should be southwest of us. This is approximately southwest according to the placement of the sun."

"But . . . we're going back for Starshine first. And to wait for Gavin, right?"

He gives me a look. "No. We're continuing on, because I have no idea where that city was or how long it'll take to get back there. We're working on limited time as it is."

I stop walking. "We have to go back. We can go back in through the tunnels. We found our way out here, we can find our way back there."

He turns around and frowns at me. "No. We're not. We're lucky we made it out of there alive the first time. And who knows what the hell we breathed in all that time we were stuck in there. It was an accident that you managed to run in the right direction and we didn't run into . . . anything that might be in there. If I'd known what that place was, we never would have stepped foot in there."

"Well, then we'll just need to take . . ." Then I hear what he said last. "Wait. What? What was that place?" A chill crawls over my skin.

"Nothing we need to worry about now. We're out and we're not going back in." Asher turns to walk away, but I rush in front of him and stop, so he has no choice to do the same or run into me.

"You will tell me." I cross my arms over my chest and lift my chin.

"You really are a princess, aren't you?" He sighs. "It's an old bioengineering outpost. The military used them in the War to design bioweapons and supersoldiers. That bed you saw? They strapped willing—and unwilling—participants to it and conducted experiments on them. Painful, appalling experiments. The straps kept them from escaping during the process."

The blood drains from my head, but I stand my ground, despite the fact that it doesn't feel as solid as it did a minute ago. "That's horrible, but that place has obviously been abandoned for years, probably decades. And we can't just leave Starshine and Gavin behind." There's a tickle in the back of my throat again.

"We can. And we will." He touches the back of his hand to my cheek. "I'm sorry, Evie. I don't want to leave them behind either, but we're not going back into that place. There are probably spores from their bio experiments just waiting for some idiot to come across them. Like I said, we're lucky we even made it out in the first place."

"So we're just going to leave Starshine out here. To die." My blood boils and I clench my fingers into a fist, holding them tightly to my body. "And what about Gavin? He'll be looking for us in that city."

"Gavin can find his own way. And we're only going to leave Starshine for now. I'll send someone back for her when we get to Rushlake. It'll only be a day, two at the most. She'll be fine."

There's a pressure in my chest and it hurts to breathe. "Is that all you ever do?" I whisper, half because I'm so mad I can't speak and half because even that is excruciating to my lungs.

Asher drops his hand. His whole face goes blank. "What?"

"Whenever something becomes too difficult to handle, you quit? Whenever someone becomes an issue, you abandon them?" He steps toward me, but I step away from him. "Don't touch me," I rasp.

His mouth firms into a tight line and anger flares into his eyes, but he doesn't say anything, so I continue, "Is that what you're going to do to me when I get to be too difficult? Are you going to leave me behind? Just like you did to Gavin? What you're trying to do to Starshine? Admit it, you're thinking of leaving me now, aren't you?"

Spots flash into my eyes and my head is tingling, like it did just before that last hallucination. I know I have to be careful or I'll have another one.

Despite that, I can see the muscle in Asher's jaw flutter and his hands curl tight into fists when he says, "Of course not! I wouldn't ever ditch you. I'm doing all of this *for* you!"

"You willingly left Gavin to die and now you're doing the same to Starshine. What makes me different?" I demand. He doesn't say anything, so I push my face into his as darkness leaks into the sides of my vision. Despite my efforts not to, I have to grab ahold of his arms to stop myself from falling. "Tell me!"

"You just are. I'm not going to ditch you, ever. Okay?" He shoves a hand through his hair. "But God, Evie, look at you!" He takes me by my shoulders and gives me a little shake. "You're standing here arguing with me and you can't even stand up straight, you're so exhausted. You had not one, but *two* hallucinations. One that almost got you killed, the other that could have. I don't even know if you're going to make it to Rushlake as it is, let alone if we take the time to go back who knows how far. I'm not going to watch you die in front of me. I won't go through that again. We're not going back." He grabs my arm and starts dragging me in the direction he wants me to go.

I wrench my arm from his and sneer at him. "I'd rather die fighting, than live as a coward."

He stops and turns. His breathing is just as hard as mine, and I'm sure my eyes are filled with the same conflicting swirls of wild fear and anger. His nostrils flare and he narrows his eyes at me. "I doubt Gavin would agree." His voice is soft and unwavering even if he is staring daggers at me. "Do you really want him to go all the way to Rushlake only to find that you're not there? And the reason you're not there is because *you're too damned stubborn to walk there?*" He shouts the last part, startling me.

Regretfully, I have to admit he could be right. Gavin's far from stupid. And I don't want to give him any more cause for worry. With a sigh, I say, "Let's go."

He spins on his heel, and starts forward again. I rush to catch up to him and he walks next to me, but doesn't touch me. We don't even talk. I don't question him again about what direction to go, I just take his word for it. I have to. I have no sense of direction, and no reference for where we are.

We walk for hours and it doesn't take long for my body to protest every movement I make. I just want to sit back onto the ground, curl up into a ball, and sleep. That, of course, makes me miss Starshine even more as I probably could have slept the entire trip if she were here. But I keep the thought to myself, not wanting to start another fight.

We pass a few trees along our route, but it's mostly just desolate desert for as far as the eye can see. And between the sand and scorching sun, I'm so thirsty that if I were still near that acid lake, I'd be tempted to drink some of it.

The worst part is Asher has not said one word to me that wasn't an answer to something I asked, or to warn me about something. I'm a little taken aback by how I've already come to rely on his all-the-time-positive attitude.

As the sun burns high in the sky, I see what looks like a lake ahead. It's blurry, but shimmering in the sunlight. I grab Asher's arm. "Asher! Water!" My throat is hoarse and hurts to talk.

He doesn't even look, he only shakes his head. "No, it's a mirage."

"No, it's water. I'm sure of it." I try pulling him, to move him faster, but he only keeps moving at his steady pace.

"No use chasing after it," he says, huffing a little himself with each step. "It's not real. You'll only make yourself more thirsty."

I ignore him, though. It's water; I know it. It's not just some delusion I've concocted in my head. Not this time. So I let go of him and race ahead. But no matter how fast I move, how hard I push my muscles, and how much my lungs beg me to stop, the water stays exactly the same distance away. I can't get to it.

Unable to keep my pace up, I slow to the point that Asher catches up to me. "It's okay," he says. "It's happened to almost every one."

I nod, feeling stupid on top of being hot, sweaty, thirsty, sore, and tired. My chest hurts again and my breath is racing as fast as my heart, reminding me that I need to stop being stupid and start listening to what Asher says.

To keep myself occupied and my mind off the never-ending and sweltering sand, I play with the sand. Of course I'm not stopping to build sand castles or anything, but with each step the sand makes this strange dry, squishy sound and I like it. So each time I step, I wiggle my foot around so it makes the sound again and again.

Asher startles me when he chuckles. I gape at him. "What?" I ask.

He shakes his head. "Nothing."

But I'm not letting him get away with that, especially since it's the first *Asher* thing he's done in hours. I slide in front of him, turning to walk backward.

"What's so funny?"

"You."

His dimple flashes when he grins at me, and a little bubble of relief floats into me, but I pretend to frown. "Me? What's so funny about me?"

"You're like a little kid bouncing around and playing in the sand. It's funny."

"I'm not a kid."

"Ah! But you *are* little." He taps my nose. "And you should probably turn around before you trip over something—"

Of course at that moment, my foot finds the only hole in the entire desert and my ankle catches, which causes me to fall hard onto my butt. Asher, unable to stop in time, follows suit and lands on top of me, pinning me to the ground underneath him.

A sharp pain shoots up my leg, but it ends as soon as my foot is free of the hole. Laughing, I try to sit up, but Asher's too busy trying to see if he hurt me and we end up bumping heads.

"I'm so sorry," we say together, and then just sit there laughing and rubbing our heads.

It's probably more the hysterical kind of laughter than anything else, but it feels good to laugh, even if it's only for a minute.

He smiles down at me and I smile back up at him, but something in his expression changes and he stares down at me so intensely, I stop laughing. I shouldn't be here, like this, I think and quickly slide out from underneath him. I clear my throat. "We should probably keep going." I turn away so I'm not looking at him.

After a minute he stands, but he doesn't hold out a hand for me this time and I'm sure we're back to silent Asher. With a sigh, I push myself to my feet on my own.

We keep going like that until the sun starts to lower in the west, leaving only a reddish pink sky and some violet clouds. The temperature starts dropping considerably the further the sun lowers.

"Any idea where we are?" I ask him when I realize we might be stuck in the desert with those dog beasts and no way to beat them this time. No way to outrun them. And no supplies or a way to keep warm through the night.

"No," he says, "but I don't think we have long. Those trees over there look familiar to me. See that tree in the front? The one that looks all twisty, like one tree is wrapped around the other? My father and I would stop there to rest every time we came this way."

I glance to where he's gesturing, and shiver. It's almost like the woods we stayed in the first night. "We're not going to go through there, are we?"

"Afraid so. No other way." He pats my arm as if to soothe my fears. Although he doesn't look very happy about our only option either.

I swallow. "But what about those birds?"

"They sleep at night, so if we go as far as we can tonight—hopefully getting on the other side of those trees—then wake up early, I don't think we'll have to worry about them."

"Are you sure?"

He looks down and at me, his eyes meeting mine. "No. I wish I was, but I'm not."

I can't help but compare Asher to Gavin in this moment. If Gavin were here, he would reassure me, even if he had to bend the truth. Asher always tells me how it is—always. Asher trusts me to be able to handle the truth. Even if it's bad. I like that. A lot. I'd much rather have the truth than have something sugar-coated to spare my "delicate" feelings.

To pay him back for his trust in me, I shrug and step forward. "Are you coming? Or are you going to stand there all day?"

We get to the tree line just as the sun is setting. I listen for the sound of wings, but the only sounds are crickets and the wind teasing the scrub oak leaves. As we walk, I wonder how the trees are getting water. Surely there has to be something nearby to keep them all hydrated and alive. I try not to spend too much time thinking about it. It's a waste of energy that should and could be spent on getting out of the small forest alive and well. But every time I lick my chapped lips, I'm reminded of exactly how dehydrated I am.

It's hard to tell when the sun actually sets, because the woods are so dark. The chill of the night is obvious though. My wheeze, which was easier to ignore in the heat of the day, sounds too loud in the tree-covered night. I worry I might cover up the sound of approaching animals, or worse yet, attract them to us.

"Maybe we should stop for the night."

"We have to keep going. Just a little bit longer, until we get to the tree line. If there are vulture-hawks, I want to be able to run into the light quickly."

"What about those beast-dogs?"

"The coyotes?" He continues before I can answer. "They *are* nocturnal, so let's try to stay quiet and move as quickly as possible."

I swallow at the lump in my throat, but do as he recommends. Hours later, when I'm continuing on nothing more than willpower alone, I hear Asher say, "Just a little further," for what feels like the thousandth time, but this time there's excitement in his voice.

I look up and gasp when I see the orange-black horizon of the rising sun just past the trees.

"Tree line," I whisper and dart forward to it, ignoring the aches and pains that cover my body.

Asher is close behind and we both make the same awed noise when we see the towers of buildings reaching up into the sky in the distance. It's probably less than five kilometers away.

"Come on!" I giggle, and tug on his arm. "We're almost there."

He allows himself to be pulled across the small plains before we get to a large body of water. A few hundred meters in is an island, where Rushlake city waits. There's a red footbridge that leads across the water to the island city with its huge buildings that sparkle and scrape the sky.

I trudge onto the bridge, nearly weeping at the thought of being so close. To sitting. To water. There's a guard station on the other side that I keep my eyes fixed on. I only have to make it that much farther, I am certain of it. But even these last fifty meters can't be easy. In my hurry, my foot catches on one of the loose planks and I crash onto the ground. I'm so exhausted I find it almost impossible to push myself up, but I finally manage, my legs shaking with the effort. The muscles in my jaw ache with thirst. I'm dizzy with it. There is water on the other side of this blasted bridge and I will crawl to it if I have to.

I take a determined step, but my energy is finished. My legs buckle, and I have a moment of thinking I might just have to crawl, when Asher swoops me up in his arms. He carries me across the rickety bridge, chest heaving with the effort. My stomach summersaults when the bridge sways wildly under his feet, but he keeps me held fast.

At the far end, two bored guards wait. Neither of them offers to help Asher, even when we're well within shouting distance. In fact, neither of them moves until we're at their station, and then it's only to demand to see our visa. Asher sets me on my feet to get out the letter from his father. The guard takes his time, inspecting each word as if he has just learned to read. I take the chance to study our surroundings. The guards' outpost is just a tiny wood building, not much bigger than the guard and his partner. It's set off to the side of a concrete platform, which has steps leading down to one of those large asphalt paths that were in the abandoned city.

When the guard is convinced our papers are in order, he lets us pass, then puts out a call to Asher's grandmother to come pick us up at the guard's station; she is going to keep us while we look for a doctor that can help me.

Asher tries leading me away toward the steps, but I pause. "What about Gavin?"

"What about him?"

"How will he get in? He doesn't have a visa. The guards won't let him in."

His eyes fill with something that looks like regret—maybe sadness—but then he sighs. "Wait here."

He turns back around and talks to the guard. His words slur in his exhaustion. "There was another member of our party. His name is Gavin Hunter." He pulls out the visa again, then points to Gavin's name. "He was separated from us in the Outlands. Will you make sure he's able to get into the city and call my grandmother when he arrives?"

"Yes, sir," the guard says. "I'll just place his name in the book. But, between you and me," he glances at his partner, "you might want to come up and check yourself for the next few days. Not everyone checks the book. . . ."

At first I'm not sure what he's getting at by letting his words trail off like that, but then the word *bribe* enters my mind. Without our supplies, we have nothing to offer the guards. Nothing to ensure Gavin's name will even make it into the book, much less earn him passage into the city.

"I understand. Thank you," Asher says, stifling a yawn. The guard appears disappointed, but says nothing.

I stare at Asher, desperate for a solution. I know he thinks Gavin didn't make it, but in my heart I know he's still out there. If I had any money, I would give it all to ensure his safety. I hate being dependent on Asher. I hate that we don't have anything to offer these lazy men. My eyes sting, but I'm too dehydrated to cry.

"I'll have someone from my grandmother's house bring them what they want," he whispers to me.

"Thank you." I press a hand to my trembling lips, grateful for even this small promise.

"Anything for such a pretty lady." Even though his voice

lacks the normal smoothness that he instills into each sylla-ble, his eyes sparkle in amusement when he says it.

I laugh, grateful for the relief, and roll my blurry eyes.

We sit at the bottom of the steps on the other side of the guard station. My back aches from the hard stone beneath my sore hips, but the relief from sitting and making it to the city is sweet and, just when I find myself starting to fall asleep, a huge hunk of metal squeals to a halt in front of us. I pull my feet away from it, gasping and pressing a hand to my racing heart.

I glance up at Asher. "That's a car," I say, astonished.

He chuckles. "Yes, it's a car. It's my grandmother's car, in fact."

"It works?" I ask, dumbfounded and continuing to stare at the big machine. It looks the same as those other ones—the ones in the abandoned city—but it's shiny and actually moving. It's kind of pretty, really.

This time he snorts and his laugh is deep, seeming to come from deep in his chest. "I should hope so, or Grandmother wouldn't be a very happy woman."

As if on cue a person rushes around to the back of the car from the opposite side and pulls a lever on the side of it. A door opens and a woman with steel gray hair steps through the opening. She smiles when she sees Asher, then turns the smile to me, but it wobbles and her eyes widen when I smile back.

She shoots a glance at Asher. "This is her?" she asks in this deep, smoky voice.

He nods and slips an arm around my waist, pulling me toward him in a possessive manner I'm not entirely sure I like. "Yes. This is Evie."

She grabs my chin gently in her surprisingly smooth hands. She stares at me and I firm my lips into a line. I don't like how closely she's studying me, as if she recognizes me somehow. Then she startles me when her lip quivers and her eyes become shiny.

"Eli," she whispers.

I peek at Asher, who knit his brow together.

"Grandma?" he asks.

She steps away with a shake of her head. "I'm sorry, dear. For a minute, you reminded me of someone I used to know." She hugs Asher and pulls me into the same hug. "Come on. You'll both be more comfortable after a hot shower and some clean clothes."

Wary, but grateful, I step forward into the car and slither onto the car's backseat next to Asher's grandma and wait for Asher to slide in after me.

CHAPTER TWELVE

Adolescent female of European descent. Extreme pallor, signs of dehydration, multiple wounds in various stages of healing. Patient cooperative, but semi-conscious, unable to provide any details of how injuries were sustained.

—Excerpt from Treatment Note of Rushlake City physician

Evie

Asher's grandmother hands both Asher and me bottles of water, but warns us to drink slowly. However, both of us are too thirsty to listen and we gulp down three of the bottles before the car even starts moving. My stomach clenches at first, but I will myself to keep the liquid down. I'm not going to waste a drop.

I'm just finishing my third bottle when we zoom away from the curb. Even though I haven't been in the car that long the heat inside makes me sleepy. It seems all the walking—stumbling—with little to no sleep has taken its toll. Even still, I can't help but gawk at the city as we pass each building. I've never seen anything like it. With the sun rising over the horizon, the sky is an orangish color that's reflected directly on the glass structures, giving Rushlake City a lost-in-a-rainbow look.

Rainbows are one of my absolute favorite things here. The first time I saw one was right after getting home—Gavin's house—after being in the hospital. Right before sunset, a double rainbow arced across the sky. It was gorgeous. I had to run to get Gavin and have him tell me what it was. The city reminds me of that moment. Impressive. Simply gorgeous. And it takes my breath away to look at it.

As we travel, Asher leans over and points out different buildings and landmarks. They're so completely different from the ones in the village. Even though it's obvious they're older than the newest buildings in the village—and much, much taller—everything is practically perfect. There are no cracks. The windows glimmer. They're actually pretty. And clean. Really, really clean. As if they've never seen a spot of dirt in their lives. With all the dirt and sand and mud I've seen just in the last few days, I don't even know how that's possible.

The tall buildings are called skyscrapers and they hold a host of different businesses. From things called banks to restaurants and everything in between. Interspersed between the skyscrapers are smaller single-business buildings. On one corner there is a smallish building made completely out of metal and glass. Asher says it's his favorite restaurant. He says it serves pizza, and the way he describes it makes my mouth water.

When we get to the city center, he points out a park. It's still foggy as the sun burns away the cold of night, but I can see the beautiful trees and shrubs. And, in the very center, a tall statue of a man.

I turn to Asher. "Is that a real statue?"

He nods, but doesn't smile like I expected. "That's Michael Rush, founder of Rushlake City." He gives me a look. "Well, he's sort of the founder. This was originally a part of a different, larger city, but during the War the main municipality was destroyed. I'm not exactly sure how the whole story goes, but he owned a lot of the land on this peninsula. When the city was destroyed, the connecting piece of land was severed and this part became an island. After the War, Michael Rush rebuilt the city and built walls around the entire island to protect it. He became the city manager and anyone who wanted to have protection from the dangerous Outlands could come here. If they could afford to pay the Tithe."

"Tithe?"

"It's basically a protection tax. You pay him a certain amount every month, or year, or whatever and he keeps you safe and sound." He looks past me, out the window. "It works, because this place is almost exactly like cities were before the War. Sure, some things are different as technology and everything gets better, but for those who wanted things to be the same—for the ones who wanted to pretend like it never happened—this is perfect for them. And they're willing to pay for it. Pay for the illusion of safety. For a false peace. Deceptive freedoms." He looks back at me, his eyes dark, hard, and cold. "Even if sometimes the cost is *more* than just money."

"Asher . . ." his grandmother says with a warning in her voice.

He clears his throat and as he does it, his eyes clear, too. "And . . . it looks like we're almost home."

I want to know more about the protection tax, but I'm sure I won't get any answers when his grandmother is around. So I turn my attention back to the passing landscape. On either side of the car are smaller buildings. They remind me a bit of Gavin's house, but they're squished closer together and they're taller, which makes them look thinner. I stare at them, but I don't pay them much attention. My mind keeps wandering to Gavin and I fight to keep it focused on what is happening now. If I think about him, I'll worry, and there's no reason to worry right now. He's coming. I know he is. He's just a little behind.

The driver pulls up in front of one of the larger houses and gets out to open the door as he did before. Asher's grandmother steps out first, then Asher scoots around me and turns to offer me his hand.

His grandmother's house is stunning. Easily the most amazing of all the houses on this street. Judging by the windows, it's three stories tall, which is the same as Gavin's house but this one seems larger somehow, more imposing. Concrete steps lead up to a set of magnificent wood and glass doors. On either side of that, two large windows jut out from the brick siding at strange angles.

"What do you think?" Asher asks in my ear.

"It's . . . it's amazing." I can't keep the awe from my voice.

"Are you going to keep the girl in the cold all day, Asher?" his grandmother asks.

He shakes himself and says, "Uh . . . no." He looks a little embarrassed, but offers me his arm to help me up the steps. "This way."

Just before I pass through the door a blast of freezing wind makes me shiver.

"Let's get you to your room," Asher says. "You can take a nice hot shower. By that time, I'm sure Cook will have breakfast ready."

I nod and let him escort me to my room. Along the way I stare, amazed at how much wood is in the house. Everything is wood. The stairs. The walls. The furniture in the rooms I pass. Even the floors.

The most surprising—in a completely fantastic way—is the bathroom. Two large wooden doors open into a large room at least twice the size of Gavin's bathroom. The walls have pretty gray tile crawling halfway up the walls. The rest of the wall to the ceiling, which is I don't know how many meters above my head and has a window in it that I can see through to the beautiful blue sky, is more wood.

Attached to this first room is another, smaller room, which has big black square tiles up the entire wall and along the floor. Upon closer inspection, I realize that the smaller room is actually a really large, luxurious shower. Glass doors section that room in half with one half being the shower, and the other holding white robes on hooks. Underneath the hooks, towels are folded neatly on a wooden bench.

In the main part of the room, there's a low-to-the-ground, egg-shaped bathtub where the faucet comes straight out of the wood paneling, allowing water to fall into the tub. It looks deliciously inviting, but I'm afraid I'll fall asleep if I use it, so I figure I'll shower instead.

Asher shows me where everything is and how it all works. It's different from the village. For one, we don't have to ration the water. I can take as long of a shower as I want. And there's a heater built into the ceiling. I don't even have to switch on a pump like at Gavin's house.

The hot water sluices away days of dirt and grime, stinging the fresh wounds on my leg and shoulder, while the old bullet wound just stirs with its familiar throb. As refreshing as the water is, I'm achy, and confused, and my heart feels heavy every time I think of Gavin. Which is pretty much always. I don't bother to look at any of the scrapes and cuts and bruises crisscrossing my body, and I specifically avoid looking at my shoulder.

When I finish, I slip into one of the robes, then limp into the bedroom. Asher's grandmother is waiting for me. She's sitting on the bed, holding something red and silky-looking in her weathered hands. She holds out the fabric when she sees me.

"Here, they're pajamas. They should fit you well enough."

With a murmured "Thank you," I take them, and hobble back into the bathroom to pull them on. They're cool to the touch and so soft I can't help but coo a little when the fabric rubs against my wind, sand, and sunburned skin.

When I come back, adjusting the top over the bottoms, Asher and his grandmother are sitting at a little table in the corner of the bedroom. There are bowls set out and when I sit at the empty seat, Asher ladles soup into the bowl in front of me.

At first I gobble it down, along with the bread his grandmother places on a plate next to me. Asher does the same and there's no other sound except the scraping of our spoons against the bowls and the occasional slurp as we drink.

But my mind keeps circling back around to Gavin. How he's still out there. Somewhere. Probably hungry and hurt. Burning under the heat of the sun as it shoves the chill of night rudely away. All of the things Asher and I were, but now aren't. I don't know what else to do about it, though, so I just keep eating. Keep feeling guilty. Keep aching for him.

Finally full, I push the bowl away and rest my chin on my palm as Asher and his grandmother get caught up. I'm trying to come up with a plan to find Gavin, but my eyelids feel so heavy I'm having trouble keeping them open. Eventually I stop fighting it and close them, promising myself that I'm just going to rest my eyes and let myself drift to the ebb and flow of their voices.

After a few minutes, his grandmother says, "Aw, the poor

dear. She's falling asleep in her soup." There's a pause before she continues, "You used to do that when you were a babe. It was so cute to see your little head bob and sway as you tried to stay awake, but couldn't."

"Grandma," Asher sighs. Then, even though I don't hear the chair move, I feel myself being lifted.

Asher grunts a little when he picks me up, then he places me in the bed and pulls the soft blankets over me. I fall instantly to sleep.

I wake in a panic, my mind swirling with images of Gavin and giant birds. Those horrible beast-dogs. I sit straight up, gasping and scanning for danger. It takes me a minute to calm down and remember I'm in Asher's grandmother's house and I'm safe. Well. Safe from anything other than myself. My mind immediately goes to Gavin and how we just left him. In the woods. With man-eating birds. To die.

"No! He isn't dead," I say aloud. He's a fighter. He's probably just slower than we were. We had a horse for most of it, after all. And we found that underground place. That probably cut off kilometers from our trip. Maybe he's just stuck outside the gates and they won't let him in.

But all my reasoning fails to silence the nagging voice in my head that tells me he's dead. And it's my fault. For being weak. For being soft. For being damaged.

Because, if I'd been none of those, we wouldn't have been out there in the first place.

There's a knock on the door and I sit up straighter in the

bed. I force a smile to my lips when Asher pokes his head around the door. "Hey, you're awake! Wonderful. I was getting worried there."

I give him a confused smile. "Why?"

"You've been asleep for almost thirty-six hours. The doctors said your body just needed the sleep, though. I guess they were right. Are you hungry?"

Thirty-six *hours*? An entire day and half of another? *Surely* Gavin's arrived by now. I peer around Asher to see if anyone else came with him. "Where's Gavin?"

His mouth draws into a straight, thin line. He picks at something on his shirt; then, when he realizes what he's doing, he shoves his hands in his pockets before looking down at this feet. "He's . . ." He clears his throat, and I want to throw something at him. Part of me already knows what he's going to say. ". . . he hasn't arrived . . . yet."

Even though part of me had been expecting that answer, I still have to stop myself from screeching *What?* "I've been here almost two days and he's *still* not here?"

He doesn't say anything, only stares at the ground as if it might swallow him whole. Maybe he wishes it would.

Unable to remain sitting, I thrust myself to my feet. Although my legs are shaky and weak, I stumble my way over to the balcony and shove open the doors with Asher not far behind me. It's cold, but I lean against the metal railing. My breath puffs out in plumes in front of my face. The balcony overlooks the house next door, but in my mind's eye I'm picturing the Outlands.

Too long. Entirely too long. No food. No water. Way too long.

Asher steps up beside me and places his hand on my shoulder.

I can't help it. I blurt out, "Do you think Gavin's just stuck outside the gates? That that's why he hasn't come yet?"

The hand on my shoulder tightens and I know what he's going to say before he does. I keep talking so that I don't have to hear it.

"Maybe we should have left the visa there with them. Maybe we should go there and see. Maybe he's waiting for us and wondering why we haven't come."

He turns me around slowly to face him, his face a mask of misery.

He can't be gone. He can't be gone.

"Evie. He's not there."

Panic rises up in me, and I try pushing it back down, but it's almost impossible. I know any minute I'm going to lose it. I'm going to fall apart. Right here. Right now. I wrap my arms around my waist as if I can keep myself together that way. "How do you know? You can't know that."

"I do. I've gone every day to check with the guards to see if he's shown."

I curl into myself. "But he could be there *now!*" I try to make it sound like I believe it myself, but even I know I'm not very convincing. "We should head over there and see if he's waiting."

He shakes his head. "He's not coming, Evie. The odds of him getting away from the vultures were extremely slim.

And even if he did," he barrels on, ignoring my open mouth, obviously knowing what I was going to say, "he'd have been hurt, with no food or water. In the Outlands it's been over a hundred degrees every day this week during the day, and near freezing at night. Not to mention the coyotes and the wolves. There's no way he made it through all that."

My heart lurches in my chest and I stagger against the railing. I have to close my eyes against the pain, but still I can see him perfectly. His golden hair blowing in the breeze from the birds' wings and his beautiful gray eyes staring into mine as Starshine raced from him. I can see, now, he knew then he wasn't going to make it. When he said "I love you," what he really meant was "Good-bye."

Suddenly I'm so angry, it wouldn't surprise me to actually see red seeping into the corners of my eyes. "And whose fault is that? *You left him!* You wouldn't let me go back for him! It's your fault. Yours!" I scream at him.

He only nods, which makes me even angrier. "I know."

I can't stop myself—I punch him in the chest. But he doesn't even stop me. Which makes me even angrier and I punch him again. And again. It isn't making me feel any better, it just makes me more irate with each hit. Because he doesn't even *try* to stop me.

Obviously I'm not hitting very hard, because he doesn't move, doesn't even wince. He only continues to stare at me with those pain-filled eyes.

That just infuriates me more. How dare he just stand there and take it? How dare he not even fight back—not even tell me I'm wrong. That it's really *my* fault that Gavin's gone. Probably dead. Why is he just standing there taking it?

My mind's a jumble of emotions and thoughts. Pain. Anger. Sorrow. Frustration. Back to pain.

It isn't until the tears I hadn't noticed blind me and I can't breathe that Asher stops me, taking my wrists into his hands.

Exhausted, I slump against him, sobbing into my hands. My heart is cracked in so many places, it's hard to imagine it ever getting put back together completely.

"He can't be gone," I whisper, not because I don't believe he's dead, but because I need him. And I know it's really my fault he's gone. He'd always been there when I needed him, but I wasn't there the one time he needed me.

Asher lowers us so that we're both kneeling on the floor. And despite the fact that I just spent the last who-knows-how-long hitting him, he gathers me into his arms and holds me. Not saying a word, simply holding me.

The doors to the room open, but he shakes his head and whoever it was leaves, shutting the door quietly behind them.

Chapter Thirteen

*Not since the Gutenberg printing press has anything had such a
profound impact on the peoples of this world as the nanorevolution. Nanotechnology, developed in part by Lenore Allen,
changed the entire course of the War in favor of those in posses-
sion of the technology.*

—Excerpt from *A Brief History of the 21st Century*,
"Nanorevolution"

Evie

After a long time, I finally cry myself out. Asher still holds
me tightly against him. I push gently away, brushing the
tears from my face with my sleeve, and look up to the stars.
I'm too tired to pull completely away from Asher and it feels
so nice, I don't really want to anyway. It's the small comforts
now. The cold wind bites and snaps at my skin, but I don't
care.

"They're not as pretty here," I say, thinking of that last
night with Gavin in the clearing. Just us two. Lying next to
each other, discussing the stars. It makes me sad. They kind

of remind me of myself with their faded lights, and I'm reminded that every day I'm fading. Without Gavin, I have nothing to anchor me to my old life. Who I used to be.

"No, they're not." His voice is soft. "It's all the lights. They're jealous of the stars, and try to drown them out."

I know it's not true, but it's a nice thought.

We sit, both of us lost in our thoughts. I know something is bothering him, but I also know that he'll tell me what it is. Especially if it has something to do with me. That's one of the things I like about Asher. His unwavering honesty. No matter how terrible—or how difficult—he will *always* tell me the truth. Even when I don't want him to.

My mind flits over to Gavin and my heart squeezes. I miss that stupid little smile he gets when he looks at me and doesn't think I'm looking. I miss the way just the touch of him makes my heart swell, and how he looks at me like I'm the only one in the world. Or at least the only one that matters. I miss how he paces every time he's frustrated, or trying to figure something out, or nervous. I even miss that he *doesn't* tell me everything. Even as frustrating as that can be.

"They did some tests. While you were out. The test results came back," Asher says, yanking me from my thoughts.

"Hmm?" I turn to face him. I'm numb now. I can't seem to find the energy to care about the results, but for Asher's sake, I try to force enthusiasm. "Oh. That's great. Any news?"

"Nothing we don't know already."

I nod and turn my face back up to the stars. That didn't

seem all that bad, but Asher still acts like something is bothering him.

"The doctor wants to draw more blood tomorrow. Talk with you, too. If you're up to it."

I sigh, but nod. That's not entirely unexpected, either. And again, I don't really care. "Of course. Whatever he thinks is necessary."

"Evie? Look at me." His voice is still low, but there's something in his tone that has fear pushing past the numbness.

I turn to face him, furrowing my brow.

"They want to study your nanos. They think that . . . that they might have something to do with you being sick."

"My . . . nanos?" Nanos were what destroyed that town. What turned living, breathing people into rock and stone. My hand shakes and I frown even more as terror makes my heart kick in my chest. "I have *nanos* in me? How do you know?"

"Gavin told me," he says without meeting my eyes. "I—I thought you knew that."

Another of Gavin's omissions. For a minute, anger chases the terror away. So, even though there's bad blood between Asher and Gavin, Gavin still told Asher things about me. Maybe even everything about me. *Asher* was good enough to trust with *my* secrets, but not me.

When Gavin gets here, I'm so going to tell him exactly what I think about that, and then I'm going to demand he tell me absolutely everything. And if he thinks he can talk himself out of this one, he's got another think coming.

But then I remember Gavin isn't here. Isn't coming. Ever. And that numbness returns, replacing the anger. Concealing the fear. And then I can only nod.

I knead my skirt in my hands, pulling and tugging softly at the fabric. "I see. So are they like the ones that killed those people? Am I going to turn into stone like they did?"

Something like sadness flashes before his eyes and he stretches out his hand. Probably to take my hand, but I slide it out of reach.

He rakes it through his hair instead and tugs on the ends. "Yes. And no. It's not the same kind, I guess. More . . . complex or something. They don't really know, but they want to find out."

"So . . . I won't turn to stone?"

He shakes his head. "They don't think so. From what Gavin said, you've had them a long time and they were meant to help . . . not hurt. They just want to do more testing to see if they're malfunctioning."

I'm grateful for the numbness I feel. Being numb is so much better than being afraid. Better than feeling your heart break into tiny pieces. Better than any of the emotions I could—probably *should*—be feeling right now.

"Of course. Whatever they think is necessary."

My voice is flat as I say it and I know Asher's worried, but he only sighs.

"You don't have to worry." He grabs my hand and squeezes it before I can pull away again. "I'll be there for you. I won't leave you by yourself. I promise."

For a minute, a spark of anger ignites in me again. I remember Gavin saying that in the village right before the trip. And, softly, in the back of my head like an echo of a memory, I hear someone else saying it.

I can't stop myself from saying, "I've heard that before." I turn away from him as self-pity pricks at my heart. "But it's a lie. It's *always* a lie."

Chapter Fourteen

The answer to our problem has fallen in our laps, gentlemen. One of my son's friends has made a marvelous find. A young girl, the heir to a throne it would seem, from a city under the ocean. I know what you are thinking, and at first I didn't believe it either, but I've watched this girl and talked with the village doctor. She is most certainly different from any young woman we've ever seen. She appears quite ill, although it's unclear whether it's emotional or physical, and I think we would find it most beneficial to bring this child under our wing and offer our help in return for hers.

—Letter from Mayor St. James to Dr. Trevin, couriered by Asher

Evie

Asher says he checks the gate, but I also know he thinks Gavin's dead, so who knows if he actually does. I'm fairly certain they're not going to let me go out on my own. I've asked twice already, and both times they've said no and changed the subject.

I don't pretend I don't know why, but I'm going to check for myself. So I plan. And I plot.

I walk slowly to the bedroom. Asher's grandmother's eyes bore into me as I do and she slowly puts her knitting to the side.

"Bathroom," I murmur, not meeting her eyes, but out of the corner of mine, I see her sit back and resume her knitting.

I slip through the crack in the door, then tread to the bathroom, making sure my steps are loud, but not so loud they sound like I'm making them that way. I open and close the door, then sneak back down the hallway. I'm still sore all over, but I grit my teeth and keep going.

At the front door, I edge out, keeping an eye out for Asher, or his grandmother, or the maid, but no one stops me. Still, I don't take a full breath until I'm blocks away from Asher's house.

It takes me a while and several stops to rest and ask for directions, but finally I find my way back to the bridge.

Panting, I force myself up the steps and to the guards' box. They're not the same ones we'd met when we first arrived, but they look just as disinterested. They don't even lift an eyebrow when I knock on the window.

"Visa," the one closest to the door says, his voice flat.

"Um . . . I actually don't have one, but—"

He points to a sign on the window.

"No visa, no admittance to the Outlands," the other one says, repeating what the sign says in a bored voice. He has red hair and skin even more pale than mine. I can't help but stare at him. He seems so strange-looking, like he has shredded carrots on his head. "Go to City Hall and get one, then come back."

I force myself to meet his green eyes. "I—I don't actually want—"

"Go get the visa and come back."

"I'm not here to leave, I just want to find—"

He leans on the windowsill and interrupts me yet again. "Look, little girl, I don't really have time for this." He points to the sign and turns around.

The way he says "little girl" sets my nerves on edge. I narrow my eyes and purse my lips. "My *name* is Evelyn Winters. I am Daughter of the People of the great city of Elysium. I am a guest of the St. James family. You will not speak to me as if I'm some foolish young child . . ." I look down my nose at him. ". . . or an ordinary commoner."

Where did *that* come from?

The two guards exchange an anxious look while I try to ignore the questions flying through my mind about my sudden confidence.

But, finally I see I have their attention when they turn back to me. "We apologize, Ms. Winters, we don't mean any insult to you or the St. Jameses, but we still can't let you into the—" the dark-haired one says.

This time I break into what they're saying, and wave them off. "I am here to see if an Outlander has attempted to enter. His name is Gavin Hunter."

Confusion crosses their faces, but the one with red hair

shakes his head. "No one has entered this way since we've been here, ma'am."

Dejection blows throw me and my legs tremble, but I force myself to remain standing. I turn toward the Outlands, squinting into the growing darkness. He's out there. He has to be. I take one step, then another before one of the guards calls out, "Ma'am! Are you okay?"

I mentally shake myself, my shoulders drooping. "Fine." I swallow and clear my throat. "I'm fine." Forcing my shoulders back again, I turn back around and slowly, achingly make my way back to Asher's.

Hours later, I open Asher's door, intending to go straight up to my room and back to sleep. But I stop dead in my tracks when I hear raised voices coming from one of the doors to my left.

"How could you just let her sneak out?" Asher yells.

I follow the voices and stand in the open doorway to see Asher glaring at his grandmother, who sits in a large wingback chair. He has his arms crossed over his chest.

"I didn't know she was going to sneak out, Asher."

"But you had to have seen her leave her room."

"Of course I did. She said she needed to use the bathroom." He makes a sound in his throat and walks to behind his grandmother. "I'm not going to keep the girl prisoner in her room, Asher." She turns to continue to watch him, then stops when she sees me. She smiles and folds her hands in her lap. "There. See? Everything is fine."

Asher spins around. His whole face lights up when he sees

· 182 ·

me. He rushes across the room, tugs me to him, and hugs me so hard, I'm certain my head is going to pop off.

"Where have you been?"

I swallow. "I went to see if anyone at the gate has seen Gavin." I push away from him and hug myself. "They haven't."

The room is silent and heavy with it until Asher sighs. "Come on. Let's get dinner." He slings his arm around my shoulders and leads me to the dining room where food has already been set out. I don't want to eat. I don't even want to think about eating. Just the thought reminds me that Gavin hasn't had food.

Several minutes into dinner, I push from the table, interrupting whatever Asher and his grandmother are talking about. I have to get away from here. From them. I need to be anywhere but here.

I make it as far as the door before Asher catches me. He grabs my wrist and tugs gently, stopping me from leaving. "It's not your fault," he says quietly. "It's no one's fault. He was protecting you." He frowns at me. "You know that, don't you?"

I rub my hand under my running nose. "But he wouldn't have *had* to protect me if I hadn't been so weak. If I hadn't forced him to come here."

"Weak?" He laughs. "You think you were weak? You totally kicked ass! The way you took care of those vulture-hawks was like something out of a comic book."

I lift my brows at him. "You make that sound like it's a good thing, when all it does is make me a . . . freak." That was one of Gavin's little brother's words. It was a word he liked to use. A lot. I'd made him tell me what it meant and, ever since, I'd known it applied to me.

Anger flashes across Asher's eyes and he takes my face in his hands, forcing me to look at him. "You are not a freak. You hear me? *Different* doesn't make you a freak. *Different* makes you special. And special is good. Special is what makes you *you*. That's who Gavin loved. He thought you were amazing and wonderful and . . . perfect just the way you are."

He's saying it to make me feel better, but all it does is make me sigh and try to look away. "My brand of perfect is what killed Gavin." I sigh and wave away what he opens his mouth to say, "Besides, I wish people would stop saying that. Everyone is always telling me how perfect I am. How beautiful. How *lucky* I am. To be this amazing, perfect person. How Mother hand-chose me, *because* I'm perfect. But I'm not. I'm not amazing. Or wonderful. I'm not perfect. I'm damaged," I whisper.

I'm not sure what I'm saying, where any of this is coming from. I don't know who told me so. Certainly no one here, but it's true. And it only proves my point . . . I'm *not* perfect.

His face blanches. "What did you say?"

"That I'm damaged?"

"No. About being hand-chosen by Mother. Why did you say that?"

I'm about to answer that I don't know when I'm suddenly not in the foyer. I'm somewhere else. Somewhere very familiar.

Glass walls and marble floors surround me. Behind the glass is another wall, one of water. I have my hand pressed against it, staring into the endless blue. I'm sad about something, but I can't remember what. Only that my heart is heavy with it.

There's a gentle tugging on my hair. It's soothing. "Evelyn," a woman says from behind me. "You mustn't worry what that child said to you. Children have a way of hurting one another by pulling out the one thing that makes you unique. Makes you special. And you *are* special, Evelyn."

I turn slightly and she tugs my head back around with my hair and continues brushing it. Instead of trying to see her directly, I focus my gaze to her reflection in the glass instead. "Am I, Mother?" My voice is younger, not quite as strong. It wobbles slightly with the tears I see running down my cheeks.

"Of course, my child. I chose you, didn't I? That alone makes you special. But I chose you because you were different. Because you were perfect. And a perfect person shouldn't worry what inferior people say about them." Her face hardens for a moment and her hand tightens on my hair, making me gasp. Almost immediately she releases me and her eyes meet mine in the glass. "After all," she smiles, "I never do."

There's a knock on the door behind us and a girl not much older than me steps in, dressed entirely in black. Mother and I both turn toward her, but the girl doesn't focus her dead eyes on either of us. "The situation has been taken care of," she states in her wispy voice.

For a second, I'm sure she glances at me, but before I can

venture a guess why, Mother says, "Excellent." Then she dismisses the girl and turns back to me, forcing my head back around again while the door closes behind us. "See? Things have a way of working themselves out."

CHAPTER FIFTEEN

Warning! Unauthorized exit from Rushlake City is prohibited. Violators will incur administrative penalty and criminal charges including, but not limited to, immediate and permanent expulsion from the city and forfeiture of all rights and property.

—Sign posted at all points of entry of Rushlake City

Evie

The next day, I sit while a doctor does everything Dr. Gillian has already done at least a dozen times before. From the way he's not saying anything, and the pinch of skin around his eyes, I know he isn't coming up with any more answers than Dr. Gillian had, either.

He shines a light in my eyes. "You're completely healthy, Ms. Winters. Apart from a minor infection and some exhaustion. In fact, you're so healthy, I'm a little jealous. I don't know what could be causing these blackouts." He steps back and takes off his glasses to rub his eyes. "I'd like to bring you in for more testing. MRIs and PET scans specifically."

"What are those?" I ask.

"Sort of like X-rays, but more precise. I'll be able to see exactly what your brain is doing. That should tell us what's going on. If it's agreeable to you, I'd like you to come in as soon as possible. Say, tomorrow?" He glances between Asher and me. We both nod—what am I going to say? No?—and he continues, packing up his equipment. "Fantastic. We'll see you then." He pats my knee. "Don't worry, young lady. We'll figure all this out."

He leaves while I just stare at my hands. Asher nudges me. "Are you as tired of being cooped up in here as I am?"

I'm confused, but answer truthfully. "Yes."

"Great. Go get dressed. I'll meet you downstairs in twenty."

"Dressed for what?"

"We're going to see a bit of the city," he says. "Dress warmly. It's chilly."

As we walk through the city, Asher keeps pointing out different things, like he did in the car when we first arrived. I try to listen, but I can't help but keep an eye out for Gavin the entire time we walk. It just doesn't feel right to be out here with someone other than him. I sigh, then wince, look-ing over at Asher. It's amazing, the contrast between him and Gavin. Asher has this . . . perfect prettiness to him that makes him look just like everyone else here. His eyes are always smiling, showing his happy-go-lucky, nothing-ever-gets-me-down-for-long personality. Even dressed casually, like he is today, he looks effortlessly put together and fashionable, like the other people I'm seeing on the street.

He's wearing a hat. His dark hair sticks out on either side of it, the blue patch just barely visible under the lip of the hat. He's also wearing a long-sleeved dress shirt with the sleeves pushed up over his elbows and a gray vest. Of course, since this is Asher, his shirt is not tucked into his jeans. But it doesn't stop him from looking great, anyway.

Gavin, on the other hand, has a rugged—almost dirty, even when he's freshly washed—look that is simply the sexiest thing I've ever seen. No matter how nice and shiny Asher looks, it's Gavin that will always take my breath away.

I feel strange thinking of him like that, especially considering I may never see him again.

But, as Asher continues to show me around, my thoughts move to the city itself. I'm amazed how different the people look from the villagers. They're cleaner, but they've got the same shiny look to them that the city has. Like Asher, only the kindness in his eyes isn't reflected in anyone else's. It's as if they're really fake. Like dolls.

I don't belong here either. I don't belong anywhere.

Asher, however, seems at home. More so than he did in the village. It makes me think of what Gavin said about not trusting him. "We need to check the gates," I say.

He doesn't even argue. Just changes direction and leads the way back to the guards. They're the same as the day before. And they have the same news. "No one has seen him."

I wrap my arms around myself and shiver. Maybe he really is dead. Maybe he isn't coming.

Asher glances over, his features as sad as I feel. "Want to go and get something warm to eat?"

I let him drag me to the closest restaurant, where he orders something that sounds like absolute heaven. Hot chocolate.

We spend the next few hours talking. He tells me about his childhood, and Gavin's, remaining careful not to tell me anything of what really happened between them, keeping to lighter things like the time Gavin and him were fishing when they were fourteen and Gavin hooked Asher instead of the fish. And how he, Asher, had gone running off, screaming, before Gavin could take it out. When Gavin finally found him, it was dug deep into his skin, and Asher squealed like a little girl when they tried to remove it. To take his mind off it, Gavin had the bright idea to break into the Mr. Pok's back room and alleviate him of the shine he kept hidden in a closet. They'd both gotten so drunk that they'd stripped down to their underpants and ran through the town square yelling something about fish. I try to ask Asher why and he just shakes his head and grins, shrugging. They'd ended up grounded for a month.

Even when the conversation moves to the other things, like me, and what I remember, and laughing or gushing over things Asher and I have in common, Gavin is never far from my mind.

Chapter Sixteen

One of the most cunning animals of those in the Outlands is the coyote. The coyote's ability to adapt is the leading reason for its continued survival. Over time, coyotes have learned to hunt in small packs and stun their kill before dragging them to their burrow for consumption.

—Excerpt from *Field Guide to Dangerous Wildlife*

Gavin

A shout wakes me, and there's a flurry of movement around me. For a second, something sharp tightens around my arm; there's another shout, and the sound of a gun going off. Finally, something yelps next to me, and the sharpness in my arm lets off.

Coyotes! my mind screams at me. *Get up. Get up. Get up.*

I try to open my eyes, but I can't force myself to do it. Sleep just grabs ahold of me and pulls me in.

After what feels like no time at all, I'm being shaken awake again. I open my eyes, immediately regretting my decision.

The light stabs my eyes like rusty knives. I groan and slam them shut again.

"Nuh-uh, Sleeping Beauty. You've got some explainin' to do," a gruff male voice says. I open my eyes again as a rough hand yanks me up to a sitting position.

In front of me is a man. From the lines in his face, the gray in his scraggly beard, and what's left of the hair on his head, he's either fast approaching middle age or time has not been his friend. He's wearing all black. It looks like some kind of military uniform.

Immediately I tense. I reach for my gun, but it's gone.

The man barks out a laugh. "Did ya think I was goin' t' let you keep yer gun?" He scratches his chin and flakes of something dribble out of his beard like snow. "Not a very bright thing, are ya?"

"Who are you? What do you want?" I force myself to my feet. I'm grateful he didn't feel the need to tie me up.

"Ah, now, see, I said you had some explainin' to do, not the other way round, boy." He straightens up and I fight back a wince when I see that not only is he taller than me, but his arms are as thick as small trees.

Shit.

"So, now. Are yeh goin' t' explain what yer doin' here?"

Where *is* here? Glancing around, I notice I'm at the lip of a sulfur lake. I recognize it from the strange greenish-yellow color and the smell. How did I get here?

Then I remember. The birds. Barely escaping with my life only to run into a pack of hungry coyotes. One of them pouncing. Falling, hitting my head on the hard ground and blacking out.

But how did I end up here?

Something my father taught me ages ago when we found the chicken coop raided pops into my head. He said that coyotes have only managed to make it so long because they're smart enough to drag their food to their dens before eating, because otherwise they'd have been hunted to extinction.

So I look around for the den, but there's nothing visible except the lake. I take a small step backward, then two.

The man chuckles. "At least yer smart enough to stay away from that." He jerks his thumb at the water. Then he frowns again. "Come on, boy. I don't got all day. What ya doin' here?"

"I—I don't know." I rub my head. "I think the coyotes dragged me."

The man frowns and scratches at his beard again, making this scratchy sound like sandpaper, and it makes me want to shudder. He continues to stare at me, his eyes boring into me as if trying to read my soul to judge the truth of my words. "Ah, yeah. I can see that. Yer lucky, you are. I stopped one of them from eatin' yer face off." He smiles, showing off several gaps where his teeth should have been. "Ye'd better get goin' though. It ain't safe here, neither." He nods a head at the lake. "That ain't the only thing waiting to peel the flesh from yer bones."

My heart beats furiously, skipping a beat here and there.

I don't know what he means by that, and I'm not sure I want to.

Obviously, he's decided I'm not a threat and is allowing me to leave. I'm willing to take it without asking questions as long as that means I get to leave here alive and intact.

I start backing up, then stop. "Can I have my gun back?"

He frowns. "Now what would yeh think I was stupid enough to hand ye back yer gun fer?"

"I didn't say you were stupid," I say.

"Nah, but if yeh think I'm jes goin' to be givin' you yer gun back, yeh must think it."

I shake my head, trying to tell him I just want the gun to hunt for food, but he narrows his eyes at me.

"What'cha doin' out here all alone fer, boy? Didn't your mammy tell yeh the Outlands is no place for tots and green horns?"

Deciding I don't need the gun after all, I bob my head quickly. "Never mind. Keep the gun." I start backing away again.

His wide face wrinkles further when I do. "I wouldn't do that, boy. I'd be stoppin' now."

I do. Immediately.

"Yeh aren't out here alone, are yeh? Yer with someone else. Aren't ya?"

I hesitate only a moment before shaking my head. Evie and Asher are somewhere out here, I hope, but it's anybody's guess where. "No. I'm by myself."

He grins, showing those dark spaces again, but it isn't a

happy look. It's mean. I've only seen that look on one other person's face—Mother. It makes my veins drip with icy fear.

"Now, why would yeh do that?"

"What?" I slide another foot backward.

"Lie to me." He shakes his head, then pulls a gun from his back. My gun, actually. I recognize the large dent in the wood stock. "Hands on your head." He gestures with the gun when I don't comply. "Come now, don't be stupid."

I lift my hands and lace my fingers together behind my head. Plan after stupid, horrible plan bounces through my mind. None of them would work. They would all leave me with a nice-sized hole in my body.

I'm pretty sure that's going to happen anyway.

Something squawks and he jumps. He turns, looking to see what's made the sound, and I decide it's now or never. I pounce on him. I hope the surprise will help me avoid that hole.

It sort of works. I *do* manage to get my hands on the barrel of the gun, but he manages to keep a grip on it even as we fall to the ground.

That squawk happens again and this time there's a voice not far from my head. "Fred? You there? Did you find the source of the alarm?"

It's a radio. It's sticking out of the sand a few feet away, next to some kind of pack and a large gun. The gun is just lying in the sand, held up by a mini-tripod. I've never seen one like this before. Between that, the mention of the alarm, and his weird uniform, I figure Fred is a guard and he's protecting something. Not that I really care. I'm more concerned with not dying. But as we roll, I realize it might just be easier to go for that other gun after all.

We continue to tussle with the shotgun, but he throws a punch with his meaty fist that connects directly with my temple. Stars explode into my eyes and my ears ring. He rips the gun out of my hands, but I jump backward, immediately falling to the ground and rolling toward the other gun.

A shot rings out. The burst of sand just inches from my head tells me he's shooting to kill. I grab the gun and spring to my feet, bringing it to my shoulder and aiming at his midsection.

"Stop!" I gasp out. "Don't come any closer." This is a bigass gun and it's going to hurt like hell to fire it. Might even break my shoulder, but a broken shoulder is better than dead.

That is, if I can actually shoot the damn thing. It's heavy, and I don't even know if it's loaded. But, maybe, I'll be able to convince him to leave me alone long enough that he won't know I've never used something like this.

He lifts his hands in the air as he pushes himself to his feet, but there's a smirk on his face. "Yeh don't have the guts, boy." He spits on the ground and my eyes take in the bloody spittle that flecks the sand.

"Fred," the radio squawks again. "You okay? . . . Did you find out what set off that alarm? . . . Fred?"

I smile, just a small stretching of my lips. "Try me." I tighten my finger on the trigger. Given the size of the gun, it's surprisingly easy to press the trigger.

The smirk falls off his face. "Now, boy, yeh don't need to do that."

"Fred? . . . If you don't answer me, I'm sending someone out there. . . ."

That seems to bolster him, though. "Even if yeh shoot me, yeh won't get away with it. They'll find yeh." Then he lunges at me, and even though I'd expected him to try something, it startles me and I press the trigger. The gun goes off and knocks me onto my ass.

As I fall, I hear three distinct shots before I hit the ground, knocking the air from my lungs.

I was right. The gun hurts like hell.

I leap back to my feet, wincing as pain rips through my shoulder. I don't raise the gun. Even if I could, there's no need to. Fred is rolling down the hill. At first he's in one piece, with three large holes in his abdomen. But then, to my horror and disgust, as he continues to roll, the skin between the holes tear and he splits into two parts.

The friction must have been too much for those thin strings of flesh. I shudder when what was inside his body comes out and tangles around him before he splashes into the water with a hiss.

Both parts sink quickly and I feel like I'm going to be sick. Actually, I *know* I'm going to be sick. I collapse onto my knees and try hurling into the sand, but nothing comes up. I'm stuck just kneeling there, gagging, until the retching stops.

What the hell kind of gun was that? I've never seen bullets that could tear someone completely in half like that.

The radio squawks again and my heart kicks. I have to get out of here.

With a lurch, I shove to my feet, then throw the gun and radio into the water. A quick search of Fred's bag produces some much needed food and supplies. I toss the whole bag over my shoulder, grab my own gun, and run. Dizzy, with a fuzzy mind, and still a little green around the gills, I don't even know what direction I'm running in. I'll figure it out later. I just run.

As fast and as far as I can.

Chapter Seventeen

Once upon a time, there was a queen who lived in an underwater kingdom. The queen was beautiful, but cruel. And although she had many subjects, they were only loyal to her out of fear. The queen did not know love, and she kept her daughter, the princess, locked away for fear that the princess would someday discover love and leave the queen and the underwater kingdom.

—Excerpt from *Surface Fairy Tale*

Evie

I wake with a scream trapped in my throat as the tatters of the nightmare drift away. The room is still dark, but I reach for Gavin. I just want him to hold me. To tell me it's all right. That they're not real. That *he's* real, that he's here. But he's not. He'll never be here.

For a good ten minutes, I stare at the ceiling, then sigh and sit up, letting my legs dangle off the side before placing my foot on the floor. But there's something squishy, and warm, underneath it. I squeal and jump back onto the bed. Whatever it is pops up and lunges at me, making me fall off the bed on the opposite side and onto my back end on the floor with a thump. It looms above me, looking down at me from its perch on the bed. It's too dark to make out what it is, but I'm suddenly sure it's the monsters from my dreams coming to get me.

I scramble back until I'm crouched with my back up against the wall. As it slowly comes nearer me, I hear that click in my head. Everything focuses, just like before.

So I can see the monster better, I reach out and grab a handful of cloth and yank it to me. The fabric rips, fueling my desire to hurt whatever this creature is and prevent it from hurting me. But even then, it's too dark to really see anything but a pair of wide blue eyes staring into mine. And, only because they look frightened, I decide not to kill it right now.

I tighten my grip on the cloth, tearing it farther and pulling the creature after me, dragging it to the lamp in the corner. With a flick of my fingers, I switch the light on and turn to see . . . Asher. He's staring at me, his eyes still wide as he watches me. His shirt is ripped practically from his shoulders, hanging by nothing but a few threads.

His tongue flickers out nervously and wets his lips before he says, "M-morning, Princess."

I scowl and release him. His shirt pools at his waist when he falls to his knees.

"What did you think you were doing?" I demand, my voice hard and hardly recognizable.

His tongue flicks out again, but he only says, "You squealed and I was trying to see what was wrong."

Things are starting to get blurry again and I feel exhausted. I let myself sink to the floor next to him as I recall what happened.

"I guess I must have stepped on you," I finally say. "I stepped on something warm and squishy and it scar . . . startled me." No need to admit I was scared. This is embarrassing enough. "Why didn't you say anything?"

He looks at me with an embarrassed smile. "I was too . . . startled."

He rubs a hand across his chest and even through my blurry eyes, I can see the distinct lines my fingernails left across his bare skin. Five distinct scratches across his chest that stretch out in a long line from his right pec to the center of his abdomen. Blood oozes down.

I touch his chest gently and bite my lower lip, wrinkling my nose. "Oh, Mother, I'm so sorry, Asher. I . . . I don't know what happened."

He takes a shaky breath, and his eyes swim with something other than pain when he takes my hand. "It's all right. My fault. Completely. I should've known better than to jump up like that." He squeezes my hand.

"Still." I try to pull my hand back. "That's no excuse. I could have seriously hurt you. I don't know what's wro—"

He cuts me off when he places his finger over my mouth. "It's okay. I'm not hurt. I'm just fine. Are you?" he asks. "Hurt, I mean? You fell off the bed pretty hard."

I take a minute to get my emotions under control—it's not like feeling guilty and angry with myself is going to change what I've done. Besides, hopefully, in a few hours, I'll know exactly what's wrong with me and how to fix it.

Gavin

I run until I collapse from exhaustion. Even lying in the dirt, my whole body shakes. My eyes are heavy, gritty and dry. They hurt almost worse than my shoulder. I tell myself I'll only close my eyes for a second. Just to catch my breath. But when I open them again, it's freezing, pitch dark, and there's so much cloud cover I can't even see the stars.

Cursing under my breath, I fight the urge to laugh, because I'm sure once I start, I'm not going to be able to stop. With my luck, the noise will tempt the coyotes back.

Coyotes. Shit.

I've got to get up. Have to keep moving, but I don't know where I'm going. I don't even know if I ran in the right direction. There's an empty, gnawing feeling in my stomach. My head swims and I'm having difficulty concentrating. I decide that I just don't care if the coyotes find me again. Maybe they'll carry me somewhere useful this time.

Until morning, I huddle into myself, trying to keep warm. By some miracle the coyotes don't find me. When the sun rises, I'm cramped and my body is reminding me how much it hates me. When I see the sun, I just stare at it.

"Damn it!" I yell and hear it echo for miles and miles—

hundreds of repeats of the word, reiterating my frustration back to me.

I went the wrong way. The completely wrong effing way. I run a hand over my face, still cursing myself over and over in my head, but I push myself to my feet and begin the long trek back the way I came.

For the next several days, I hike with the sun at my back in the mornings and follow it to its horizon in the afternoons. Nights are for lie-downs and fitful sleeps, while I try to keep one ear open for carnivorous wild animals and one hand on my gun.

Every day my muscles get heavier. It requires more and more effort just to keep walking. Even my bones feel like they're made of lead. Several times, I'm certain I hear voices. And once I even hear Evie's laugh. I spin around looking for the source; I even backtrack a few steps looking for someone, hoping it's Evie and Asher, only to find there's no one there. Which only fills me with bitter disappointment and makes it even harder to keep blundering my way forward.

Finally, I stumble upon another set of footprints. Two sets. One is about my size; the other is much smaller. It can't be them, though. They have Starshine. There'd be horse prints. Unless they ran into coyotes like I did.

It's impossible to know for sure, but I follow the prints anyway. Wherever they lead, there will probably be people on the other side, and I hope that means Rushlake, too. My thoughts are fixed firmly on finding Evie. She must be so worried about me. It's been days with no contact, and she has no way of knowing if I made it away from those vulture-hawks. I keep her face in my mind and put one foot in front of the other, knowing each step takes me closer to seeing her in person.

I panic a little when the footsteps lead into another set of trees. The vulture-hawks prefer forested areas, but they're diurnal. Thank God. I'll wait them out and slip into the trees while they sleep.

As soon as the sun sets completely, I step into the woods, keeping the shotgun drawn and cocked, but nothing happens and I push through the woods as quietly as I can.

The footprints disappear in the slightly marshy under-brush of the woods. There's not enough light, but I remember from the map that the city is just on the other side of a set of woods. So I just keep heading as straight as I can, hoping that I'm almost there. Then, as if I willed it to appear, I find myself on the other side of the trees and staring at Rushlake City.

Evie

I sit in the waiting room, my knee bouncing up and down and my heart beating almost in rhythm to it. I grasp my necklace and run my fingers over the edges of the rose. Whatever happens here at the medical facility, I know it's going to determine everything. I just have to hope that this time these tests will tell me exactly what I'm supposed to do. And the possibility of knowing the answers scares me almost more than not knowing them.

Asher puts his hand on my knee, but he's shaking almost as much as I am. For some reason that makes me feel slightly better. To know he's just as nervous as I am.

The door pushes open and the doctor stands there, silhouetted by the bright lights coming from the room behind him. My mind goes entirely blank and my mouth goes dry. Like I'm back in the Outlands.

"Subject 121!" a voice calls through a set of speakers set in the walls.

That's me. I know it's me. I know I have to follow the person in the shadows, but I can't make my legs move. I really want to cry and I really want my mom.

The woman next to me stands up. "Come now, Evelyn. That's you." She smiles down at me, but even I know it's fake. She doesn't want to be here either. That doesn't help my nerves.

"Mother does not tolerate dawdlers." She yanks me up. "You are not just any three-year-old, you are an Enforcer. And you are not off to a good start. If you wish to impress Mother, you need to follow orders implicitly."

I swallow and nod, forcing my legs to push me toward the dark person in the doorway. To the moment that changes every-thing.

"Evie, are you all right?" Asher asks right next to me, causing me to knock the top of my head into his chin.

He spins away, cursing, while I clutch the top of my head with both hands.

I jump up. "Are you okay?"

"Yes. Fine. You?"

"Yeah."

"I knew you were hardheaded, Evie, but I didn't realize how hard." He grins at me, still rubbing at his jaw.

"Evelyn Winters?" The woman at the door says, and not for the first time if her tone is anything to go by.

"Coming." My voice cracks and I clear my throat. "Coming."

Feeling faint and not a little nauseated, I walk through the door, letting it flap shut behind me. The room is completely white, and directly in the center, taking up most of the space, is this . . . well . . . I don't know exactly what it is, but it reminds me of Snow White's casket in the storybook I found in Gavin's house.

The image does nothing to help my fluttering stomach and heart palpitations.

I take a step backward, away from it, bouncing into someone. I twist around to see the doctor—the same one that had spoken with me at Asher's grandmother's house—peering down at me.

He explains the procedure, which consists of me lying in the glass coffin—wonderful—with it closed—even better—while they watch from another room. Fantastic.

"Ready?" he asks.

I don't answer. I only suck in a deep breath through my nose and settle myself into the tube.

The nurse places headphones over my ears, then presses a

button on the side of the box. The glass draws over my head and instantly I feel claustrophobic. As if it's not just glass crawling over my head, but thousands and thousands of liters of water.

Mother is speaking, droning on and on about etiquette and manners and my duty. Stand this way. Push your shoulders back. Head up. Make sure you smile!

I'm standing on a little pedestal while the Dressmaker walks around me, mumbling around a mouthful of pins.

"Evelyn, that pink is a wonderful color on you."

I smile even though I'm sure the color washes me out. "Thank you, Mother."

"I knew that it would." She tugs on her own sapphire blue dress. "I think that it's a little too short, though, don't you?"

It's just barely above my knees, but I nod. "Yes, Mother."

She nods at the Dressmaker, who starts pulling pins and adjusting the hemline.

Mother goes on about my schedule for the next week. Meetings I'm to attend with her to take notes. Another request day. My appointments with Dr. Friar. Another ball. Violin lessons. Vocal lessons. Suitor tea party. An event at the theater. A dinner.

"Ouch!" I call out when the Dressmaker pokes me with a needle.

Mother glares at me. "Evelyn. Do not interrupt me."

"Sorry, Mother," I mutter and the Dressmaker sends me a look of apology.

The glass top opens and the doctor peers down at me. "Everything all right?" he asks.

"Yes."

"Fantastic. Now we need to inject you with some dye. I'd like to see what those nanos are doing. We're going to stick a needle in your arm, okay?"

My stomach drops and I know this is a bad idea, but if it helps then I'll do whatever it takes. I nod.

He signals the nurse to come over and I roll my head to watch her. She walks over slowly with something in her hand, but keeps out of my sight. When she's next to me, she takes my arm and says, "This is going to sting a little. You might want to close your eyes."

I do as she says, but my stomach churns and my entire chest tingles. This is a bad idea. A very bad idea. I open my mouth to object, but a sharp pain stabs into the crook of my elbow. My eyes fly open, but I'm not staring at the white walls of the medical center.

The walls are a pretty light blue that instinctively I know is supposed to be calming, but it's not. It's terrifying.

Medical equipment beeps and buzzes. Air hisses from somewhere nearby. The room is bustling with Medical Technicians. Their droning voices circle around me. "She's dangerous. Unpredictable. A killer . . . worse . . . a monster . . . a risk . . . must be eliminated."

Misery is my cloak and I wrap it around myself like a blanket. I deserve this.

I am a monster. A murderer. Betrayer.

A Technician leans over and sneers at me. "Traitor," he whispers into my ear, then pushes some sort of mask over my nose.

"This is too good for you." Straps are yanked across my body, biting into my skin, causing tears to prick at my eyes. But I don't cry out. I deserve this. I am a traitor.

My pulse beats a tattoo against my throat and my head swims. Black spots form in front of my eyes and no matter how much I blink they multiply and grow, so I let my eyes drift closed.

"Stand clear," a soft voice says.

Something pierces the skin inside my elbow and a deep aching fills my bones. The aching turns to gnawing, then to pure agony that travels from the marrow of my bones to the tips of my nerve endings. Within seconds every square centimeter of my flesh is being devoured slowly by fire. I scream out, but it doesn't sound like me. It's as if something primal has taken control of my body.

I thrash against my restraints, while people rush around me. Another needle is plunged into my other elbow. And yet another in my neck. With each assault the torture grows worse, until I'm nothing more than a writhing mass of torment.

Just when I think I can't take any more, there's a soft click in my brain and a mist films over the agony. I rip my arms from the straps, tearing the needles from my arms. Blood squirts across the nearest Technicians.

Shouts yell for someone—anyone—to get me under control before I hurt someone. Two Technicians advance on me and sink into a crouch. When they get near enough, I lunge forward, grabbing each by the arm and tossing them aside like dolls in turn. I'm moving before they even hit the wall to either side of me.

Another Technician jumps on me from behind, his arms tight around my neck. I flip him over my head. He lands hard on his back at my feet and his breath whooshes out all at once. I leave him there gasping as I run for the door.

As I wrench it open, two Enforcers appear on the other side of it. I strike out with my foot, kicking one in the chest. She flies back, hitting the wall on the other side of the hallway, but the other dashes forward and tackles me, shoving me into the ground and knocking the wind out of me.

Before I can even get my breath back, more people are crowding on top of me. My legs are tied together behind my back and to my arms. I have a moment to think that my limbs are going to be torn from my body when they lift me up and toss me onto the bed again.

They strap me to the bed again, this time facedown. A new voice speaks from the doorway. One I'd know anywhere.

Mother.

"What a mess. I told you to sedate her first."

My mind goes blank and my body seems to lose its connection with my brain as I blink and stare at the scene in front of me.

I'm not lying on my stomach restrained to a bed. I'm standing. Blood trickles down my arms from the slashes across them. Two men lie in a heap on the floor at my feet. The only sign they're still alive is the slight rise and fall of their chests.

The doctor stands only a few feet from me, another syringe in his hands. The nurse that talked to me just a few minutes ago is standing next to him, pulling jars of liquids from a cabinet.

Asher pushes past the two people in the doorway and we stare in shock and horror at each other. I don't have to ask to know I'm the one that did this.

CHAPTER EIGHTEEN

It's been a year to the day. I have to think that Eli's not coming back. To be honest, I probably knew from the beginning that Mother wouldn't let him get away with what he did, but even if my head knew it, my heart wouldn't believe it until now.

—EXCERPT FROM LENORE ALLEN'S JOURNAL

Gavin

I'm not sure how to get in. I'm almost positive the guards won't let me in without that stupid paper, so I'm working on coming up with another way. It takes me a moment to realize that the bridge across from me is only large enough for foot traffic. That means there's another entrance. There has to be. How else do they get supplies in?

I wander around until I find the bigger entrance, and then I wait, hiding in the shadow of the concrete wall. Watching. Studying the patterns and duties of the guards at this gate.

After a few hours, I realize that they don't even look inside the large supply wagons. If I can somehow sneak over to one, I can slip underneath it and hang on until it drives into the city.

Finally, a horse-drawn wagon comes rumbling up to the gates. One of the guards comes out and speaks with the driver. Seizing my chance, I sneak over to it, then slide underneath the wagon and wrap my ankles around part of the wagon's frame and my arms around another part. It hurts to be stretched out like this, and my shoulder is screaming at me, but I can't think of another way.

They have an eternity-long conversation that I try to block out, and my legs and arms start to cramp from the exertion of holding on to the undercarriage. Eventually, though, the wagon pulls through the gates and into the city.

When the wagon stops at a crossroads, I let go, dropping to the ground and rolling out to the side, before jumping up and strolling away as if I didn't just drop out from underneath a supply wagon. After a few blocks, I stop and massage the knots in my arms and legs.

I may not know the exact layout of the city, but I remember listening to Asher talking about it when we were kids. I know about where Asher's family lives. It's just a matter of finding out exactly which house is the correct one. It's not like I can just go up to the people and ask them if they know where the St. Jameses live. I'll be reported for being an Outlander and arrested faster than I can blink.

But there's no way I'm going to be able to find Evie without some kind of help. Maybe I should just take the chance and ask one of the police. I *can* prove that I'm supposed to be here. What harm could it do?

Then I shake my head. Nope. Bad idea. The people of

Rushlake dislike outsiders almost as much as Elysium hates Surface Dwellers. Except they don't go quite so far as death to punish people for "breaking" in. Still, I don't feel like getting booted out. Even though when they find the St. Jameses, they'll see I have a visa and it'll be fine. Of course, that would depend on *if* Asher actually showed them the visa.

Maybe I could surreptitiously ask a few people, saying I'd come with the St. Jameses and went for a walk and got lost and need help finding my way back. I glance down to my filthy clothes. Nope. That'll just send me back to talking with the police.

I'll just have to take the chance and try asking a servant. They're less likely to care that I'm an Outlander. But it's not like I can just pick a house and ring the bell. I'll have to wait until someone comes outside.

Even that proves to be difficult. When I get to the area where I know Asher's house is, I manage to catch three servants on their way out of various houses, but only one even acknowledges I'm talking to him, and he just points down the street, which doesn't help me. At all. Apparently even the servants think they're better than Outlanders. Figures.

Evie

I don't suppose it's much of a surprise they decide not to let me go home. Considering what I did, I guess I should be glad they didn't have me arrested. They still don't know what caused it, despite all their fancy equipment. And they don't know how I knocked out two grown men at least twice my size with my bare hands. So, now I'm stuck in yet another hospital room while they try to figure out how dangerous I am. While Asher talks with the doctor, trying to find out how long they're going to keep me here, I let my eyelids drift closed. All the panic is making me exhausted.

After what feels like only a few minutes, Asher gently shakes me awake. When I blink my eyes open, his grandmother is there, watching me with a sad expression.

She takes the seat across from the bed, while Asher settles onto the chair to my left. I can see she's bracing herself to tell me something. It's quiet and I try not to fidget while I wait for her to speak. She seems lost in her thoughts and Asher and I exchange a look before he clears his throat. She startles and then her eyes focus on Asher.

She gives him a look of apology. "It's always hard to know where to start, but as with everything it's probably best to start with the beginning." She moves her gaze to mine, then gives me a small smile. "You and I, my dear, have a lot more in common than you think." She takes a deep breath and then looks into her lap. That's when I notice her hands. She's holding a small piece of shiny paper.

She gives Asher one more apologetic glance before handing it to me. I take it, dread curling in my stomach. Whatever this is, I don't want to look, but I do. Then furrow my brow.

It's just a picture of a group of six people smiling into the camera. They're all wearing lab coats and smiles. There are six of them. Four men, a woman, and a girl about my age, maybe slightly older. All have blond hair. The four men are split, two on either side of the woman, who has her hands on the girl's shoulders. Behind the group is what looks like the window from that creepy underground lab in the Outlands, or from the rooms in my hallucinations, only the water behind them is lit with lights and is dark blue—almost black. It's only recognizable as water because of the colorful fish swimming in it.

It's pretty, and . . . I feel like I know where it was taken. Like I've been there. The strangest part is that the two females and the youngest man look familiar. I'm sure I know them for some reason.

I look back up at her. "I don't understand."

"That's me." She points to the woman.

I go back to studying the picture and Asher leans against my knee to get a better look himself. And while at first I didn't get it, I can see the resemblance now. It's in the shape and color of the eyes—the same as Asher's. The picture must have been taken years ago, when she was much younger, because her gray hair is blond in the picture and her face is smooth and free of wrinkles.

"You were very pretty," I blurt out. I realize quickly that was probably very rude. As if I'm saying she's not pretty now, which isn't the case. She's a very handsome woman, for someone of her—

She smiles at me, cutting off the mortified rant inside my head. "Thank you."

Asher looks up at her. "Who are the rest of these people?"

She returns his look, then turns back to me. "Do you know? Does anyone look familiar?"

I slowly shake my head. "I feel like I should, but I can't figure it out."

She points to the girl. "That's the woman you know as Mother." Asher freezes and his eyes lock on to his grandmother, but she ignores him and continues. "And, as I'm sure you've guessed, this picture was taken in Elysium. It was taken right after we cracked the puzzle to the greatest scientific advancement of that time. Permanent sentient nanobots." She looks up to meet my wide-eyed gaze. "I'm one of the scientists who invented the nanos that took away your memories, Evie."

I can only stare at Asher's grandmother. "*You* invented them?" I finally ask. She nods and I can't help but blurt out, "All of this is your fault? I don't know who or *what* I am because of *you*?"

She shakes her head, then pauses and nods. "Ultimately, I suppose this is my fault. They were never intended for what Mother eventually used them for, but . . . yes, I, and the others in my group, created them, and in the end that's all that really matters."

Asher doesn't even look shocked.

"Did you know about this?" I demand of him.

He shakes his head. "Not until a few hours ago. I . . . I didn't know how to tell you . . ." he trails off, looking at his hands.

My hands clench into fists as my anger turns to burn at his grandmother. "You didn't think it was important to tell me right away when we arrived? Or when the doctors said it may be my nanos making me hallucinate?" She doesn't answer, only looks away from me. I slam my fisted hand onto the bed. "Answer me! Why didn't you say anything?"

She sighs. "Because I didn't want to. That part of my life— the fragment of time I was there—is over, and I wanted to keep it that way." She looks at Asher. "I wanted to keep that part of my life from touching you, but it seems that fate has made it your problem too. I've been responsible for enough people dying. I wasn't going to let my selfishness harm an innocent girl. I couldn't keep it a secret anymore." She gives Asher an apologetic look, then sends me one as well.

Still furious, I shake my head and try to connect the dots. If she invented them, she knows how to fix them. I lean forward, the first flicker of hope fluttering in my heart.

"You know how to make me better."

She shakes her head. "No, they've made a few improvements to the 'bots that I don't know how to fix. I've already spoken to the doctor about it. But I might know someone who can help."

"Same thing," Asher says. He gets up and stalks toward the window.

Her eyes follow him. They're sad when they turn back to me. "Eli and I—we were partners." She glances over at Asher before turning back to me. "More than partners, really." She sighs. "But that's neither here nor there. As I said, I'll start from the beginning.

"I was recruited to work in Elysium shortly after the War. She—Mother—hired me because of my work with the military here and my knowledge of nanite technology. Apparently there had been an outbreak of disease in Elysium and it had killed over half her people. She wanted to prevent it from happening again. She'd read of my success with sentient nanobots and had hoped by injecting nanobots, they would act like an immunization. That is to say, they would work along with the body's immune system to get rid of germs and viruses, on a permanent basis, so she wouldn't have to worry about something like that again.

"I took the offer almost before she stopped speaking. I saw it as a real opportunity to help people. After everything that happened during the War, I thought it would be a good way to repent for my sins."

I frown. "Sins?"

Her chuckle is full of derision, but I'm certain it's not directed at me. "A way to make up for things I thought I'd done wrong. And for a while, I thought I'd done it. I spent months with the others there, experimenting with the military tech I'd brought along, and finally came up with something that would keep people from being sick.

"I was so young, barely into my thirties. And stupid. But I never dreamed what happened would happen. I never realized what she really wanted the nanos for. Or what she would do. She was so young herself. A baby really. Too young, I suppose, to be running an entire city all by herself."

"How old was she?" Asher asks.

"Seventeen, eighteen. Twenty at the most. She said she was twenty-five when I met her, but it was obvious she was lying. I suppose that should have been my first clue. But I didn't think I had anything to worry about. If only I'd known, even though she was so young, what she was capable of."

"What?" I ask, but I don't think she even hears me. Her eyes are far away and I'm certain she doesn't even see me anymore. I glance to Asher, who returns to sit next to me, his uncertain expression telling me he doesn't know what she's talking about either.

"Eli and I both came from the Surface, but he'd already been down there from . . . before. Apparently she trusted him more than anyone else. She put him with me mostly to supervise because I was a Surface Dweller."

For the first time, she smiles at me as if we're sharing an inside joke, but while the phrase makes me nervous, I don't know why. When I don't smile back, she turns her attention back to her hands. "And, for a while, it worked out well, and she began to trust me. I liked her almost from the beginning. She seemed so sweet, and she was so *young*, barely older than you and Asher. I almost saw her as a kid sister. And Eli . . ." Her eyes take on that faraway look again. "He was so smart. And sweet. Attractive. He had fantastic ideas. We quickly became partners." She looks back up; her eyes darting back and forth between Asher and me. "Both inside the lab and out."

She shakes her head as if amused when Asher makes a disgusted sound in his throat. "We continued working on our project and everything was falling into place easier than I'd hoped. I'd never been happier. I was doing something I loved, helping people, living in the prettiest place on earth, and I was falling in love with a wonderful man. Life couldn't have been more perfect."

My life is just about perfect. The thought comes out of nowhere. I don't know why I thought it, but it startles me and reminds me of the way Gavin had reacted in the village when I'd said something similar.

But before I can think further on it, Asher is talking and I lose the thought.

"So what happened?" His voice is rough, but he doesn't seem angry anymore.

"Fate had other plans," she says, quietly. "What neither of us knew was that Mother—we knew her as Abigail then— had fallen in love with Eli, too. And while he never did anything to encourage her, she developed an entire relationship between the two of them in her head." She meets my eyes. "If I'd known how . . . not right . . . in the head she was, I would never have taken the job. Never."

She pauses and seems to be waiting for me to respond. As if she needs me to believe her because maybe she doesn't believe herself. But I nod, because I want to know the rest of the story. It's the most information I've ever had about the place that was my home for sixteen years.

She lets out a breath. "Then, a few months after we found

success with the nanos and finished injecting them into people, we saw they were working. *Really* working. Just like they were supposed to. Sure, all the data and tests we'd done said they would work, but we didn't know for certain until we actually put them into people and tested them on a large scale. People weren't getting sick, even when directly exposed to diseases that should have killed them. It was fantastic. We'd found a cure for almost any disease we'd ever faced, and with no side effects. It was a huge medical breakthrough. I couldn't wait to share it with the rest of the world. However, one night, when Eli and I were . . . um . . . celebrating . . ." She blushes and I almost smile. "She caught us."

"Then what happened?" Asher asks, without even batting an eye at his grandmother's admission. He's leaning forward eagerly, and I have to admit I'm dying of curiosity.

"Abby went crazy. She was sure we'd done it on purpose. That we'd known she loved him and were laughing at her behind her back, which of course we didn't and hadn't. But she didn't believe us. She yelled about paying us back and then ran off.

"She was only a child, really. What was the worst she could do? We thought she'd get over it. But we should have known better. There had been rumors—that I ignored or just flat-out didn't believe—that the people who she said had died of diseases had really died at her hand. Because they didn't fit her ideal vision. But I blew it off as ludicrous. She'd lost her entire family in the War, but she was still only a child. And even though people always seemed especially careful not to upset her, I didn't put much stock into any of the rumors. But she instituted a new law. Unmarried—un*Coupled*—people weren't allowed to touch, and she was the only one who could permit people to become Coupled. It was her way of making sure Eli and I couldn't continue our relationship."

"UnCoupled." The term rolls around in my head. Coupled. UnCoupled. *Touching between unCoupled people is forbidden.* I glance at Asher, wondering if that's why I'm so nervous when anyone new touches me. But his grandmother is still talking and I force myself to listen.

"So, we just figured we'd leave. There was no reason to stay. We'd finished our task. Sure, Elysium was pretty and peaceful, but that was it. We had the nanos inside us, and we knew how we'd created them. It'd be easy to share that knowledge with the rest of the world. So we got ready to leave . . . except she caught us. And then we realized what *else* the nanos could be used for. Torture. Control. Not all of the military tech had been stripped from the nanos, and she used that against us. She tortured us until I agreed to let her have him." There's a tremor in her voice.

Asher and I exchange a glance and he squeezes my hand. I have no idea what Mother did to torture her, but if Lenore loved Eli as I love Gavin . . .

Asher's grandmother takes a deep shaky breath. "The minute she left us alone, confident she'd made her point, we ran away. Eli and I snuck out using one of the submersibles. When we got back to the Surface, he told me he loved me, but he was worried about the rest of the innocent people. That he didn't want her to use the tech we built to hurt others, but he wouldn't be able to live with himself if she killed me, which he was certain would happen if I stayed. Then he kissed me, and jumped back into the submersible before I could stop him. I never saw him again."

"Why?" Asher asks, voicing the question in my head.

"No way to get down there. No one believed me that it existed, and I couldn't find a different way to get that deep on my own. Eventually, I met your grandfather and it didn't seem to matter as much." She looks off into space. "I'd begun to wonder if I hadn't just been making it all up myself. A city underwater? It didn't seem possible. How could they be there without anyone knowing about them? So I just did the easiest thing and pretended to forget about it." Her eyes meet mine. "Until I met you, my dear."

"Me? How did you know?"

She gives me that soft smile again. "You reminded me of Eli. Then Asher told me where you'd come from and I knew."

"Knew what?"

She opens her mouth, then closes it and sighs. "Knew I couldn't pretend anymore."

"But . . . why didn't you use your technology to help people here?"

She gives me a level look. "Twice unscrupulous and murderous people corrupted the technology I invented to help people. Twice I was ignorant and naive enough to be used to hurt innocent people. I promised myself never again. I would never again be manipulated or let my knowledge cause pain for any reason."

"So . . ." I say, still not understanding.

She closes her eyes, and I get a sick feeling in the pit of my stomach when she reopens them and focuses directly on me. "I think you need to go back. To Elysium."

"You want me to go back?" My voice cracks with surprise. I don't know why, but I never saw that coming.

She nods. Then pauses and shakes her head. "No, I don't really want you to go back, but I think it's the only way. Go to Eli. He'll help you. If he's even still alive. . . ." Her voice trails off and she goes back to twisting her wedding ring around and around on her finger.

Asher turns to me. "You don't have to go back, but it sounds like it's the best bet. Even if we can't find Eli, there has to be *some*one there who knows how to fix the nanos."

When I hesitate, thinking of everything Gavin feels about the place, Asher's grandmother speaks up once more. "I know you want to go back, Evie."

"No . . . I . . ." I sigh. What's the point in lying? Despite everything Gavin said about it, I do want to go back. I want to go home. "Yes. I want to go back." Looking first at Asher and then at his grandmother, I say, "Thank you for helping me."

She gives me a sad smile. "It isn't just for you I'm doing it. It's for me, too." Without any further explanation she stands and walks from the room, leaving Asher and me to stare after her.

Chapter Nineteen

I found a letter today. From Eli. From . . . back then. I found it in one of the books I haven't looked at since then. I don't even really know why I looked now, except I needed to clean out that room. The baby is due any day now, and she'll need it. Anyway, the letter warns me to never go back. Not until he gives the signal. I can only assume he never got the chance to send one.

—Excerpt from Lenore Allen's journal

Evie

Exhaustion pools into me and I let myself fall back into the bed. Asher turns toward me, but I wave him off. "I'm fine. Just tired." I'm beyond tired. I feel like a husk of myself. Every time I feel that click in my head, or have a hallucination, or wake up somewhere other than where I thought I was, it's followed by this crushing fatigue. I feel as though I'm being dragged to the floor by invisible hands.

He watches me for a minute, then nods as if he just came to a decision. "We're going to have to leave tonight," he says.

Shock makes me speechless and he continues, either not noticing or not caring that I'm completely flabbergasted. "They're not going to just let you walk out of here. Not after you KO'd everyone in that room. And if we go late, there won't be as many people walking around. We should be able to sneak out."

Sneak out? Gavin's stories of Elysium dig at me. "I don't know. Maybe we should wait and see what your doctor comes up with."

He blinks at me. "No. They're not going to come up with an answer, Evie. You've intrigued them. They want to know more about *you* and how *you* can do what you did. You'll be nothing but a lab rat now. I can't let that happen, which means we need to leave tonight."

"But . . . why? What's the hurry? Why can't we wait?

He sighs. "Remember those errands my father wanted me to run in exchange for helping you here?"

I'm not sure what that has to do with anything, but I only say, "Y-yes . . ."

"Well, one of the errands was to take a letter to someone in the city. I'm not stupid enough to give someone a letter without reading it first, at least, not anymore." He looks extremely sad for a minute, but when he continues his voice is just as strong as it was. "Well, I read it and it was about you. To someone I know very well." The way he says it suggests that he may know him pretty well, but liking is another matter entirely. "My father wanted this person to find out as much as they could about you. To do some tests and everything to figure out just what you could do. He said you could be useful to the city in ways we could never imagine."

"I-I don't think I understand. Are you saying that *you* gave a letter to someone to have them *experiment* on me?" I can't decide if I'm angry or shocked or some other emotion all together.

"No!" he says forcefully. "No. I didn't give it to him. I ripped it up and threw it away. My grandmother made sure we could trust the doctors who were helping you. But after your testing today, I went to find the doctors to figure out what our next step was. I heard them talking with someone really familiar. The exact person I was supposed to give the letter to. And they weren't discussing treatment plans. They were talking about what tests to run and they were excited about what that could mean for Rushlake's security force and technological advances over the other cities."

This time I don't have to have him explain to me what he means. I get it, and besides, the quicker I get to Elysium, the quicker I can get my memories back. It's not like they can really do anything for me here anyway.

"All right," I say. "What's the plan?"

"I'm not exactly sure, but I've got some ideas. Give me a little time to pull things together and get everything ready," Asher says, pausing at the door. "Rest until I get back."

Left with no choice, I stay where I am, but I don't want to rest. Even as spent as I feel, my body is tingling with nerves and anticipation. If I weren't so exhausted, I'd probably be pacing the floor like Gavin used to do all the time.

My thoughts are filled with him. What if he's really gone for good? What if he's not? What if he shows up after we leave?

For the next two hours I sit in the chair, dozing while I wait, while Asher runs around getting things ready. I consider writing a note for Gavin, but what would I say? He'd never support returning to Elysium. I don't even know that he'd ever get it. If he's alive *to* get it.

Finally Asher steps into the room. "Everything's set. We should go."

"What's the plan? How are we going to get to Elysium?"

He looks over his shoulder, before stepping closer. "When Gavin came back with you, he had a submarine. I guess that's what he used to escape with you. My father confiscated it, for safety, of course." He rolls his eyes.

"Of course," I say.

"Anyway, I know where it is and I know it's still working. We're just going to steal it."

"Your father doesn't have it protected?"

Asher gives a cynical laugh. "Yeah, right. My dad's too sure of himself to think anyone would steal from him right under his nose."

It's not perfect, but it's the only plan we've got. We're going to have to make it work . . . but there's just one more thing I need to know. "What if Gavin is still looking for us?"

He gives me a sad look, but his eyes are determined. "We don't have time to wait. My friend is guarding the gates right now." He glances at his watch. "For only another twenty minutes. If we're going to go, now's the chance. We can't wait for a slim-chanced maybe."

My stomach lurches. "But . . ."

He leans down so his face is close to mine. "Evie . . . you know as well as I do, he's *not* coming. We've been through this and we have to leave now before it's too late."

I don't say anything and he turns and starts walking toward the door.

"But what if he's right? What if it is far worse to be there than here?" It's barely a whisper.

Asher spins around. "Evie! You do not have a choice! I wasn't kidding when I said Dr. Trevin would use you as a lab rat. Sure, they probably could fix your problems. But then they'll perform experiments on you. Just to see how well they work. They'll cut you open to see how long it takes you to heal. Give you different poisons, bring you to the point of death, only to revive you and bring you back. Force you into situations like what happened today, but maybe next time you won't pull back. Maybe you'll kill someone, Evie." I look at the ground. I know all too well, that's a definite possibility, but he doesn't stop. "Then, when they have all that, they'll torture you to get information about Elysium. Information you don't remember. And do you think they're going to believe you don't know the answers to their questions?"

Again I shake my head, as visions of what he's talking about play in my mind. My breath hitches, but as much as I don't want that to happen, I'm almost positive that if we leave, Gavin will show up. I'm not sure why I'm so sure. Maybe it's wishful thinking.

"I don't know, Asher—"

"Evie!" he yells, startling me into shutting my mouth. He's never yelled at me before. "If we don't leave in the next five minutes we won't get another chance until tomorrow night and by that time it may be too late."

I close my eyes and nod. He's right. Gavin's not coming and if I wait, it may be too late. Not just for me. For everyone around me.

Asher leads the way out of my room and around the corner to a stairway. He was right about there being no one around. It's almost as quiet as that horrible empty town we rode through. The clatter of our footfalls on the concrete stairs terrifies me as we run down them. I'm sure someone is going to hear, but then we're bursting out into the moonlight.

He glances left and right, then jerks his head to the left. "Come on. This way."

We run through the streets and I'm glad he knows where he's going, because by the time we've turned three times, I've no idea where we are or how to get back to where we were. Finally, a building looms in front of us, large enough to be at least two levels, but I can see through the open doors that it's just one large one. A smell that reminds me of Starshine blows out and I feel my stomach sink. I still don't know what happened to her. Lights suddenly blaze out as we approach, blinding me. Someone's going to see us. I try ducking back out of the path, but Asher lunges at me and yanks me back before I can.

"Relax," he says with a half smile. "The lights are automatic. They turn on when someone walks near them." He drags me into the building, which I can see now is lined on either side and as far as the eye can see with horses in boxes.

In the aisle between them, four horses are already prepared and tethered to the bars of the closest boxes. The leather of their saddles creaks as they shift from foot to foot. Almost the instant we step in, the horse on the left makes a familiar whinny sound and stomps at the floor. I can't help the grin that slides across my face. It's Starshine. I race toward her, and wrap my arms around her large neck.

"Told you I'd send for her."

At that moment, two men step out from an aisle. They're dressed in black with two guns crisscrossed on their backs. I can see the barrels peeking over their shoulders. I instantly tense when I see them and try backing away. I'm not letting them put me back in that hospital.

But Asher touches my shoulder. "It's okay, Evie. I hired them to protect us in the Outlands." He glances at my leg. "I'm not taking any chances this time."

I'm still a little wary of the guards, but I grin at Asher. For the first time in days I feel like maybe this will be all right. That everything is going to get better.

Starshine makes another sound and picks at the back of my shirt, tickling me. Giggling, I say, "I missed you, too."

Asher laughs. "Long way from the girl who was terrified of her just a few days ago."

I just shrug. "Transportation?" I put my foot in the stirrup and try to hitch myself up.

He gives me one quick nod and pushes on my butt to shove me into the saddle. "Transportation."

Chapter Twenty

They came again today. Somehow my past has caught up with me, but, as before, I've told them nothing. Even if I have a few bruises on my person for my troubles. I don't know where they heard about Elysium or why they want information on it, but it can't be anything good, especially when they're willing to resort to torture of an old lady to obtain the information.

—Excerpt from Lenore Allen's journal

Gavin

I've just about given up. Despite my careful rationing, I'm out of food, and I've been hungry for hours already. I've just made up my mind to come up with a new plan when the door in the house across from where I'm sitting opens and Mayor St. James emerges.

I glance around, sure this is some weird set up. It couldn't be that easy. Could it? And why the hell is Asher's dad here? He jogs down the steps, then gets into a car that's waiting at the curb. The car pulls smoothly away, moving in the opposite direction from me.

I wait until I'm sure he's gone to rush up the front stairs and knock on the door. It takes a minute, but when the door opens, I recognize Asher's grandmother. At first she looks shocked to see me, but then she opens the door wider. I can't help but notice that her eyes don't look all that friendly.

"Gavin, isn't it?" She firms her lips into a thin line.

"Yes, ma'am."

She leads me into the warm kitchen. It's uncomfortably hot compared to my hours outside in the cold, but I forget all that when she introduces me to the cook, who beams at me and plies me with cookies and milk to eat while she cooks me something warm.

While I appreciate it all, and I *am* starving, I really just want to see Evie.

"Is Evie sleeping?" I peer around her to the door that leads to the living room. "I'd really like to see her."

Mrs. St James doesn't answer right away and I shift uncomfortably in my chair. Something's wrong. Something is very wrong.

"Eat, then come find me," she finally says, and leaves the room before I can argue.

I don't want food, I want Evie, so I try to follow, but it still takes me a few minutes to find her. She's sitting in the parlor and reading a book. I feel awkward going in—I'm pretty sure she doesn't like me very much—and even more so when she looks up at me. It's as if she's appraising me and I'm not up to her standards.

Nothing I'm not used to.

"They were here five days," she says at last. I open my mouth, but she gives me a look—one that tells me to shut my mouth, so I do. She continues, "In those five days, we've hired only the best physicians to work on her case. Asher has spent practically every waking moment with her making sure she was comfortable and happy. Despite all this, the hallucinations did not improve. The doctors were, for lack of a better word, stumped."

I lift an eyebrow. I'm so confused right now.

"She never gave up hope on you. She either snuck out to see if you made it to the gate or forced Asher to go with her to check. Every day. She cares for you very much."

This time, my eyebrows wing up. Evie snuck out to look for me? I have to grin. Of course she did.

She leans forward, the book falling to the floor, forgotten. "It's obvious she loves you and you love her." She pauses as if expecting me to argue, and a tiny bit of warmth creeps into her eyes when I don't. But there's sadness there, too, when she says, "Keep in mind you're not the only one."

That's not surprising really. My mom fell in love with Evie almost immediately. So did my sister, and my brother. Evie just has that way about her. I don't even know what it is exactly.

Maybe it's how strong she is despite everything that's happened to her. She's a fighter. That's for sure. And she's nice and polite to everyone, even when she's pissed. Especially when she's pissed. It's like she's trying to actually kill you with kindness.

I realize Asher's grandmother is still staring at me, waiting for my answer, so I nod.

"They went back to Elysium."

The blood drains from my face. I can feel it. My head spins and I have to catch myself on a chair next to me to prevent myself from falling. I lower myself to it slowly.

"No. Absolutely not." It's all the words I can muster. I can't seem to remember how to form sentences.

She finally meets my eyes. "The nanos are malfunctioning. It's probably what's causing her issues. Her memory loss. Her blackouts. Her hallucinations. If they don't get them fixed and/or removed, she'll die."

I shake my head. "The nanos are only in her to prevent pressure sickness and to promote healing. That's what she told me when we were in Elysium. They're not making her sick." I pause at her expression. "What?"

"No. They're not. That's not at all what they're for."

"How do you know?"

She won't meet my eyes. And that bad feeling comes back with a vengeance. "I helped invent the nanos. I lived in Elysium. For a time."

My whole body trembles. And black spots swim in front of my eyes. *No. That's not possible. That can't be possible.* "You're from Elysium?"

"I am."

He betrayed me. Again. And I trusted him. I clench my hands into fists, red spots replacing the black ones. I can't believe I fell for it again. I knew better! Damn it! I strike the arm of the chair so hard my entire arm aches from the force. I shove up from the chair.

"Where are you going?"

"To get her back. I'm not letting her go to Elysium." I say it like I'm challenging her, and I think I am. Challenging her to stop me from going after Evie.

She sighs. "I understand why you wouldn't want her to go back, but it is her only option. Eli—my partner—can help fix her."

"That's a lie," I shout. Then something even worse occurs to me, making my stomach roll with terror. "That's why Mayor St. James was here. Why Asher was so willing to help us. He knew. He *knew* from the beginning and he had *no* intention of really helping." I glare at her. "You're one of *them*. One of those . . . those monsters, and you're going to get Evie killed. Just like my father."

Her voice is soft in comparison to mine. "Yes, Kristofer was here. And yes it was because of Evie. But I would *never* let them hurt her, especially my son-in-law. You don't live this long, with the secrets I know, by being foolish, boy. Even though Kristofer thinks he's calling the shots, I always have strings to pull and an ace in the hole. I wouldn't have sent her back to Elysium if I didn't think it was the only option." She shakes her head. "I'm not one of them, but your ranting sounds just like them . . . Surface Dweller."

I stop and spin around, my heart thudding in my ears like a drum. "What did you say?"

"I lost someone important to me, too, because of *her*. I

know how horrible Mother is. I don't think anyone but you and I know exactly how much of a monster she is, Gavin. But you have to understand how important this is. Going back is Evie's *only* chance. *Eli* is Evie's only chance. He made those nanos what they are; he'll be able to fix them to get her back to normal."

"I don't believe you."

"I don't blame you," she says with a sad smile. "I wouldn't believe me either." It's said so matter-of-factly, I'm suddenly sure it's the truth. I blink dumbly at her. "Do you even know what nanos really are?"

I shake my head.

"Sit. Please. You make me nervous when you hulk over me like that." She laughs softly, but I don't. I don't find anything funny about any of this. She sighs and gestures to the chair again. I lean against it instead, crossing my arms over my chest.

"Nanos are short for nanorobotics. Robots so small you can't see them unless you have a microscope. They're built on a nanoscale, which is why they're called nanobots. A nanometer is something like one billionth of a meter."

"Okay, so they're really small. I got that already."

Her entire face pinches, and I think she's finally going to lose her temper, but she takes a deep breath and continues. "Yes. They're really small. They were originally invented long before the War for medical purposes. At first simple things like site-specific medication delivery, microsurgery, and diagnosis. Then certain electronic companies started experimenting to make them smarter by adding propulsion systems and the ability to control them remotely."

"I don't get what this has to do with Evie. . . ."

"I'm getting there. Mostly, nanites were used for peaceful purposes. And while they were important, most funding went to less . . . out-there . . . programs. So, as you can imagine, progress was slow. But then the War started and the old governments realized that nanotechnology wasn't just for science fiction. They started an arms race with each other. To find the most cost efficient, yet effective weapon possible to turn the tide and win. They spent billions on technology and scientists and engineers. I was one of those engineers. Hired straight out of engineering school. I'd invented the nanites that were used in the warheads that took down almost every major city in the world by the time I was twenty-five."

I plop back into the chair, because my wobbly legs can't hold my weight anymore. "Holy shit."

She cracks a smile. "Indeed."

"How . . . how did that happen?"

She shrugs. "Vanity." She waves her hand at me. "But that's not important. What is important is that technology is the same technology I took to Elysium when Mother hired me."

"She hired you?"

"Yes. She wanted me to develop permanent sentient nanites that would protect her people from disease. I did it, too. With the help of Eli, my partner. But Mother turned it against us. She didn't want to prevent diseases, or not totally. She wanted control. Complete control, and she got it. All because of me."

I'm more confused than anything. "I don't get it."

"The nanites do whatever they're programmed to do. Prevent disease. Repair body tissues. Destroy them. Rewrite neuropathways." She gives me a meaningful look. "But the program only works if it's functional. Something broke Evie's. She needs it fixed, and I'm fairly certain Eli's the only one who can do it. Before something worse happens."

I stare at her. I can barely wrap my mind around what she's saying. This is insane. Then again, maybe I shouldn't be surprised. If there's one thing I know for sure, it's that Mother is insane.

Then another thought hits me. I remember this story. And I remember exactly where I heard it. Elysium. In the journals Evie found in the secret room in the abandoned sector. Except the story came from a different person.

Eli.

Who was killed. By Mother.

He's not even there. They're going back to Elysium to get help from a guy who's been dead before Evie was even born.

I shove to my feet, the chair falling over with a clatter.

"When did they leave?"

She frowns at me. "An hour or so, I think. I don't know. They snuck out."

I curse under my breath and rush to the front door.

"Where are you going?"

"To stop them."

"Didn't you hear what I said about the nanos?"

I don't even turn around. My mind is swirling with ideas of how to stop them. "Yeah. I heard you. And I also know that Eli is dead."

"Wait. What?" Her breath catches. "How do you know?"

Grimacing, I turn to look at her. "We found his journals. And then we found Mother's. He tried to start an uprising." I swallow and lick my lips. "Mother put a stop to it."

Her shoulders shake and her lips tremble; then her eyes grow wide. "You have stop them. Mother will kill them, and with Eli gone . . ." She shakes her head.

I yank open the door.

"You'll never catch them on foot," she calls out to me.

"I don't plan on running all the way there."

"Then how?"

"I'll figure something out." I push out the door.

"Good luck."

Whether or not luck is on my side, I will do whatever it takes to get to Evie before she leaves for Elysium.

CHAPTER TWENTY-ONE

When traveling the Outlands, it is highly recommended to travel in groups of no less than three people. Should you need to travel in smaller groups, make sure to pack appropriately in case of emergency situations, keeping in mind the severe climate changes that take place in the Outlands. Travelers would also not go amiss carrying firearms to protect themselves from the wildlife.

—Excerpt from *Safety Guide to Traveling the Outlands*

Evie

The thud of the horses' hooves and the jingling of their reins and saddles are the only sound as we rush back to the village. We've been riding all night and I'm exhausted and sore and my skin is completely numb from the cold.

Asher is riding next to me and he looks just as tired. "How long?"

He sighs, and looks at the rising sun. "A few more hours until we stop to eat and rest the horses."

My stomach growls at the mention of food and he laughs. "Maybe only another hour."

The entire time we're riding, I try not to think about what's waiting for me under the ocean. There are too many unknowns. So instead, I let my mind drift.

It's so different from the trip to Rushlake. It's freezing for one. Plus the two guards with their guns and whatever else they have in those large packs. And we're moving much faster than a walk. Not as fast as when we were running to get away from the coyotes, but fast enough. Also, the air is so much drier. Even though our packs have water and food in them, my mouth and nose feel caked with sand.

Despite my discomfort, it doesn't take long for me to be dragged down into another dream. But this one is different. It starts as so many of them do, with me covered in blood and terrified, my mind filled with pain and misery. Something horrible has obviously happened, but I can't remember what as I sit on the floor of a shower stall and let the freezing water sluice over me.

I'm hoping the water will wake me, but even when I'm completely clean and shivering, I still feel weighted down. The water soaks my bandage and burns the wound, but I can't make myself get out. I just sit in the corner of the granite stall and bury my face in my hands. I've cried myself dry, but that doesn't stop the sorrow.

Eventually, Gavin comes to check on me. He knocks at first, but I ignore it, hoping he'll just go away. I should have known better, because when he receives no answer he pushes into the room. Then rushes across the bathroom, practically ripping the curtain from its hooks in his hurry to check on me.

His expression changes from worry to sadness when he sees me curled into the corner. He turns off the water with a flick of a wrist, then bundles me into a fluffy white—and dusty—towel and carries me into the bedroom. Then he starts chafing me with the towel, trying to rub warmth into my freezing body.

Even when I stop shivering, I still feel cold. I wonder if I'll ever feel warm again.

"How are you feeling?" he asks after several minutes.

I jump. I hadn't expected him to talk. "I don't know," I say. "She was my best friend. And she died because of me."

"Not you. Never you. Mother. She's the one who started this."

"I'm an Enforcer," I say without any emotion. "A monster."

"No, Evie. Not a monster," he says quietly.

"I killed those people. I've killed lots of people. All in the name of Mother's 'peace.'"

"Because Mother programmed you to do it. And Nick. Apparently." He takes my chin in his hand and forces me to look at him. "You also saved me. And you tried to save Macie. You only killed the guards in self-defense and you stopped yourself from killing the innocent people in the hallway. That's not a monster."

There's nothing to say to that.

"You're not afraid? Of me?" I ask finally, averting my eyes.

He waits until I look back up at him before he shakes his head and smiles at me. "No. Never."

Gavin pulls me into his arms again and kisses me. Gently at first, then more aggressively. As if he can't help himself. And the minute of panic fades as if it was never there. The kiss has the effect that nothing else has—it warms my blood and soothes my soul. I don't want it to stop.

Starshine veers and bumps into Asher's horse, who nips at her and startles me awake. I stare around for a minute, lost as to where I really am. The dream felt so real, I could swear I'd really been there and not here.

And then I realize.

It wasn't just a dream, it was a memory. A real memory. Not the stitched-together ones.

And I still remember it.

I smile as I savor it. It's the first memory I've been able to keep. And it's of him. My Gavin.

The smile fades when I remember I'll never be able to tell him.

The final two hours are a misery. No matter what I do, I can't get comfortable and we've only stopped long enough to rest the horses and fill our bellies and theirs before moving on again. I have no idea how they can keep up the pace, but they don't so much as neigh a complaint.

When we finally pull up to the village, it's dark with only the stars and moon to guide us. It looks just like it did before we left, and I almost expect to see Gavin waiting at the gates. But, of course, he's not.

Asher jumps out when we get to the gate to talk to the

guards. I watch as something passes between the two men; then the gates open and Asher signals me forward. The gates shut again behind us, while the guard stubbornly looks in the other direction and we continue into the village. Asher guides his horse to a stable like the one in Rushlake.

He helps me down and turns to our escorts when they step up to us. He talks with them for several minutes and, like with the guard, he hands something to the two of them. More bribes.

They promptly put it into their pockets and take the horses from us, while Asher guides me gently but firmly away.

It's still quiet, with only the occasional howls from outside the gates that I now recognize as coyotes. I shudder, remembering how vicious they were and how lucky we'd been to avoid them this time. Then again, Asher had a shotgun like Gavin's, so maybe it wasn't luck at all. Maybe they just knew better.

Asher leads me through the village, past Gavin's house. I don't look at it; I do not want anything to stop me from what I've decided to do. It doesn't take long before the lights from the village fade and our path is only illuminated by moon and starlight again. I glance up and watch the stars twinkle in their black canopy.

I'll miss this. I stop and take a few minutes to savor it.

Asher turns when he realizes I've stopped and returns to my side. "We'll see them again." He sounds so sure, I almost believe him.

"Of course we will." I shift so I'm looking at him.

He watches me for a moment, then turns and continues on. "We'd better hurry."

Without saying a word, I follow.

We're quiet the entire way to another large building. "Welcome to our boathouse," he says, tossing out his hand in a grand gesture.

"Boathouse?"

"Well, that's probably giving it too much credit." I have to agree. It's not much of a house at all. The wood has rotted away entirely in places. I'm not entirely confident the whole thing won't collapse on top of us the minute we step inside.

The door is unlocked and Asher pulls it open with a squeal of hinges. The sound is deafening in the quiet. We hold our breath as we wait to see if the sound has given us away.

After a few minutes, it's obvious no alarm has gone out, so we slip into the building. There, next to a rotting dock, is a shiny silver vehicle. It glows in the moonlight streaming through the holes in the roof.

"Here it is," Asher says. "Dad hid it away in here after you and Gavin showed up in it. He had a bunch of guys from Rushlake studying it, but they never could figure out how to open it." He shrugs.

Hesitantly I reach a hand out to the sleek silver machine and feel the cool metal and glass under my touch. I'm not sure what I expected, but nothing happens. Not even a hint of a memory.

Asher is watching me expectantly, so I shake my head. He lets out a breath. "Let's just get this show on the road."

"Road?" I frown. "Elysium is underwater."

He laughs. "Just an expression."

I turn my attention back to the boat, trying to locate the mechanism that will open the door. Asher kneels next to me, his thigh bumping mine as we run our fingers over the glossy surface.

After a few minutes, he straightens in triumph. "Here it is." The glass top opens with a hiss.

I lift an eyebrow and he grins at me. "They never figured out how to open it, but I did."

He turns and holds his hand out to help me up. I grasp it and let him haul me to my feet, wobbling slightly as the blood rushes from my head. "Why didn't you tell them?"

"They never asked." He looks away from me and I know that's not the real answer.

"Evie!" a voice says behind Asher. Asher spins and I peer around him, my heart somersaulting in my chest.

Gavin is standing there, his skin pale in the moonlight.

I tug on Asher's clothes. "Please, *please*, tell me you see Gavin, too. Please tell me I'm not just hallucinating." My voice has a pleading, almost hysterical, edge to it.

Asher stares if he can't believe his eyes, but then he shoves his hands into his pockets. He gives me this smile that I can't decipher before he nods.

"I see him. He's real."

Even then, I can't seem to make my legs move. Gavin's breath is coming out in ragged gasps and he's leaning over as he drags in more air, but he takes another step forward, tripping a little over his feet. "You're all right. Please tell me you're all right."

This time I can't stop myself—the desperation in the plea breaks through the shock and I rush to him.

He tucks a strand of hair behind my ear before cupping my cheek in his hand. I lean into it, letting my eyes drift closed and breathing his scent like air. Then his lips brush mine, and my stomach flips, like it does every time I kiss him. There's just something about that initial touch.

Then I'm pressing my lips harder against his and pulling him closer to me, as if even the tiniest space between us is too much. Tears flow down my cheeks, and he just keeps brushing them away with his thumbs.

Asher clears his throat, but I'm not ready to let go yet.

"Where were you?" My voice is still thick with tears and muffled in Gavin's chest. "We thought you were dead. *I* thought you were dead."

He's silent for a long moment, but his voice is filled with emotion—regret, pain, terror—when he finally says, "I'm sorry, Evie. I'm so sorry." He pulls me tighter to him and I don't have the heart to make him tell me the whole story right now.

"How did you get here?" I decide to ask instead.

He rests his forehead against mine. "I thought I was going to be too late," he whispers.

"I'm —" I start, but he interrupts me.

"I can't believe you just took off with him." He glares at Asher. "What were you thinking? I told you what it's like down there. You can't go down there. *She* can't go back. Mother will *kill* her. The nanos—"

Asher cuts him off. "Grandma told us about them. They're broken. And Eli—"

"Eli is dead," Gavin says. He glances down at me. "We saw him die, Evie. In Mother's diary. There was a link to a video. It showed the lead scientist, Eli, being killed by his nanos. Him and the majority of his sector."

I knit my brows together, my eyes searching his face. "That can't be true."

He hugs me. "It is. I'm sorry."

"Even if it is," Asher says. "There has to be someone there that can help."

Gavin gently pushes me away. "Are you stupid? There's no one there to help her. The only thing you'll find there is death." His eyes are wild. I can see his pulse racing.

"Gavin, calm down."

He takes me by the shoulders. "No. Not until you say you're not going to go."

I want to say I'll stay. For him. To make him happy. But I can't, because I'd only be staying for him. And that's not right for either of us. Closing my eyes, I say, "No, Gavin, I'm not. I made up my mind and I'm going to Elysium. They're the only ones who can help me."

"There's not anyone who *can* help you. Eli's gone. I wouldn't be surprised if Mother killed everyone who worked on nanos. The minute you set foot back in that freak show, Mother is going to be all over you like white on rice. We barely escaped last time. I'm not letting you go."

Anger makes my heart beat faster. I lift my chin. "Letting me? You don't *let* me do anything. I choose. Me. Not you. And I *choose* to go to Elysium." He opens his mouth, but this time I don't let him speak. "I *have* to go back. I'm tired of having bits and pieces thrown at me, and not being able to hold on to any of them." I take his hands in mine. "I just . . . I don't belong here. I've felt lost since I got here."

He squeezes his eyes shut. "I know. But going back isn't going to help you."

"It might. I have to try."

Gavin turns to Asher, his eyes feverish. He starts pacing, his movements short and jerky, to Asher and then back to me. He's muttering something to himself, a look of intense concentration on his face, and it terrifies me. I've never seen him like this.

I don't see it coming until it's too late. Gavin throws himself at Asher. The two fall onto the wood dock and it makes an ominous creaking sound. Before I can do anything more than avoid being pulled down with them, Gavin swings his arm back and throws his fist into Asher's face.

Despite the shock of being tossed onto the ground, Asher throws his own punch, and pretty soon the boathouse is filled with the sounds of Gavin and Asher fighting.

"Hey. Stop!" I whisper-yell. Of course that doesn't do

anything, so I step closer. "Asher! Gavin! Stop it. You're going to give us away. Stop it!"

Nothing. Hoping for the best, I step into the fray and try to pull them apart. But it's as if they don't even see me, and I get a fist to the side of my head for my trouble. My vision swims with red and black spots. I'm not sure which one did it, but Asher immediately stops, his eyes glued to my face.

"Evie, are you okay?" he asks, but Gavin evidently hasn't noticed what happened, and takes advantage of Asher's distraction to hit him in the face again. Asher tries to brush him off and stand, but Gavin keeps coming.

Suddenly there's that click in my head again, and all the pain I'm feeling disappears. My vision clears and the hatred on Gavin's face is clearly visible. *Surface Dwellers are dangerous.*

I grab him by the shoulder and spin him around. Shock widens his eyes when he sees me, but before he can do anything more than that, I punch him in the stomach. His breath whooshes out with an *oomph* and he bends over, clutching his abdomen. Then I straighten my hand and chop him in the back of the neck. Not too hard, just enough to knock him out.

He immediately falls to the ground, out cold. It's as if a light is switched off, and I fall to my own knees as all the strength and energy I just had pours out of me. Asher kneels next to me.

"Are you all right?" He presses a hand to the side of my face and I hiss. He makes a face. "That's going to bruise. It's already turning colors. Come on." He shoots a disgusted look to Gavin. "We'd better go before he comes to."

Repulsed by what I did, I say, "We can't just leave him

here. He could be hurt. *I* could have hurt him." My stomach rolls. What is *wrong* with me?

Asher opens his mouth like he's going to say something, but then stops when he sees my face. He sighs. "Fine. He'll just have to come with." He smirks. "Boy is he going to be pissed when he wakes up and realizes where we are."

That only makes me feel worse. Asher sighs again, then helps me to my feet. "Let's get you in first." He helps me into the seat next to the driver's seat, before unceremoniously dragging Gavin through the hatch until he's crumpled onto the floor behind us.

"Asher!" I chastise, but he only skirts around Gavin to go to the console.

I rush to Gavin and kneel beside him, adjusting him so he's not just piled onto the floor like so much unwanted rubbish. Brushing the hair out of his face, I see dark shadows under his eyes, not to mention a slew of other bruises, cuts, and scrapes, some of them in the process of forming because of his altercation with Asher just now. And there's an ugly yellow bruise peeking out from under the collar of his dirty and torn T-shirt. I tug it down to see that the bruise covers pretty much his entire shoulder and upper right chest. Guilt tears at me for knocking him out, but it wars with relief and utter joy at seeing him again. Alive. Knocked out because of me, and pretty beat up, but alive.

"Better get buckled up, Evie. This will probably be a bumpy ride," Asher says, startling me. I'd all but forgotten he was there.

At first, I consider ignoring Asher, but then I realize if I do lose my balance and fall, I'll land on Gavin, causing more harm.

I press a gentle kiss to his forehead and run my fingers along the side of his face, before sighing and pushing myself up to walk to my seat and buckle up.

Seated behind the console, Asher frowns and pushes a button, but nothing happens. He pushes another. No response.

Finally, his face lights up. "This *has* to be it," he says, and tries one more. The glass top shuts over the top of us and he leans over the console, more confident now, before pushing a lever forward. We move, the nose dipping down so we can pass under the broken doors leading to the open water.

Soon we're completely under the surface. My breath catches in my throat when it closes over our heads. For a terrifying few seconds I'm dead certain that we're going to drown, but then Asher says, *"With hands held high into the sky so blue, As the ocean opens up to swallow you."*

"I'm sorry?"

He turns to me, and shrugs. "It was from a song back before the War."

"Ah."

He turns back to controlling the sub and the way he's competently pushing buttons I have to think he knows what he's doing. I turn to ask how, but he only smiles at me, obviously anticipating the question. "I . . . ah . . . kind of played with this when you first got here."

I laugh, roll my eyes, and shake my head. Of course he

did. "Didn't your dad know you were playing around with this thing?"

He gives me a look. "My dad doesn't know anything unless his assistants tell him. And he doesn't know anything of what I do, unless I screw something up."

I wrinkle my nose and go back to staring at the water. I try to control the flutters in my stomach that seem to grow stronger with each passing air bubble.

It's hard to tell how fast we're going since it all looks the same and I don't know how long it'll take to get there. I decide to ask Asher, since he seems to know where we're going. He's probably gone down there a lot while "playing around."

He shrugs. "Don't know."

"But . . . you *do* know where we're going, don't you?"

He shakes his head. "Not a clue."

I lift an eyebrow and sit up straighter. "Then . . . what . . . how are we going to get there?"

Even in the dim light from the console, I can see him blush. "Uh . . . the buttons are labeled and this one here says 'autopilot.' When I pressed it, it gave me a list of choices. I chose Sector Three."

I stare at him for a minute, then burst out laughing. "Cheater," I say.

Asher winks at me, then goes back to studying the panel, while I look over at Gavin. He's still breathing, so that's a good thing, but I'm worried about him. He's been out awhile.

But I can't find it in me to feel too bad about it when I

think how close I am to answers. To getting my memories—and my mind—back.

Asher looks over. "You okay?"

"Just excited." It's not *entirely* a lie.

From the look he gives me, I can tell he doesn't really believe me, but he only says, "Okay, just let me know if you need anything."

I don't respond, but when I turn to face out the window, I gasp and stand to walk closer to the front of the sub and get a better view. Asher gasps behind me.

There, rising in the murky depths, like Atlantis, is Elysium. I've never seen anything more beautiful. The feeling of rightness returns with a vengeance and I smile.

"I'm home," I say and press a hand to the glass in front of me.

CHAPTER TWENTY-TWO

Evie

The computerized voice of the submersible says to have a seat and buckle up to prepare for docking, and while I do sit, I can't stop staring openmouthed at everything as we drift slowly down a trench. From a distance, it looks like an overgrown, lopsided octopus. In the trench, though, you can see one entire side is lit up like a strange glow-in-the-dark honeycomb. Directly below us I can see more lights. The sub slows and I have a minute of panic about what we'll meet when we dock. A memory pushes into my brain of a glass-walled room filled with blue-eyed, blond-haired girls, all wearing the same thing.

Black dresses and hooded capes, with black gloves and black boots covering up every square inch of visible skin.

Enforcers, my brain supplies not so helpfully, and I shiver. Something about them makes my blood run cold.

Another flash: I'm standing in the center of the room and all around me are the charred remains of the girls . . . the Enforcers.

I blink when I hear the computer voice again reminding us to remain seated. That was the same memory I had in the Outlands. So that was probably real, too!

My breathing is ragged and I recognize the signs of an impending attack. Despite the ominous computer warnings, Asher pushes himself up, leaps over the few centimeters separating us, and tries to shove my head between my knees. I push him away.

"I'm fine," I rasp, trying to swallow the cough away. "I'm not having a panic attack. Promise."

"Then what's wrong?" he asks.

"I remember them," I whisper. "We were there, trying to find a way into the submersible, and they were trying to break down the door." I look up to meet Asher's eyes. "Mother. I think. Her Enforcers. And, before that, these strange, murderous men. Gavin was right." My heart speeds up. Oh Mother. Gavin was right.

I shove my own head between my legs this time.

"It's okay, Evie. We'll be fine. It's been weeks. It's doubtful they're still there. I'm sure your mother took care of them.

No way she's going to let murderers run around and destroy her perfect city, right?"

After a minute, I nod. "I hope you're right."

We're all jolted as the submersible docks to what, according to the computer, is Sector Three. The seat belt digs painfully into my ribs, but Asher gets the worst of it when he flies into the front of the submersible, then back. He lands on top of Gavin, who groans.

Poor Gavin.

Asher quickly shoves himself to his feet and brushes himself off, before giving me this cocky grin that says, "I meant to do that."

Snickering, I disconnect myself from the seat belt and turn to face the rear of the sub, where another door I didn't know existed is open. I can see what appears to be the room from my memory.

I exchange a look with Asher, who takes a deep breath and starts forward. "Stay here," he says. "The big red button on the console closes the door. If I shout, shut the door."

I narrow my eyes at him. "I'm not letting you go out there alone."

"But I—" He points to himself, then hesitates and adds helplessly, "And you . . ."

I use my best no arguments voice. "I don't seem to recall you tearing vulture-hawks apart with your bare hands."

He flushes. "You're injured."

"So are you." Gavin gave him a good walloping on the dock. There's still a bit of blood trickling from his nose.

He sighs. "Will you at least let me go first?"

"A gentleman always lets a lady go first." I push out of my seat and lead the way onto the concrete deck.

There are bloodstains and burn marks on the floor. I don't even know what could have left the divots in the concrete, and I don't think I want to.

"Nobody's here," Asher whispers from behind me.

I scan the room, wishing I could have the clear vision I experienced every time I've had to protect myself. "Yes, but *something* happened here."

"Obviously," someone says behind me, and I whirl around, my heart flying into my throat.

Gavin stands just inside the submersible, rubbing the back of his neck. "Damn it, Evie. Did you really have to knock me out?"

I open my mouth to apologize, but Asher beats me to it. "You should know better than anyone that she didn't mean to. Besides, if you hadn't attacked me like a maniac, she wouldn't have had to subdue you."

"'Subdue'? Fancy word for coldcock." Gavin glares at him, then turns his attention to the room. He shudders and gets that wild look in his eyes again. I swallow and worry that he's going to do something to Asher again, but he takes a deep breath and his eyes focus. He looks around, zeroing in on the doors. "Looks like someone did some clean up." He turns his attention to me, his eyes traveling up and down my body. "How are you feeling? Anything different?"

I assess myself, then shake my head. "Everything feels the same."

He gives Asher a smug look, even though it's easy to see the worry lines spreading across his brow. "See? Nothing has changed. Now let's get the hell out of here before Mother figures out we're back."

He takes a step back into the sub, but Asher says, "Nice try. We have to find someone to fix Evie."

"No one here can help her. Everyone here is *trained* to *hurt* her," Gavin points out. He shifts slightly to one foot and almost instantly transfers his weight back.

"Someone here has to know *something* about nanos. They wouldn't keep using them if no one here knew how to make them work or fix them if they malfunctioned." Asher tilts his head to the side, his expression saying, "Just try to argue with me."

Gavin stares daggers at him and I'm terrified they're going to get into it again.

"Come on, Gavin. We made it this far," I say. "We can't quit now." And I have no plans of doing so either.

He crosses his arms over his chest. "We need to go back."

Asher looks at me, then shrugs. "Then go. No one is stopping you." Then he turns back to the door. "Come on, Evie, let's go find some help."

Gavin still has his arms crossed, but he's watching me now, his eyes pleading with me. I look back to Asher, who has his hand on the door, then back to Gavin.

I let out a breath and give Gavin a look of apology. "I have to." It tears me up inside to do it, but I go to Asher, who opens the door and glances around quickly before stepping into the hall. Second-guessing and regretting every step I take away from Gavin, I follow Asher into the hallway.

My mind whirls with déjà vu, but I can't remember what exactly is familiar about it. Other than it reminds me a bit of that strange complex Asher and I got lost in, back in the Outlands. My body tingles a bit as I wait for some kind of panic attack, but when nothing happens, I release the breath I didn't know I was holding.

"Where to?" Asher's voice echoes. There are only two options, but it's pitch-dark one way and the other dead-ends several meters up ahead.

"I guess this way." I start moving down the pitch-dark hallway.

Asher follows, and we're a ways down the hall when we hear a door open. Because of the echoes it's hard to tell where the door is, but when we hear footsteps, we push ourselves tight against the wall and try to breathe as shallowly as possible.

The footsteps tread slowly, and a light flicks on to our left—the way we came from—but I can't see who's holding it. I hope it's Gavin, but I doubt it. Where would he have gotten a light?

The light sweeps from side to side as it continues forward and my heart pumps furiously. I wonder if anyone else can hear it. I'm afraid to move, but if we stay where we are we'll be caught for sure.

Finally, I decide I have to move. I slide my foot out, then move my body to join it.

The light immediately swings in my direction and shines in my face, blinding me. "Evie?" Gavin says, the same relief I feel in his voice.

"Oh, thank Mother," I say, wrapping my arms around him in a strangle hold as he steps next to me.

"I'd rather not, actually," he says, but he holds me just as tightly. The stuff in his hands presses painfully into my back, but I don't care.

"You stayed," I say, my voice muffled by his chest.

He pushes me away a little and tilts my chin up with his finger. "I won't ever leave you again."

"Promise?" I ask.

"Promise." He smiles, but before I can smile back he's kissing me. My stomach flips and my heart trips, but I kiss him back, breathing in his scent like air and holding on to him as if my life depends on it. And it might just. I don't think I could handle it if he were gone again. Thinking he was dead had just about killed me, too.

Behind me, Asher clears his throat and regretfully I peel myself from Gavin, but I wrap my hand around his forearm. I'm not letting him go again, either.

"Where did you find that?" Asher cuts in, gesturing to the light in Gavin's hand.

"It's from before. We needed it the last time we were here because the Enforcers cut off the power so the murderous monsters running around the Sector would have an easier time killing us. Thankfully we had plasma and machine guns." He shoves something at Asher. "I left them in the submersible. I guess it's a good thing, too. If I can't persuade you not to go, at least I can try to offer some kind of protection."

"What is this?" Asher stares at the silver contraption in his hand.

"It's a gun, dipshit. It's called a Reising and it's fully automatic. You do know how to work a gun, don't you? I'm all out of knives."

"Knives?" Asher asks. I'm a bit perplexed myself.

"I figured with all your backstabbing experience a knife would be your weapon of choice, right?"

Asher makes this sound in his throat and I step between the two of them, trying to prevent another fight. This isn't the time or the place.

"Great! We have weapons. Let's keep moving, shall we?"

At first no one moves, and then Asher puts a hand on my shoulder. "Lead the way. I'll be right behind you."

Gavin snorts. "Typical. Hiding behind someone." He slings the Reising over his shoulder by the strap and palms the smaller one, holding it and the flashlight in the same hand and taking my hand with the other, before he starts walking, leaving Asher to follow or not.

Gavin

The Sector is so quiet it's almost creepier than the first time we were here. It's hard to believe that it *is* the same place.

But I don't drop my guard. I'm sure those . . . things are still here somewhere and the minute I turn in the wrong direction they're going to jump out and claw my face off.

I don't want to be here. What I really want to do is grab Evie in a football hold and run straight back to the submarine. But Evie is nothing if not stubborn, and with Asher feeding her stubbornness, there's no way I would win. So it's on to plan B. Which . . . I haven't quite figured out yet. Being here makes it almost impossible to think.

The dark is playing tricks on my mind. There are times that I'm positive something is right next to me, so close it could breathe on me, but when I flash the light, there's nothing there. And then there's the horrible creaking sounds. It reminds me of when I used to climb around the old wrecked warships as a kid. The sound was unnerving when I heard it then; it's even more terrifying now. It's making me jumpy, and my nerves are so tight I'm afraid they're going to snap at any minute.

We turn down another corridor and I pause, trying to remember which way to go to get to the elevators. I focus on bringing up the map I have in my head from when I was here last, and I'm concentrating so hard I don't see what I'm walking into until my foot catches on something and I land with my nose just inches from something that smells incredibly disgusting. Evie tugs on me to help me up, asking if I'm okay. I quickly shove to my feet, thinking the worst of what I almost landed in. A body. *Part* of a body? Something worse? I don't want to look at whatever it is but I know I don't have a choice.

I expect to see blood and body parts, like last time. But what I see when I shine the light down totally confuses me. It's definitely a puddle of something, but it's a greenish color instead of red.

"What's wrong?" Evie asks.

"I almost fell in something weird." I squat down to examine it and she does the same, placing a hand on my thigh when she teeters a bit. She reaches out, but I grab her wrist. "Don't," I say. "Who knows what this stuff is."

Asher peers over her shoulder. "Yeah, it could be acid or something. We wouldn't want you to lose a finger."

She yanks her hand away and I peer at him over my shoulder. "Really, Asher? Really? Do you just say every little thing that pops into your head?"

"Not everything."

Even though I can't really see him in the dark, the smirk in his voice is obvious and it sets my teeth on edge.

"Well, the next time you want to open your mouth, use that tiny thing in your head that passes for a brain, will ya?"

"I think you're confusing my brain with your—"

"Enough!" Evie says, and the heat of her gaze burns my face. "Can you two just pretend to get along until we get back to the Surface? *Please*."

We both mumble "Sorry," but I'm sure we both know she's asking for too much.

"What do you think this is?" I can feel her watching me again, so I'm pretty sure she's talking to me.

"I don't know. I don't want to touch it."

"Does it really matter, guys? I mean, it's green goo. So what? Let's just keep going so we can get somewhere there's light," Asher says.

"What's the matter? Afraid of the dark?" I say, smiling.

"Gavin," Evie warns. "Asher's right. Let's keep moving." She places her hand on my thigh again to push herself up.

I stand and hop over the puddle, before turning to shine the light on it so Evie can see her way around. As soon as she's over, I turn around and start walking away, keeping her hand in mine.

"Hey!" Asher says. "What about me? I don't want to step in that stuff."

I pretend not to hear him and keep going. A few seconds later I smile when I hear, "Ugh! Gross!" Music to my ears.

But then, Asher says, "Uh. Guys? I'm stuck."

I laugh as I turn back around to see him pulling on the leg that's supposedly stuck in the puddle. "Seriously, Asher? Now's not the time to pull that shit. Stop kidding around."

He looks up at me and I don't see the glint of amusement in his eyes, I see anxiousness. "I'm not joking. It's really stuck."

"Really?" I stare closer at his arms pulling on his legs. He's definitely straining to yank his foot out.

Releasing Evie, I bend down and start tugging too, but it's really stuck. No matter how hard I pull, it doesn't even budge. Then I realize something that sends chills down my spine. The muck is actually creeping up his shoe.

"Take your shoe off. Take it off now," I shout, yanking at his laces now instead of his leg.

He starts pulling at them, too, and for a minute we're battling each other for the laces until we finally get them loose enough for him to wrench his foot from the shoe. The three of us share a glance, but can only stare in horror as his entire shoe is consumed.

"What. The. Hell?" Asher says, still staring at the spot his shoe was.

"I have no flippin' clue," I say, more shaken than I want to admit.

"Those were my favorite shoes." Asher rips off the other shoe and throws it at the crap. It floats on the surface for a minute before it too sinks. "Damn it."

Evie grabs my hand and tugs on it. "We should get away from here." Her voice is soft, but I can hear the nerves underneath and her hand is sweating. She's never shown her nerves this much. She really must be scared. If she can keep going, as scared as she is, so can I.

I nod and start forward again.

We continue walking, every so often running into more puddles. We're careful to avoid them, each of us working with the others to make sure everyone makes it over them, especially the larger ones. And especially Asher. It's bad enough he has to walk around barefoot; we don't need him to lose them, too. The puddles are strange, though. It's too dark, even with the flashlight, to see them completely, but I've never seen liquid pool in the shapes that these are collecting in. There's no sign of a source, so we ignore them as much as possible and keep going.

It's entirely too quiet again, the only sounds the scrape of our shoes against the concrete, that odd groaning sound, and Asher's occasional mutterings about me purposely getting us lost. And while it's definitely not purposeful, I have to admit we probably are. Lost, that is. I'd only traveled this way once, and we'd gotten a little distracted running for our lives from the insane cannibals. It's a wee bit hard to remember where to turn.

Eventually, with more luck than anything else, when we turn yet another corner—I'm *sure* we didn't turn this much last time—I see a tiny bit of light peeking around a corner.

I rush forward, reaching behind me to grab Evie's hand and tug so she'll follow me. As unrealistic as I know this is, my mind begs for the light because light equals safety. Her feet drag a little until she sees why I'm rushing. She speeds up a bit and I don't feel so much like I'm dragging her behind me.

"Hey! Wait up!" Asher calls from behind us, but we ignore him. I stop only when I get into the light. The hallway looks just like I remember it. Long, and empty. Concrete walls with the occasional door. Every so often down the hall there are more piles of gunk, and their shapes are starting to click in my head. They almost look like bodies, or parts of bodies, but I'm almost positive my memories of this damned place are making me imagine it, like when you see shapes in the clouds. This makes me especially grateful for the light.

I follow down the corridors with the lights working until *finally* I see a set of elevator banks. I rush to the button and press it, then press it again a few seconds later. Then again. Over and over again, until Evie places her hand on mine, stopping me.

Come on. Come on. Come on.

Inside the shafts the car clangs and bangs as it gets pulled up. My mind flashes on those monsters from the last time. I shudder as I remember how the whole hallway had been filled with blood. Sprays of it on the walls, dripping from the ceiling. And a carpet of bodies strewn across the floor. It dawns on me that I should be more careful. Just because, so far, we haven't seen hide nor hair of them, doesn't mean they aren't waiting. An elevator would be just the place to hide.

I usher Evie and Asher back to wait behind a corner, where I watch for the elevator to arrive while they both stare at me like I've lost my mind. Maybe I have. I've never been more terrified in my life.

Asher shoves past me. "What are we waiting for? Let's go."

I grab him and yank him back. "Stay still," I hiss. "Those things could be in there."

Evie and Asher exchange a look and he wrinkles his nose. "You've lost it, dude. We haven't seen anyone in the entire time we've been here. There's no one here."

He steps forward again, and I snatch him back, shoving him to the wall so hard his head smashes against it. He yelps.

"Gavin!" Evie says, tugging on my arm.

I ignore her, shoving Asher into the wall again. "Damn it, Asher. Just flippin' listen to me for once. You're going to get us killed."

He scowls at me and rubs his head, but doesn't say anything. When the doors finally slide open and no one steps out, I palm the plasma gun and double-check to make sure it's loaded before stepping out into the hall.

It's a relief to see there's nothing in there. Not even any of the green goo. I signal for the others to come, and while Asher glowers at me when he gets to me, he gets into the elevator without saying a word. I ignore the concerned looks Evie keeps shooting me and press the button for the bottom floor. I'm pretty sure that's where the Tube station is anyway. I can't really remember where we'd started from when we were here before. I just know it was a relatively long elevator ride. But it's not like we can't start at the bottom and work our way up until we find the right floor if I'm wrong.

Snakes roll around in my stomach as my nerves act up. I *really* don't want to go back to the other side of Elysium. It makes the most sense to go there, but I don't know how we're going to get past the turrets and cameras. Even if we're not shot, the cameras will catch our every move. Evie might have been able to delete us from the targeting systems last time, but it seems unlikely Mother hasn't had her little trick undone by now. And there's no way Evie can get us back in the system now. Not without her memories.

We'll just have to use those maintenance tunnels again and hope we don't set off any of the turrets as we run from the Tube to the tunnel. Of course, the problem with that is, Evie has no memory of how to break the security on the doors. Maybe it'll come to her. Maybe just being in the area will spark some of her memories.

The way she's looking around like she's never seen an elevator before, I don't hold out much hope for that.

When we're finally about to hit the bottom level, I step in front of Evie and hold the plasma gun out in front of me. This is where our luck runs out. I'm sure of it. Evie makes a frustrated noise, but doesn't argue. Behind me Asher cocks the Reising, and steps up next to me.

I lift an eyebrow at him.

He shrugs. "You're not the only one who can protect her."

Evie makes that sound again. "I don't need protecting," she says, but her voice wavers. There's no doubt in my mind that if she was herself right now, this wouldn't even be up for discussion. She'd be in front of both of us, strapped to the teeth and ready to take no prisoners.

I grunt in response, but turn my attention back to the doors as they slide open. I'm not sure what I expect, but it isn't what I get: freezing cold water flooding into the car. It gushes in so fast the only thing I can do is inhale a single breath before it closes over my head.

Chapter Twenty-three

Evie

As the water closes over my head, the memory of something similar flashes in my mind, but I shove it away. There's no time and it's not like it'll help. I force my eyes open, then wish I hadn't when the seawater sears my eyes, but I have to be able to tell which way is up.

Something tugs on my hand, pulling me out of the car, and I almost scream, but manage to clamp my lips together to keep from letting loose and losing the much needed oxygen. The familiar roughness of the hand tells me it's Gavin and while I try to look around for Asher, it's a lost cause. It's too dark and I can't see anything.

My lungs burning, I kick as hard as I can, letting Gavin pull me. Just when I can't hold my breath any longer, we burst through the surface, our heads hitting the ceiling. Seconds later, as Gavin is practically begging me to tell him I'm okay, Asher surfaces next to us, gasping for breath. He frantically looks around and when he sees me, I can see him relax. He swims closer, panting a little.

"You okay?"

Coughing, I nod and ignore the pain in my chest. "Just in a little bit of shock."

He turns to Gavin. "What the hell, dude? Are you trying to kill us?"

Gavin only gives him a look. "If I'd known that was going to happen, I wouldn't have brought us down here. It wasn't like this before. I don't know what's going on, but we have to get out of here," he says.

We all turn around in circles, but I can't see anything. None of this looks familiar to me, though I'm starting to get small flashes. Gavin running, me slung over his shoulder. Shooting some kind of blue light at people running behind us. Clouds of ash where the people stood.

Something brushes my leg and I scream as my imagination forms the image of one of those blood- and gore-covered brutes, wrenching me under the water. Then, because I still haven't caught my breath, I break into harsh coughing.

"What?" Gavin pulls me behind him and looks around frantically.

"Something . . . brushed my leg. I don't know what it was." I accidentally inhale a mouthful of water in my panic and nearly choke.

Gavin shoves a wall of water at Asher. "Come on. Stop playin' around."

Asher holds up his hands before slamming them back into the water to paddle. "Don't look at me. I didn't do it."

"What the hell was it then?" Gavin's eyes are taking on that frenzied look again, but it doesn't take long to find out his answer. An obviously dead body floats by just under the surface, its eyes wide and unseeing. We all watch as it continues its meandering path past us. And I'm pretty sure the reason it's moving is because wherever the leak is, the water is still coming in.

"Oh Jesus," Gavin says, while Asher starts gagging and flapping his arms around in an obvious attempt to get away from it. He only ends up drawing the body closer.

My body feels numb and there's a pressure deep in my head as it buzzes from the shock.

Gavin focuses on me. "Can we go back to the Surface now?"

I want to say yes. I want to say forget this, forget all of it, but I shake my head. "I can't. I need to find the answers."

He sighs, but looks resigned. "Well, we have to get out of here at least."

"If this is like any of the buildings in Rushlake, there should be stairs near this elevator," Asher says, trying to stay calm, and Gavin nods. "So who wants to look for it?"

Another body floats by and I shudder so hard I bite my tongue.

They both stare at each other; then Gavin holds his

hand out in a fist. I open my mouth to tell him he can't force Asher to try and find it, but then Asher holds his out too, just short of touching Gavin's. I watch, completely confused, as they lift and lower their hand three times; then Gavin splays his hand out flat at the same Asher brings out his index and middle finger in a sideways V.

Gavin nods. "Right." Then he takes a deep breath and his head disappears under the water before I can say anything.

I paddle over to Asher. "What was that?"

"Rock, paper, scissors. The ultimate decider." He manages a shaky smile and I shake my head and wait, metaphorically holding my breath until Gavin's head appears again.

He pops up, sucks in a breath and goes back under before anyone can say anything. He does this five more times, taking longer and longer and making me more and more anxious until he finally comes up with a look of triumph.

"Found it!"

Relieved, I swim over to him. He takes one hand, and Asher takes my other. We all suck in deep breaths, and go back under, letting Gavin guide us to the stairwell.

It takes both Gavin and Asher working together to open the exit door, but then we're slipping through the crack and swimming up. This time when we surface, we're in a much smaller space and there are stairs leading up.

We swim over to where the stairs meet the water, and start climbing. I go much slower than them, though, because no matter what I do I can't get these visions out of my head. They're just flashes. I can't make out what they are, but they slow me down, nonetheless. Gavin and Asher pause to wait for me, and so I suck in breaths and go as fast as I can.

Each time we reach a new floor, Gavin pokes his head out the door to check if we're at the floor with what he calls the Tube station. According to him, he'll know it when he sees it because it's the only floor that is completely open. That kind of terrifies me. Open to what? We've already been almost drowned. I don't really want to try that again. Maybe Gavin's right. Maybe it *is* time to head back to the Surface. Between the stuff that almost ate Asher's foot and now practically drowning in a sea of dead bodies, I have to admit that Gavin was right about it being dangerous. He was probably right about a lot of things. Yet . . . we're so close to the answers I want. The answers I *need*. I can feel it. If we leave now, I'll never know who I was. Who I am.

So I don't say anything about turning back. I keep going, but when we stop for what feels like the hundredth time, a huge wave of déjà vu hits me. My head swims and I have to lean against the wall.

Asher turns around to smile at me, and a hallucination hits me so hard, I stumble.

The hallway is so dark I can't even see Timothy, but I know he's there. His uneven gasps blow across my cheeks.

"Are you going to tell her?" he asks.

"First thing in the morning," I reply, feeling a familiar tickle in my stomach, and smiling.

"You won't forget," he teases.

Before I can reply, he kisses me again, pressing me back

against the cold concrete. I push harder into the warmth of his body, closing my eyes.

When I open them again, I'm back in the stairwell, gasping for breath, those black dots back in my vision. Asher is watching me warily.

"Everything okay, Evie?" he asks. Gavin must have slipped out of the stairwell to do his quick look-around.

I wave Asher away, not wanting to waste what little breath I have to assure him I'm fine when I'm not completely confident I am.

His brows furrow, but he doesn't say anything. He only continues to watch me. Gavin returns and I push quickly off the wall, as if I've only been biding my time and not trying to figure out what in the world that was all about. He shakes his head before heading up the stairs to yet another level.

Between the ordeal at the hospital in Rushlake, the race back to the village, and now almost drowning, exhausted doesn't even begin to explain how I feel. I want to groan, but I still haven't caught my breath and I'm sure even that would be too much, so I just put one foot in front of the other. I stumble when I don't lift my foot up high enough. I put my hands out to catch myself, but Asher catches my arm and pulls me back up to my feet. I give him a grateful smile before I turn back around to try that step again and notice Gavin watching us.

That hallucination—me, pressed against another boy—makes me feel incredibly guilty, and I duck my head and start trudging up the steps again.

I can feel Gavin's curious gaze, but he keeps moving after a second or two.

At the next landing, Gavin looks out the door and whoops. "Found it!" He dashes out the door.

"Finally," Asher says, and follows.

I follow, just at a bit slower pace. When I step out the door, I can definitely see the difference between the other floors and this one. It's absolutely gorgeous, for one. The floors are all concrete, but the walls! The walls are floor-to-ceiling windows, the outside is all lit up and I can see the ocean. It's so peaceful, I think, walking over to it. I press my hand against the cool glass, and watch as a school of brightly colored fish swim by.

A grouping of brightly colored and strangely shaped rocks gather on the bottom of the window sills. *This.* This feels right. *Finally*, I think. The glass feels so marvelous against my hand, I decide to press my face against it too. A moan escapes me at the feel and I hear a chuckle behind me.

"That good, huh?" Asher asks.

Gavin clears his throat from the other end of the large hallway and I open my eyes to see him smiling at me. "If you're done molesting the glass, we should get to the Tube."

Asher chuckles and, flushing, I push away from the wall, but keep a hand to it as we walk toward where Gavin is.

Just before the hallway turns, there are more splashes of that green goo again. Almost the entire floor, from wall to wall, is spotted in the strange pools. But when I get close to them, I shudder. Each one looks like a body. Flat, green, liquid bodies. As if someone painted them onto the floor. Some are larger than others, like some are children and some are adults. Some have their arms close to their torsos; others have them stretched out as if reaching for the puddle next to it. I don't know why, but the scene has a lump forming in my throat and tears stinging my eyes.

Gavin frowns down at them. "This is so weird."

"What is?" Asher asks.

Gavin looks up at me and I blink the tears quickly away so he can't see them. "This is where all those people were, re-member?" he asks.

"No," I say flatly, trying not to let it bother me that he obviously forgot I don't remember *anything* from here except those flashes.

His eyes close for a minute. "That's right. I can't believe I forgot." I shrug and he stands, brushing his hands together. "Never mind. It's not important. Come on, let's get to that Tube station."

I stare at the green bodies for a bit longer, letting his words tumble through my mind, trying to remember something, anything, so I can begin to understand, but nothing comes and Asher tugs on my arm to get me to go. I have to practi-cally run to catch up with Gavin in the next room, but when I do, I stop short.

I remember this room. Or at least one similar.

I'm waiting in the dark, peering out over a thousand faces. I'm leaning against a brick wall. The area around me looks like the streets in Rushlake City, only with short squat one-story buildings lining each side of the street instead of the several-stories-tall buildings that were in Rushlake. The street in front of me is filled with people with identical faces, all staring up at a woman. The woman who frequently stars in my nightmares. Mother.

She's making a speech on the platform in the Square about working together and how everyone is just one cog in a giant machine. A commotion to my left draws my attention. A man close to me is arguing in whispers with the woman next to him. She's vigorously shaking her head and glancing in my direction.

In response, I step out of the shadows and up to the couple. The crowd around them disperses quickly, watching me as carefully as I watch them and the pair I'm walking to. They're both taller than me, but when they see me looking up at them, they freeze, identical expressions of terror on their almost identical faces. I don't say anything, I don't have to and I know it.

But the man suddenly glares at me. "Monster," he whispers. The woman's face goes completely white.

I signal the two guards next to me to apprehend him. They each take an arm, but he shrugs them off, and follows me into the dark of the shadows. We walk into a maintenance tunnel and behind a stairwell. I lift the weapon on my side. He only lifts his chin as I press the trigger. The click of the hammer hitting the cylinder echoes throughout the stairwell.

Oh, Mother. I think I killed someone. Not accidentally, either.

Gavin starts swearing at something, but I don't look up.

My chest is squeezing like it did in the stairwell and my heart won't slow down. I can't seem to catch my breath. I bend over and shove my head close to my knees like Asher had done in the sub, but I still can't breathe.

"Are you okay?" Asher places his hand on my back and crouches down to look me in the face.

"Fine. Fine. Just need to sit and catch my breath," I wheeze out, but that proves too much for me and even as I suck in more air, my head spins. Then I feel like I'm falling right before the darkness comes.

When I wake, it's as if I'm hearing things from underwater. Their voices echo, bouncing around each other until they finally come together as they're supposed to.

"Did she hit her head?" That's Gavin.

"No. I caught her right as she fell forward." And there is Asher.

Slowly I open my eyes to see them both staring down at me. I try pushing myself up, but only manage to feel like a turtle on its back. Gavin and Asher help me up, then ask me what happened. I hesitate. Gavin doesn't want to be down here at all. If he knows I've hallucinated twice in less than an hour, and that I think I'm one of the monsters he was talking about, he's going to insist we go back, or worse, go back without me, leaving me.

But I'm sure these hallucinations, these flashes of memory, are proof I'm doing the right thing. So I lie. I tell them I couldn't breathe and that it must be left over from almost drowning. And instead of insisting we go back, they decide I need a short break. I try to insist that by passing out I already *had* a short break, but they won't listen.

"Besides," Gavin says, "we've kinda reached the end of the road." His voice is relieved and his eyes are bright. For the first time since we got here, his entire body seems relaxed, not rigid and tense. "In order to get where you need to be, we have to use the Tube. That's the track." He gestures to the sloping floor with the strange metal plates on it. Then he looks at me. "The last time we were here, we shut and locked the door to prevent Mother from sending anyone else over. But it didn't work. And now it seems they've sealed them back up." His lip twitches and I can tell he's trying not to smile.

I push myself to my feet. We've come this far, and I can *feel* we're getting closer. I walk up to the door and press on the red button on the side, but it doesn't budge. Make a noise. Anything. Frowning, I stride back up the sloped floor and cross over to the booth. I didn't make it all this way to give up so easily.

Inside it is a bunch of levers and knobs, but I don't know which does what. Gavin, on the other hand, does this indecisive little back and forth motion with his body before sighing, then taking my hand and pressing it against the cool glass plate. I jump when a light flashes underneath my palm, but he won't let me take my hand from it. He keeps it pressed against the glass. As soon as I realize it doesn't hurt me, I turn to watch Gavin, who is in turn watching the door, obviously expecting something to happen.

"Access denied," a computer voice says, startling all of us.

Gavin swears again under his breath and I can't hide my own disappointment. This can't be the end. "There has to be some other way to get to where we need to go."

Gavin shakes his head. "If there is, I don't know what it is. We came through here before and at the time, you said it was the only way. Considering how dangerous it was, I have to believe you were right." Again, I can't help but notice that he doesn't seem all that disappointed by the turn of events.

Asher kicks the console hard enough for an alarm to start screaming on it. I slam my hands to my ears, while Gavin punches Asher in the arm. He yells something at him, gesturing wildly, but I can't hear him over the shrill alarm.

Then, the entire thing turns off and a computer voice speaks. "Due to unauthorized tampering, this console will shut down until re-activated by an authorized service technician. Any further damage to the machine will result in harsh punishment. Vandalism will not be tolerated at the Elysium Resort and persons accused of such an act will be fined and sent to the Detainment Center until you are relinquished to Surface authorities. Have a nice day!"

We glance at each other, but before any of us can react to that, there's a mechanical humming sound. Gavin and I dash out of the booth to find where it's coming from, only to see that a wall is being lowered from the ceiling, blocking the way back to the stairs.

"They're locking us in!" Gavin exclaims. "Come on! We've got to go."

He yanks me down the hallway and to the corner and Asher is right behind us. I wonder if we'll make it. Considering how heavy that wall must be, it's moving fairly rapidly. When we get to it, we have to slither underneath. With no time to hesitate, I slide under followed by Gavin, and then Asher. Not even ten seconds later the wall slides into place and there's a loud clang of what I'm sure is a lock clicking.

Across the way, another wall slams, effectively locking us, and at least a half a dozen bodies of goo, between them in a square approximately ten meters by ten meters, with no way out, and nowhere to hide.

Chapter Twenty-four

CAUTION: THIS SECTOR UNDER QUARANTINE
DUE TO BIOHAZARDOUS MATERIAL.
TRESPASSERS WILL BE PROSECUTED.
—Painted on sign next to the Tube

Evie

Gavin and Asher each take a turn shoving at the wall while I look for some kind of button or lever that'll release it, but none of us are successful.

"Way to go, Asher," Gavin says between clenched teeth. He's adopted that tense, ramrod-straight posture again. "Now either we've alerted Mother that we're here, or she'll find out when she sends someone to check out what's going on."

"Me?" Asher says with a pinched laugh. "I'm not the one who shoved everyone in here! You're the one who decided it would be the smart thing to run under a *wall*."

"I didn't know there'd be another wall right behind it doing the same thing." He throws his hands in the air, prowling along the wall. "I was hoping to get back to the stairs or elevator!" He glances over to me and I try to give him an encouraging smile, but I can't hold it. I wrap my arms around myself instead.

"Maybe she'll just ignore it altogether," Asher says. "It's obvious this sector isn't used anymore. She could think it's a false alarm."

"Like that's better?" Gavin's voice sounds like he's fighting back a scream. "Then we get to starve to death or suffocate. I'm not sure which is worse." Gavin kicks the wall, even though that's exactly what Asher did to get us in trouble. "I told you this was a bad idea. I told you guys not to come here, but no. Does anyone listen? Of course not!"

I'm relieved when Gavin stops shouting and starts pacing. I thought for sure I would have to break them up again.

Asher looks to the floor. "I'm sorry. I didn't realize—"

Gavin spins around to glare at Asher. "That's exactly the problem, Asher. You didn't think. You *never* think. You just *do*, and ask questions later."

"It's better to beg forgiveness than ask permission," Asher shoots back.

"And screw anyone who happens to get hurt in the process, right? As long as Asher's happy, no one else matters."

"That's not true and you know it!" Asher practically yells. "This? All this? We're only here because I was thinking of Evie. Because *she* needs to be here. I didn't do this for me. I did this to help *her*."

"And this is helping her? We're trapped. And we're going to *die*! No matter what happens from this point out, that's going be the end result because Mother is going to *kill* us. And Evie is going to get the worst of it because she betrayed Mother to help me."

I stop twisting my hands together to gape at Gavin. "I did *what*?"

He winces. "You betrayed Mother. To get me home." He rushes on, his sentences running together. "But it's a good thing, because she was going to turn you into breeding stock, and there were those murders, and she was going to kill you eventually. I'm sure of it. You were much safer up there." He goes back to glaring at Asher. "Until *some*one decided to bring you back."

"I was trying to *help* her," Asher starts.

"You weren't planning on helping her! You were planning on using her. Like you do with everyone."

I shake my head. "You don't know that."

"Yes I do! I know him more than you ever could. And I know for a fact that he's just using you."

Asher butts in, face flaming. "When are you going to realize what happened was an *accident*? A horrible mistake. My mistake. I trusted someone I shouldn't have. He's a liar and a cheat. He gets people to trust him, only to turn around and not only stab them in the back, but take away the people most important to them. I lost my best friend because of it. Because in trying to help him and his family, I ended up betraying them, and not a day goes by that I don't regret it. And you want to know something else? The reason I was even helping you and Evie in the first place was because I was trying to make up for what I did to you."

"That's a lie," Gavin says, but he doesn't sound convinced. "You've said numerous times that you *weren't* doing this for me."

"For pity's sake, Gavin! I couldn't exactly *admit* I was doing this for you or you'd never have let me. You're as stubborn as a damn mule and have never taken help from anyone. I knew that the only way I was going to be able to prove anything to you was to take care of your girl. You'd have to be blind not to see how much she means to you and I knew you'd do anything, including letting me help you, to help her."

I gape at Asher, shocked. He's standing with his fists clenched at his sides, his whole body shakes with indignation and anger. I want so badly to ask what exactly happened. It's not hard to see it was bad—bad enough to split up two best friends—and my heart breaks for the both of them, but I don't know what to say. I wouldn't even know where to start.

Gavin doesn't say anything either, but at least his anger has left him. Instead, he looks thunderstruck. He lowers himself to the ground, staring off into space. Asher watches him for a few minutes, but when Gavin doesn't seem intent on saying anything to anyone, Asher turns back to me.

"So," he says as if he hadn't just been yelling at Gavin for the last few minutes, "what do you think that stuff is?" He points to the closest "body."

I watch Gavin a second more before turning to Asher. "I don't know. Maybe it was something they used to clean up the deceased Gavin said were here. They *are* in the shapes of bodies."

"But why did it try to eat my foot?"

"Maybe it likes the taste of chicken," Gavin mutters.

I have to stifle a laugh, but Asher ignores him completely.

"Hmm." Asher tilts his head as he focuses his attention on the green sludge. Eventually, he stands and leans over it, then kneels next to it. He rubs his hand against the floor, picks up a handful of debris and starts throwing it into the puddle.

Even from here I can see it suck up the pieces like a sponge.

"Hmm," he says again, then looks around.

"What are you looking for?" I ask.

"Something else to throw in it."

"Why?"

"Got any other plans to keep busy?"

I shake my head.

"Well, then, this is as good as any."

Since he's got a point, I dig into my pockets to see if I have anything hiding in there. I come up with a pen, a couple scraps of very wet paper, and a paper clip.

Asher takes the items. One by one he throws them in, only to have them get sucked up. Which is odd, because the muck can't be more than half a centimeter thick. The pen, at least, should be touching the floor and still visible. Instead the puddle looks completely unchanged. It seems to have eaten the items, just like the other mass ate Asher's shoe.

"I guess they're not coming," Gavin says when we run out of things to throw. "It's been a while. I'm sure if they were going to come, they'd have been here by now."

"I don't know whether to gloat, or be upset that I was right," Asher says, worry clouding his face.

What was it the computer said about being arrested until surface police get here? Asher's focused on me, but it's Gavin who answers.

"I think it's a holdover from when this was a resort. The journals Evie found made it really clear her dad had built this whole complex as a rich man's playground. It was never meant to be a self-sufficient city. Not until Mother killed him and turned it into one.

"She killed her own dad?" Asher asks. "That's sick."

Gavin presses his lips together and nods, not saying anything.

I decide I don't want to continue this conversation and step closer to the green stuff.

I step as close to the goo as I can without getting a foot full of whatever it is.

Just as I squat down to look closer at it, the whole puddle lurches toward me. Screaming, I fall back onto my butt at the same time Gavin and Asher shout, "Whoa!"

Asher, the closest to me, yanks me away, shoving me behind him. I peer around his shoulder.

"What was that?" Asher asks.

But Gavin doesn't get a chance to respond before it moves again, its arm stretching toward Asher and me.

All three of us run to the other wall, as far away from it as possible, but it doesn't do anything else.

"What the hell was that?" Gavin asks.

Asher shrugs. "I have no clue. I have never seen anything like that before."

They both turn toward me. "Evie?" Gavin asks.

I shake my head rapidly. "How should I know? I don't remember seeing anything like that. I don't remember *anything*, remember?"

Gavin steps up to it again, but when he apparently gets too close, its arm lunges at him again and he jumps back with a yelp.

"Okay, I take it back," Gavin says. "Mother isn't going to kill us. That thing is."

Asher and I both nod, our eyes wide as the arms of several of the piles slide slowly across the floor toward us. But before we can do more than think about reacting, the walls start to rise. The three of us exchange a terrified look. It appears Gavin was wrong again. Mother did come, and she is going to kill us.

Asher slides underneath the still rising walls and pulls me toward the stairwell with Gavin close on our heels, but before we can get there, a male voice yells, "Stop! Don't move any further."

We keep running, but the voice yells, "Evelyn! Gavin! Wait! Please."

Both Asher and I stop in our tracks and Gavin plows into the back of us. "What are you waiting for? Come on!"

"He knows your names," Asher says. His face is crumpled into a look of confusion and I'm pretty sure he feels the same warring emotions of fear and curiosity as I do.

"So . . . we were here before, it's not surprising," Gavin says, tugging on my arm.

I start to turn away, to listen to Gavin, but the voice shouts again. "I'm not here to hurt you. I promise. I know you don't trust me, but I promise I'm really here to help you."

I'm not sure why I turn around, but when I do there's an older man with blond hair streaked with gray coming toward us. He appears to be in his sixties or seventies, but he carries himself as if he's younger. He looks . . . familiar.

"Who—who are you?" I ask, narrowing my eyes.

"Don't you remember me, Evelyn?" the man asks. I shake my head and he sighs. "It's me. Father," he says with a smile.

I exchange a look with Gavin, who purses his lips and says, "Father is Coupled with Mother. He's the second-in-command, which means he's lying about not turning us in."

But Asher steps forward, his eyes narrowed. "Eli?"

Chapter Twenty-five

Due to the recent infiltration of a Surface Dweller and subsequent kidnapping of my daughter, Elysium is now under a mandatory curfew. All Citizens, minus those designated by Mother, must be in their residences no later than 8:00pm. All doors will be locked and will be checked nightly. Anyone with their door unlocked or caught outside their residences will be persecuted to the full extent of the law. We understand that this is an inconvenience and appreciate your cooperation.

—Letter sent to all residents of Elysium

Evie

My mind instantly goes back to the picture Asher's grandmother showed us and I realize why the man looks so familiar. He's one of the men from the picture. The one that was closest to Asher's grandmother. Asher's right. It *is* Eli. A huge weight lifts from my shoulders as I realize we actually found the man we were sent here to find. And he's alive! Now to see if he can actually do what Asher's grandmother thinks he can and help me get my memories back.

Eli, who's been staring at me, turns his full attention to Asher. "Yes. Yes, but that is not a name I've heard in a long, long time."

"But . . . you're dead!" Gavin bursts out. "We saw the video. We read the journals. Eli was trying to escape, but he was betrayed by someone and Mother killed anyone who tried to escape. She *killed* Eli. You can't be him."

Eli raises an eyebrow. "Well, she tried anyway," he says, but before Gavin can argue further, Eli turns his attention back to Asher. "Who are you and how do you know who I am?"

"I'm Asher St. James. My grandmother—Lenore Allen—sent us here to ask you for help."

Eli stares at Asher for a long time. There are so many emotions flickering across his face you can't even make one out before another is flashing into place.

Finally, he steps forward, bypassing the green goo, which has stopped moving as if it never had started. His eyes are focused completely on Asher, who shifts as if uncomfortable. When Eli gets within touching distance, he stops and tilts his head this way, then that, studying.

Gavin and I exchange a look. A smile slowly spreads across Eli's lips. There is definitely sadness in his expression, but relief as well.

"You have her eyes," he says after a minute. He presses his lips together and I think for a minute he's going to say something or do something else, but then he shakes his head. "No time for regrets."

Eli catches the look Asher sends me and raises his brow at Gavin, who only stares back at him, distrust clear on his face. Then Eli turns his attention to me. And this time, I can make out the emotions running over his face. Relief, happiness, and, finally, sadness. Gavin slides his hand into mine and squeezes. I squeeze back to let him know I'm fine.

It's not exactly true. My head feels like it could explode at any moment from all the stress, but he doesn't need to know it.

Eli reaches out toward me and both Asher and Gavin shout and block his advance. Gavin draws his gun and Eli puts his hands up, palms out.

"I just wanted to touch the necklace." He keeps his eyes steady on mine. "I meant no harm. I can't believe you still have it. I meant no harm."

Gavin jerks his head around to face me and there's understanding in his eyes. He lowers the gun and steps back. "You're the one who gave it to her?" he asks.

Eli hesitates for a moment, lowering his hands to let them hang at his sides before saying, "No, not I. Her mother . . . her *real* mother. But I gave . . . I'm pleased to see she kept it."

He's not telling us everything. I don't know how I know, but I know. From the expression on Gavin's face, I can see he's thinking the same thing.

"But the scents? You're the one who gave her the perfume bottles, right? You're the one who helped her every time she got her memories erased?"

Asher jerks his head around and narrows his eyes at

Gavin, even as I watch Eli and Gavin wide-eyed. I had my memories erased before? This isn't the first time? Why didn't Gavin tell me? If it happened before and there was a cure, why didn't we come to Elysium earlier?

Eli nods. "Yes. I did what I could at the time. Even if it wasn't nearly enough."

"But now you're here to actually help us?" Asher asks, his face scrunched up in confusion.

Eli looks around. "Yes, but not here. There's a place in the Residential Sector that I can take you to. I assure you, it's safe. Then you can tell me what you need help with." He turns to me with a smile. "There's someone there who really misses you and wants to see you again."

"Oh no," Gavin says, and all of us turn to him. He crosses his arms across his chest. "We're not going anywhere. We came to find you and you're here, so you need to help us now, so we can back to the Surface."

Asher nods, agreeing with Gavin for once, but I ignore it and ask, "Who's waiting for me?"

Both boys turn to me. "Evie . . . ," they warn, but I ignore them.

"Who?" I demand.

Eli takes a deep breath. "Your mother. Your *real* mother," he says, quietly.

My heart trips in my chest and I raise a hand to my necklace again, trying to remember something about the woman who birthed me, but nothing comes. Not even the tiniest of memories.

But . . . I do feel *something*. And I want nothing more than to meet this woman.

I open my mouth to tell him we'll go, but Gavin interrupts. "Nice try, but no. We came to get her memories back. That's it, and then we're gone."

Eli turns toward me, his eyes really focusing on me again. "You lost your memories?" I nod. "What happened?

I don't think Gavin will tell him anything—after all, he was dead set that coming to this place was the wrong idea—but he surprises me. "I don't know. She was having issues when we left. Small things. Like how to work the Slate, and where things were. But it wasn't until we got to the Surface that I realized she'd forgotten everything." He looks at the ground. "Including me."

"It's the nanos," Asher shoves in. "Grandma said that you and she developed the nanos, but they've changed. She couldn't help Evie, but she was sure you could."

Eli's face darkens. "They've changed all right. After all, we couldn't have our little prize giving anything away, could we?" he mutters.

Gavin and Asher exchange a look. "Huh?" Asher asks.

Eli shakes his head. "Nothing. Never mind. I can help her, but not here. She needs to come with me."

Gavin raises the gun and aims it at Eli. "I'm not sure if you're hard of hearing or just dumb, but she's. Not. Going. With you. Whatever you need to do, you can do it here."

Eli shakes his head. "You don't understand. What needs

to be done is . . . quite complicated. I *can't* do it here. Believe me, if I could, I would. It's going to be hard enough as it is." He looks at me. "I promise you I won't let anything happen to you. I *can* help you, but you have to come with me."

Gavin is about to say something, but I know it's another argument, so I start talking before he can. "The nanos? Are they what's making me forget everything?"

Eli hesitates, then nods. "Yes."

Gavin and Asher look between Eli and me as I say, "And will I get my memories back if you fix them?"

Eli at first doesn't respond, but then he starts firing questions at me. "Have you been able to recall anything at all?"

"I-I don't know. I'm not sure."

"How about any dreams that seem more real than usual?"

I share a glance with Gavin and nod. "Y-Yes."

Eli makes a hmm-ing noise. "How about hallucinations? Sleepwalking? Sleeptalking? Fugue states?"

I nod quickly, getting more excited with every question. "Yes! Yes, I have. All of those."

"That's the major reason we're here, actually. She's almost killed herself a couple of times with sleepwalking and the fugue states," Gavin interjects.

Eli's eyes widen. "Please explain."

Gavin tells him the story of me walking into his weapons room and then of me almost drowning myself, while Asher explains about my hallucination in the Outlands.

Eli tilts his head back and forth, obviously considering all of the information. "Yes," he finally says. "The memories are still there, they're just blocked. It's part of their programming for Enforcers. We've never tried to get memories back, but I think I can."

He doesn't seem confident, but I've heard all I need to hear. He can help. Probably. Before I can respond, Gavin asks, "How are you going to get her memories back if you've never done it before?"

"Well, we're going to have to reset the nanites."

"And how are you going to do that?"

Eli shakes his head. "We don't have time for explanations right now. It's not safe here. I'll explain everything when we get somewhere secure."

"Then let's go." I push past Gavin and Asher.

They grab at my arms, each saying something to try to make me change my mind, but they speak over each other and I can't understand.

Besides, I don't want to hear it. Eli says he thinks he can fix my memories. That's good enough for me. I pull away and step closer to Eli before looking over my shoulder. "I'm going. You can come along if that will make you feel better, or you can wait here with the goo."

Then I turn back around and start walking toward the Tube station again.

Eli laughs as they run to catch up after a long pause. "Still the same Evelyn, I see. Good. We'll need that spunk." Then he steps in front of me, leading the way.

Gavin

I don't know what to do. I can't say I'm surprised Evie made us follow Eli, but nothing good is going to come of this. I'm certain of that. I can sense Asher's unease as he walks behind me, and serves him right. He's the one who brought us down here. My only comfort is that even if Evie doesn't remember Father, I remember the way she'd talked about him and how he'd helped her stand up to Mother in the past. If anyone can help her now, it's probably him.

Of course, that doesn't mean I completely trust him.

"The train itself is out of service," Eli explains as we quickly walk through the Tube. "Due in part to a mysterious malfunction that ended up causing the entire tunnel to flood, killing six people." He gives me a knowing look.

I clear my throat. "And the other part?"

His look doesn't change, but it darkens. "I'm sure I don't have to say, but it has something to do with some . . . failed experiments, and that marvelous substance you were trapped with."

Asher dances in front of Eli, walking backward to face him. "What was that stuff, anyway?"

Eli shrugs and shakes his head. "We don't know yet. We're still studying it. It's been a bit of a challenge. It resists all our attempts to gather it by somehow mutating anything that touches it into its matrix."

"And that doesn't bother you?" I ask, shuddering as I think how close *Asher* came to "being mutated into its matrix."

"Of course it does. We've had to quarantine Sector Three." He passes by Asher, shutting down any further questions, while the three of us exchange a look behind his back. Just another reason on the long list of them: murderous experiments, entire floors flooded with seawater, green mutating goo—to get the hell out of here as soon as possible.

When we enter the Tube tunnel, dread hunches my shoulders. I expect the sound of rushing water and the icy chill of the ocean to pour over my head. Mother'd tried to drown Evie and me—not to mention the family that had been unlucky enough to have been in the train with us—the last time. There's no evidence of any of that now. It doesn't surprise me that the train—and bodies—are gone. Mother strikes me as nothing if not efficient. Even so, I'm glad Evie doesn't remember any of it. She doesn't need any more anguish right now. It's funny to see her gaping around at the water that surrounds us and the lava flows below us that turn the water orange. She's the one who grew up here.

Asher is doing the same and I have to wonder if that's what I looked like when I first came. I hope I didn't look as stupid as he does, with his mouth hanging wide open. I can't imagine I did. Evie wouldn't have tolerated it.

Then again . . . I chuckle to myself as Eli barks at Asher to stop gawking and keep up. *That* sounds exactly like what Evie had said to me.

The tunnel slopes upward and for the first hundred or so feet, everything seems to be okay. But then Evie stumbles.

I rush to help her up, but she says, "I'm fine. Just a bit

tired." Her voice is all breathy and her tone confused. She had another hallucination. I know it. I can see it in the way her eyes aren't completely focused.

Eli looks over her head at me with worried eyes. He turns his attention back to her. "We can rest if you need to, but we really need to get you somewhere safe as soon as possible. You'll probably experience more and more of your . . . hallucinations the further we go. Especially back in Sector Two. The more familiar surroundings are likely to act as triggers, and we can't risk you doing something to endanger yourself."

I know what he didn't say, "and us." Then something he said clicks in my head.

"Wait. If she'll get her memories back just by being here, why do you even need to do anything?"

"I didn't say she'd get her memories back by being here. I said here might *trigger* more *hallucinations*. And the hallucinations, as you well know, are dangerous. She's been lucky—mostly because of you—up until now, but there's no guarantee that she'll stay lucky. Without my intervention, she could end up injured or worse." He gives me a steady look until he's satisfied I understand what he means, then he turns back to Evie. "Again, we can stop if you need to rest, just let me know."

She must see how worried he is, because she shakes her head. "I'm fine. Let's just keep going."

We do, but after another couple hundred feet, she stumbles again. When I reach for her this time, she just leans against me. Her body is shaking, and even through that I can feel her chest heaving with each breath she takes. Whatever she's seeing, it terrifies her.

"Are you okay?" I ask.

She nods. "Yeah. Perfect."

Asher shoots me an uneasy glance. He knows as well as I do how far from perfect we are right now.

"Do you want me to carry you?" I ask. I don't know if it'll help, but at least we'd be able to keep going.

She looks up at me with the look of "Are you insane?" She shakes her head. "No. I've got it."

For the next several minutes we continue up the constantly sloping floor until even I'm winded. The last week of running all over the Outlands has taken its toll. At least for the trip from Rushlake, I had a horse. Even if I did have to steal it. My whole body aches and I just want to collapse right here and sleep for a month. But I don't trust Eli enough to close my eyes even for a second. Looks like sleep is off the menu until we leave.

And then we come to the open doorway that leads into the main part of Elysium. Up ahead, I can see the pools of light in the center of the Square, though the shops and businesses around it appear dark. Closed up for the night. It looks peaceful, like my own village after dark, but I know it's nothing like that. Everything in this place is manufactured. False peace. Fake plants, a fake moon overhead, and a weird smell like baked goods. But even that isn't quite right. It's more candy-like—a sickly sweet—instead of real spices and sugar.

I have to fight not to turn and run in the other direction as every cell in my body warns me of the danger. Eli gestures for us to get into the shadows made by the lights just outside of the tunnel, so we slip around the corner and press ourselves against the walls as he goes on ahead. My mind screams that we can't trust him, that he works for *her*. He's not bringing us to help, he's bringing us to Mother.

With a small shudder, I push the thoughts away. I don't have a choice. Evie is determined Eli can help and Asher's the classic case of curiosity killing the cat. Even as I think it, he steps into the light to look closer at *something*. I bark at him to get back into the shadows. Which he does with an "oops" expression, but doesn't look all that concerned. I have to remind myself, he doesn't know what could be watching him. Literally. And he doesn't realize that his silver tongue isn't going to be able to talk him out of any trouble he's gotten into.

We wait and I look around, trying to find the turrets, but I can't see any from my angle. I take slow, deep breaths to calm my own unease. What if Eli's going to get an Enforcer? Or Mother? What if he doesn't come back at all?

It's so quiet around here. Last time we were here, this street—the whole Sector—was filled with people. So much so we couldn't walk from one end of it to the other without having to weave between them. Where are all the Citizens? The Enforcers? Guards, even?

Something's wrong. I can feel it.

A few minutes later, Eli reappears, alone, and gestures for us to follow him. "Keep quiet. The city is under curfew."

"Curfew?" Asher asks with raised eyebrows and Evie knits her brow together as if that doesn't quite make sense.

Glancing at her, Eli says, "Mother instituted it shortly after you . . . left. In fact, she started a lot of new, more restrictive laws using you as an excuse."

"Wonderful," Evie murmurs. Guilt drips from every syllable and I can't help but feel for her. She shouldn't be here. She shouldn't know what happened after we left. This isn't at all what *should* have happened. I clench my fists, then force myself to relax them.

Just then Eli curses under his breath and yanks Evie deeper into the shadows. I immediately do the same, knowing better than to take longer than a second. When I turn, my back pressed as tightly as possible against the wall, I see someone that makes the blood in my veins turn to ice. An Enforcer stepping out of the shadows. I thought—wanted, hoped—I'd never see one again, but she's unmistakable with her all-black clothing. The short dress that falls to just above her knees. The long boots, the tops hiding under the skirt, and the gloves and cape that cover the rest of her exposed skin. She's looking right at us. Right at Evie.

Her eyes flick to Asher, who was the slowest of us getting to the wall, and I want to hit him when he whispers, quite loudly, "What's going on?"

"Enforcers." I barely breathe the word. It's probably still too loud, but if I don't answer him, he'll just keep questioning. Next to me, Evie shifts from one foot to the other, and grasps my arm tightly. She's shaking. Or maybe that's me.

The last time I saw an Enforcer up close, she was trying to put a bullet in me.

But then she—the Enforcer—steps backward into the dark. It's almost as if she's melting into them, becoming part of just one large Enforcer shadow. My muscles spasm at the thought.

Eli narrows his eyes, but doesn't say anything. After a minute, he continues forward. Cautiously, I follow, sticking like glue to the walls. Last time, the shadows meant for the Enforcers kept us safe from the turrets. Not that running into more Enforcers is on my list of priorities—that last one is still causing my nerves to spit sparks throughout my body—but maybe with Eli here, they'll ignore us.

I won't get my hopes up.

I think he's going to lead us to the maintenance tunnels Evie and I used the last time we were here, but instead he walks right past them.

"We aren't going to use the tunnels?" I ask, tense.

He doesn't even spare me a glance. "She's too weak to crawl up the ladders on her own. Now hush and keep up."

I glance nervously at a section of the ceiling that has a black pole protruding from it. "What about the turrets?"

This time he stops, but only long enough to give me a look. "Do you think I didn't already think of that, Surface Dweller? I would not let harm come to my daughter, even if that means protecting someone like you. Now hurry, before another Enforcer sees us and all my precautions were for naught."

I bite back a nasty comment, because he's right. While

the Square appears to be deserted, it doesn't mean we can drop our guard. Enforcers could be anywhere. Didn't Evie teach me that?

We move quickly through the spookily quiet city. Every once in a while an Enforcer steps out of the shadows, and every time they look in our direction, I think we're busted. That it's all over. But they just slide back into the shadows.

"What the hell," I whisper.

Eli turns to me with an equally confused look, but his eyes are filled with worry and not a little fear. He mutters, "That's not good." Then he speeds up, but it still feels way too slow for me.

If Eli is worried, "that's not good" is an understatement. My heart gallops in my chest and I feel cold, like I've just drunk an entire gallon of ice water in one shot. The only thing not stopping me from running straight back to the sub is Evie. Even though it's obvious she's terrified with her wide eyes and colorless face, she also looks resolute. There's no way I'd get her out of here without a fight. Which would only draw more attention to us.

"This is insane," I say as quietly as I can. "We're going to get caught. The Enforcers *know* we're here. I know they do."

Eli only nods. "We must hurry. It's safe where I'm taking you. I assure you."

I'm not "assured," but Evie follows, leaving me no choice unless I hit her over the head and drag her back with me. I have to admit, that's looking more and more like a good option.

Suddenly, there's a giggle and shout.

"Meredith! No. *Stop!*"

A little blond-haired girl darts by, and we all stop in our tracks. Eli's face goes from worried to full-out terrified. He lunges forward, trying to grab the child, but she only laughs harder and slips right out of Eli's outstretched hands. I reach for her too, but she only twists her body around, dodging me, still giggling.

"Meredith!" a woman calls. We can't see her yet, but I don't need to see her to know she's in a full-out panic.

I focus in on Eli. The panic he's obviously feeling is practically pouring off him in waves, which makes the dread pooling in my stomach weigh like a stone. He seems torn—undecided—but then he straightens his shoulders and takes a step out of the shadows. Evie makes a short squeaking sound, then slaps her hand against her mouth, her other hand reaching out to him. As if she's willing him to come back.

But it's too late. An Enforcer has beaten both of us to it. Eli steps back into the shadows almost instantly.

The Enforcer is holding the girl, who isn't giggling anymore.

Somewhere in me, I know what's about to happen.

A woman rushes around the corner, then stops in her tracks at the sight in front of her. Her eyes shut and even from here, I can see her swallow. But she straightens her shoulders and walks calmly forward. I have to admire that even though she's obviously terrified, she doesn't turn tail and run.

"That's my daughter," she says, her voice only wavering slightly. "I apologize. She just learned how to open doors. She doesn't understand the curfew. It won't happen again. I promise."

The Enforcer doesn't say anything. She looks down at the child, who is shrieking now.

The mother is still blabbing on, stepping forward, but Eli is mumbling something too and I can't make out what either is saying. I want to do something, grab the girl and run, but I know what would happen. I'm a Surface Dweller. She'd probably kill the girl, then come after me next.

But Eli could do something. Right? He could stop what's happening. Why doesn't he?

Without warning, the mother's body jerks as red spreads across her chest. Her eyes widen, but I can see the light in them die before she even hits the ground. I turn back to the Enforcer to see the glint of a gun in the Enforcer's gloved hand.

Her voice is as dead as the woman on the floor when she says, "Curfew is for the safety of all Citizens. Failure to comply will result in severe punishment."

Then she turns and disappears with the girl into the shadows. The girl's howls slowly fade away.

Chapter Twenty-six

Citizen Evangeline Summers, you are hereby summoned to report to the Medical Sector, tomorrow, March 15, to initiate fertilization treatments.

—Summons for Procreation Duty, dated seventeen years prior

Evie

The memory comes so fast and so hard, I almost feel like it's pulling me from one world to another.

"Congratulations! Evelyn has been chosen for Mother's special program." The woman behind the desk smiles. *"You two must be so proud. It isn't every family that gets the privilege of serving our city so completely."*

"Special . . . program?" My mom, my real one, clutches me tightly to her chest. Dad is staring at my mom like something horrible has happened and it's all her fault. I can see him clearly, but when I look at her, her face is just a smudge of smoke.

She turns back to the woman behind the desk. "But—but we thought Evelyn was meant to be a scientist, like her father and I."

I fidget in my seat and try not to look at the woman, but fail. She makes me nervous. I want to suck my thumb even though my mom says big girls don't do that.

"Mother requested her personally," the woman says, her voice notably cooler. Then she laughs and her blue eyes sparkle with fake happiness. My parents don't join her. They're too busy having one of their silent conversations. "Her genomes have proven superb." She forces her face into a serious expression, one that makes me even more scared of her. "Of course," she says, "you will be fully compensated for your contribution."

As if summoned, a young woman slips out of the shadows, startling my parents and terrifying me. I cling to my mom's neck as the shadow woman walks directly to me.

"She is in my charge now," the new woman says. Her emotionless voice causes my little body to shudder and I cower even more into my mom's chest.

"Now?" my mom asks. "But—"

"She must begin immediately. There is no time to waste." The monster takes my hand and rips me from my mom's lap.

"Mommy," I yell, tears rolling down my cheeks. But she doesn't get up, and the monster doesn't even pause as she removes me from the room.

When I come out of it, I'm staring at a woman's body and the small pool of red forming around her. I feel like I'm going to be sick.

Everyone is still gaping and Eli looks shell-shocked. After a second he yanks me down the hall in a full out run. Gavin is pushing me from behind as if he's terrified I'm still not moving fast enough. Finally we reach what Eli calls—and a little voice tells me is—the Residential Sector without further incident.

I can tell Gavin thinks this has been too easy, despite the scene we just witnessed. He's watching Eli warily as if he thinks we're being led into a trap, but I hope he can shove down his paranoia enough to let Eli help me. If it is a trap, then we'll just have to deal with that when the time comes. I don't have to tell Gavin to be prepared. He's got his fingers wrapped tightly around the gun.

We take a set of stairs and by the time we make it up the half dozen or so flights, I think my heart's going to explode the way it's banging against my ribs. Finally we reach the right floor and go through a door and down a hallway. We stop at a door at the very end and Eli knocks loud enough to startle everyone.

"What's he trying to do?" Gavin whispers to me. "Wake the dead?"

I wince. Not exactly the right wording there.

A few seconds later, the door opens slowly and blue eyes peer out from the crack. Then it jerks open slightly more as those eyes catch slight of Eli.

"Father?!" The woman bows her head, the only part of her body I can see, but her hair covers most of her face besides her eyes. "To what do I owe the pleasure of seeing you so late this evening?"

"Evangeline." His tone—one I've heard Gavin use when talking to me—has everyone glancing at him, before Eli shakes himself. Suddenly he's all business. "Evelyn has returned. These Surface Dwellers have brought her back to us, but her memories are wiped clean. The nanobots have done their job. Too well, it would seem."

The woman's eyes widen; then she follows Eli's gaze over to me, and the door flies open, banging against the wall. It makes me jump, but the woman ignores it.

She leans against the door and I'm surprised to see how familiar she looks to me. As if I've seen her before, but I can't remember where.

"Come, come. Get in here before someone sees you," she demands.

We step inside, and she immediately shuts and locks the door behind us. She starts toward me, but Eli brushes her off. "No time for that now. We need to get her memories back or she'll never be able to help us. Where's the best place?"

She gives him a bland look. "The Medical Sector," Evangeline says.

"You know we can't risk that," Eli says.

She gives him another look, but sighs. "Follow me." She pushes past him, leading the way down a hallway painted a pretty lavender with wood wainscoting on the bottom. It reminds me a little of Asher's house in Rushlake. Pictures of a little girl are framed on the wall and I tip my head to the side to study them closer. I think I recognize her from somewhere.

Eli clears his throat. "Come on, Evelyn. We should get started as quickly as we can."

I follow him, though I keep glancing back at the photos until I get into the room. It too is purple with the wood wainscoting. The pictures in this room are all of flowers. Disappointment pricks at me. The answer to where I've seen that girl before had been just at the edge of my memory.

"Lay here." Eli gestures to the bed. "I'll be right back. I need to get some things. I hadn't been expecting to do this."

He starts to walk past me, but I place a hand on his arm as the question I should have asked first finally comes to mind. "How did you know we were here?"

"The nanite substrate."

"Excuse me?"

"The nanite substrate. The green substance? It moves. I'm sure you noticed." He lifts his eyebrows. "Mother has me studying it. I told you. And we've been trying to figure out what it is. We've figured out it has something to do with the nanites of the deceased bodies, but we're not sure exactly how they went from"—he glances at me—"human bodies to that substance. We'll figure it out eventually. Anyway, it sets off the alarms in the Sector. As you can imagine, Mother hated that the alarms were going off every time the stuff migrated." He shrugs when Gavin scoffs. "So I rerouted them to send an alert to my slate. That included *all* the alarms for the Sector. Including when the sub docked, and the alarms for the Tube station. I knew the minute you came back." He glances at Gavin. "You weren't as secretive as you thought you were."

"I wasn't trying to be secretive. Just stay alive," Gavin mutters.

"Anyway, as soon as I realized you were back and got over the initial shock of that," he smiles at me, "I made sure I'd be able to get you into Sector Two and up here without setting off the other alarms. Then I went to find you and ensure you made it to safety without causing the uproar you caused before."

"And the Enforcers? What about them?" Gavin asks. His arms are crossed over his chest.

"That, young man, is the exact reason we can't be sitting here talking." He focuses back on me. "Sit tight. I'll be right back."

Before we can ask any more questions, he rushes out the door and the four of us—Asher, Gavin, Evangeline, and I—sit there in an uncomfortable silence. Gavin is studying her. She's studying me.

I nudge Gavin—hard—with my elbow and give him my "stop staring" look. He gives me a "what?" look in return. Evangeline grins at me.

I shift my gaze to my hands while Gavin sits next to me, still watching Evangeline while trying to look like he's not. Asher walks around the room, picking up picture frames and putting them back down before moving on to the next one.

After a few minutes, he says, "So? Evangeline? How are you involved in all this?"

Before she can answer, Eli bursts through the door. "I've got everything here to help you." He swallows and I see how nervous he is. "But there's a problem."

"What? What's the problem? I thought you said you could fix this," Gavin demands, his voice and movements panicky as he jumps from the bed.

"I can," Eli says. "But she . . ." He focuses back on me. "You'll have to be awake for the procedure. I'm sorry, but I don't have the equipment I need to put you to sleep. I'm sorry," he finishes weakly.

"Mother," Mom says, and presses her hands to her mouth. "There's nothing you can do?"

"I'm going to give her a sedative, but there's no guarantee she'll stay asleep during . . . everything." He looks over at Gavin. "You need to keep her still. Can you do that? If not, I'll have to tie her down. It's bad enough that I have to gag her; I don't want to do that, too."

Gavin blanches. "Why does she need to be held down? What *exactly* are you going to do to her?" His voice has a hint of panic in it, which makes me feel a little panicky.

Eli sighs as if he really doesn't want to spare the time telling us, but he says, "I'm re-injecting her with working nanites, or nanobots. They'll go in and they'll repair the bots that aren't working and hopefully restore the parts of her neuro-network that have been destroyed to access those memories again—"

"Hopefully?" Gavin interrupts, disbelief tainting his voice.

"You've said repeatedly you could fix her and we're actually working with a hopefully?"

Eli glares at him. "I've never promised anything. I've promised to do the best I can, and I'm fairly confident this will work, but there's never any guarantee. We're working with human biology here, not machines."

"Well, actually we are," Asher says. "Aren't nanobots tiny robots?"

"Yes." Eli sounds exasperated. "But the main part we're actually restoring is her neuronetwork inside her brain. So yes, we're working with machines, but the machines are working on the biology. Now are we going to sit here discussing what we're going to do or are we going to do it before Evie has another hallucination that could kill her?"

I finally pipe up. Ultimately I don't really care what's going to happen as long as I get my memories back. "Let's get moving."

Eli gives me a grim smile, then turns his attention to Gavin. "Can you hold her down? Or not?"

"I can."

"Are you sure? I can't—"

"I said I could do it," Gavin says between clenched teeth.

"Me, too," Asher says, swallowing hard.

Eli nods and turns back to me. "I'm going to give you a shot. Okay? It's going to sting, but it should make you sleepy after that. It should . . . help."

I'm about to nod when Asher says, "Uh . . . maybe we should hold her down for this? She kind of took out like six full-grown men at the hospital back home when they tried taking her blood."

"What?" Gavin demands. "Really?"

Eli's eyes grow wide, but there's something in them that makes me think he's happy to hear this. "There's no need. It's not a real needle. Just a pressure syringe. She won't feel it."

I look away anyway. I really don't want to hurt the people in this room. But Eli was right. I don't feel it. I don't even know he's done it, until he says, "Done."

Eli disappears and comes back again with an armful of supplies. He lays them all out on the dresser next to the bed. It's a handful of syringes that make my mouth dry. I recognize those syringes for some reason and they terrify me, but the shot he gave me already is masking it and I watch with an increasing amount of numbness as he lays out different machines, vials with a silvery liquid in them, and other things that I don't recognize. Then he removes his jacket and rolls his sleeves up past his elbows, before turning to me with a piece of cloth all twisted together. "I'm sorry, Evelyn, but this has to go in your mouth. If anyone hears . . . anything, we'll be in trouble. Okay?"

I know I should feel something. Panic. Fear. Anxiety. Something. But all I feel is an odd floating sensation, and so I do as he asks and open my mouth without even so much as a question.

He places the cloth in my mouth and ties it behind my head, then disappears from view again while the pungent smell of rubbing alcohol scents the air. When he returns, he peers down at me. "Scream all you want. Okay?" he says, and looks away.

My eyes widen. Something in his tone makes panic tingle in my veins for the first time.

I shake my head rapidly back and forth. But they all ignore it and it's only moments before a sharp pain tears through me. My chest, lungs, shoulder, leg. They're all on fire. I jerk, trying to scream, but the gag prevents it. There are voices in the background, but it's hard to understand over the screaming inside my head.

I struggle harder, but they're pinning me down. I open my eyes to see Gavin with a determined look on his face. Asher stands at my side, leaning over my chest, holding my arms down. More pain rips through my body and it jerks. My head spins opposite of my stomach and I think I'm going to be sick, but neither Gavin nor Asher will let me up.

Without warning, I feel bugs crawling over my feet, burrowing into my skin, slithering across my muscles and nerve endings. I try pulling away, but it only gets worse and worse. Those nasty little bugs crawling up over my feet, past my ankles, my shins, knees, until more than half my body feels like it's infested with the horrible burrowing insects. I scream, wiggling and struggling to get away. But the firebugs continue to ravage my body, over my chest, up my neck, until I'm gagging on them, fighting to breathe.

Voices crowd around me. Shouting, whispering, rising and falling around me like waves.

Then, just when I think I can't take any more, it stops and I feel nothing. No pain. No burrowing insects. Nothing but the strange floatiness I felt before. My eyes drift closed.

My eyes fly open. Every bone in my body aches. Sweat clings to my skin and blood bubbles on my mouth where my teeth tore into my lips. My whole body feels like it's encased in ice.

I'm lying naked in a room of all white, strapped down to the bed, Technicians floating around me, murmuring.

"Excellent candidate," one says. "Procedure went perfectly. Tell Mother. She'll want to watch this one."

One of the female Technicians helps me sit up, wrapping a robe around my shoulders. She smiles at me. "Congratulations, Evelyn. You're officially an Enforcer."

I kneel, careful not to get too close. He's quite obviously a Surface Dweller and therefore unpredictable.

"Hello," I say softly. "I won't hurt you."

He shrinks away from me and narrows his eyes, but adjusts his body, bracing his legs. It's obvious he's positioning himself to run again.

"Yeah, right." His voice is scratchy, as if he's swallowed too much saltwater.

*I try again, using a smile this time—*a woman's best weapon is her smile, unless there's a loaded Beretta 9mm nearby. *I frown. What an odd thought. "I don't blame you for not trusting me. You don't know me, but I assure you, I mean you no harm. My name is Evelyn Winters. I'm the Daughter of the People."*

"Gavin Hunter," he answers warily.

I smile again, a real one this time, and he blinks, as if surprised.

"Gavin. It's a pleasure to meet you."

"Faster," the woman says, mashing a button on the box in her hand.

Suddenly my blood's on fire and I scream, collapsing onto the ground. Almost instantly the pain stops, but I'm still gasping for breath, even as I lurch to my feet and jump onto the rope swinging from the ceiling, pulling myself up hand over hand. Even as I push the button to ring the bell at the top, I know it's my fastest time yet. I let myself drop, bending my knees as I was taught to absorb the force of my weight.

"Good." The instructor smiles. "Faster." She presses the button again.

"Aren't you coming?"

"Of course not. Why would I leave? This is my home. I'm just going to make sure you get back to the door that leads to the Surface. You're all healed, so you should have no problems getting out okay after that."

"But what about the Enforcers? Won't they kill you for helping me?"

"A chill tickles my spine and I suppress a shudder, but I say, "I'm the Daughter of the People. Mother will never believe it was me who helped you."

He doesn't look convinced. "I'd feel better if you came with me," he says.

"If you're really concerned about me, you won't argue with me. The clock is running and the sooner you get out, the less chance they'll figure it out."

"But the guards saw you."

"Who will Mother believe? The Guards? Or her own daughter? Now come on!"

"Fine, but this conversation isn't over," he says, and I fight the urge to roll my eyes. "So, we're on the run now, right?"

"Yes."

"Great." He grabs my arm and spins me around, and then pushes me back with his body so I bump into the wall. Before I can say anything he leans down so his mouth captures mine.

At first I freeze, afraid of the punishment that's surely coming. I start to struggle to get away from him, but then, as my mind fogs from his scent and taste, I melt in his arms. If not for his hands holding me steady at my hips, I would be a puddle on the ground. His lips are sweet and soft, but insistent. The kiss makes my head spin. As far as first kisses go, I can't imagine a better one.

A girl lies at my feet, her face covered in blood, her arm twisted by her side at an awkward angle. She's older than me and almost a complete Enforcer. Sweat covers every inch of skin and my body is bruised and battered, but I held my own. I stand there as straight as I can, wanting to pant as my body craves oxygen, but I will maintain control over myself. No one will know how I almost lost. How winded and exhausted I am. Especially not Mother.

She watched the entire thing, and now she strolls over to us both, flicking a gaze down at the girl who's trying to push herself up on her good arm before turning her attention to me.

My lips want to pull up in a smile as she inspects me. Instead, I pull myself straighter, ignoring the excruciating pain in my ribs from where the girl kicked me. Mother's gaze travels from my head to my feet and back again, before she turns away without saying a word.

I close my eyes against the dismissal and let my shoulders droop.

I struggle to remain standing. I'll kill him before I go down. Again, I raise the gun, aiming for his head. I won't miss this time. I won't fail again.

He closes his eyes and steps forward, pressing the gun to his own head.

"What are you doing?" I ask. Panic is tearing through me and I don't know why. I should be grateful he's doing my job for me.

"Making it easier for you. With that arm, you wouldn't be able to hit the broad side of a barn."

"Are you crazy?"

He nods and there's a small ghost of a smile. "Yeah. I think maybe I am. I've fallen in love with a girl who's programmed to kill me. Not a very sane thing to do, is it?

My jaw drops. *"What? What did you say?"*

He looks straight into my eyes. "I love you, Evie."

"This is your chance, Evelyn. You won't get another one like it to-day. Failure will not be tolerated," my mentor says. We're stand-ing in the Square, waiting for Sorting. The water is dark blue over our heads and I can hear the low moaning of the whales in the distance. The Square is decorated in black and purple.

"I understand," I reply, determined that this time, Mother will notice me. She won't be able to ignore me this time.

My mentor leaves me to wander the slowly growing crowd and takes her station somewhere on the other side of the aisle left open for Mother. For a loud few minutes, people talk around me, not even noticing me. I don't look like an Enforcer. Not yet, I think. But soon. Very soon.

Excitement boils in my blood. Butterflies flutter in my stomach but I squash all emotion. Emotion won't get me no-ticed. Success will. I will *not* fail.

Then a hush draws over the crowd. Mother walks through the crowd, and on either side of the aisle, Citizens bow their heads in reverence. Except the Citizen right next to me. An older man. He refuses to bow his head. The Citizens next to him are hissing at him to do it, but he stares straight back at Mother without so much as a nod. She lifts an eyebrow and stops for the briefest of seconds before moving her gaze to me.

I know what I'm supposed to do. It makes me sick to think about it, but failure will not be tolerated. I sneak behind him, then grab him by his arm and pull him into the shadows.

Although he struggles, it's a simple matter of injecting him with the syringe of medication Enforcers use to calm the unwilling. I place my hands around his head and twist. The popping sound his neck makes leaves me nauseated and for a minute, I lean over, pressing my sweaty palms on my thighs.

After a few minutes of breathing shallowly through my nose, I leave his body for one of the disposal crew to clean up. They should be around any minute. I rejoin the crowd with my stomach still rolling. They part for me now and when Mother sees me, she smiles from the stage set in the middle of the Square. I'm disgusted and queasy, but I fight a smile. I've been waiting five years for this.

Memories flash by in an endless series of bodies and blood and pain. The minute one ends another starts, filling my body with sorrow, regret, disgust, and anger. For myself. For the woman who did this to me and for the one who let it happen. But there are certain memories I'm grateful for. Ones that make up for every single one of the bad ones. Memories of Gavin.

Chapter Twenty-seven

It is a privilege and an honor to serve as an Enforcer, Elysium's most prestigious designation . . . Conditioning is the ideal training method as it is safe, quick, and completely painless.

—Excerpt from *So Your Daughter Has Been Chosen to Be an Enforcer. Congratulations!* pamphlet

Evie

When I wake, my whole body is sore. Just like in the memories. This is a pain I know well. How many times did they do this before? Too many to count. Enough for me to lose myself, though. Enough to turn me from a normal little girl who wanted to play with dolls and have tea parties to a monster who killed people to impress a different monster. To make *someone* proud of me.

I open my eyes and survey the people grouped around me. My eyes land on Evangeline. The woman I now realize is my mother. My real mother. I must have been an idiot not to see the resemblance between us. It's there, slapping me in the face in the color of our eyes. The tilt of our mouths. The upper lip that's slightly fuller than the bottom. Her face is almost identical to the one I see every time I look in the mirror.

Unlike my reflection, though, she won't meet my gaze. She knows that I know and that's just fine with me. I firm my mouth into a straight line. "So, where's my real father?"

Evangeline's eyes widen and stare daggers into Eli. "You didn't tell her?"

Eli looks down at the ground and mumbles, "I thought we should tell her. Together."

Evangeline—I don't know if I can think of her as my mom—shakes her head. "You mean leave it to me." She lowers herself to the bed and tries to stroke my hair, but I jerk myself away from her. She sighs. "Father *is* your real father."

I don't know how to respond to that. Evangeline is obviously my real mom. Eli, on the other hand . . . I tilt my head to study him, but looking at him, there really isn't anything physical we share. But . . . there is something similar. Our mannerisms. Our facial expressions. Even the way he's looking at me, obviously trying not to let me know how nervous he is about what Evangeline just told me, is something I would do, and I doubt anyone else would even know he's nervous.

More than that, there's some kind of connection between us. More of one than I feel toward my mom, and enough of one that I trusted him to get us here. My memories are like leaves fluttering on the wind. No order yet, but something tells me I still don't have the whole story of what happened between Eli and Evangeline.

I sneak a look at Gavin, who doesn't seem that shocked. But Asher is gaping at Eli, and a considering look crosses his face when he turns his attention to me.

I frown at him, wondering what he's thinking, but I say, "This isn't right. He's not my dad." I focus back on Evangeline. "I remember someone else. I never met you until . . . until after I became an Enforcer."

Eli has this half smile on his face, but Evangeline shoots a worried look at him. He nods at her to continue, and for a minute she looks like she's going to refuse, but then she sighs and stands as if she's too nervous to just sit and do nothing.

"You're right, Evie. This is all very complicated, but there *was* someone else. His name was Nathaniel. We were Coupled and he . . ." She stops and closes her eyes, taking a shaky breath before continuing. "He's the one who raised you, but he wasn't your real dad. Not genetically."

My heart starts pounding in my chest and I know I don't want to hear the rest of the story, but I can't make myself tell her to stop. It's as if my body knows I need to hear the rest.

"I was so young. Just barely sixteen. But Nathaniel and I were in love. I was already approved as a breeder, so it was simply a matter of obtaining the license to Couple. So we went to Mother and applied for it. We were approved, but there was a stipulation." She looks at me, and lets out this short, humorless laugh before glancing down to her hands. "For me, anyway. But I didn't know it. Not until after Nathaniel and I were Coupled. Nathaniel and I decided we wanted to start our family right away. We said it was to do our duty for Elysium, but we really just wanted to have children." She smiles at me, but I can't smile back, so she looks back at her hands. "I remember that day perfectly. It was two months after our Coupling and I was in what was to be your nursery. Getting it ready in the hopes that it would give me good luck." She looks at me. "I'd failed to conceive up until this point and she—Mother—came to find me personally. She told me that my genetics were a perfect match for something she was hoping to do. She'd chosen me to be the mother to a new breed of Enforcers. A breed designed specifically for the task. At first I was flattered. Who wouldn't be?"

She smiles at me, but I'm not amused. She was *flattered*? Really? How fantastic for her.

She clears her throat. "Um . . . it was short-lived. She went on to say that the father of the baby I would carry would not be Nathaniel, but would be her own partner. Father."

Everyone looks at Eli and he shifts from side to side, looking at the ground.

"I don't understand." Gavin moves his gaze back to Evangeline. "If she wanted you to Couple with Eli, why did she allow you to Couple with Nathaniel?"

"To force her to agree," Asher says, and I shift my attention to him. He's looking at Evangeline. "Right? She gave you what you wanted, then threatened to take it away if you didn't do what *she* wanted."

Tears fall from Evangeline's eyes, but she nods. "Yes.

Exactly. When she told me that she wanted me to breed with Father—" She looks at each of us in turn. "Not Couple," she clarifies. "Coupling would mean she would have had to give him up. And there was no way she was going to allow that. No, she only wanted him to breed with me. Anyway, when she told me, I refused. I said that I was Coupled and that I wanted children with Nathaniel. So she threatened me. She told me that Nathaniel was sterile. A failure. He wouldn't be able to breed, but she had allowed me to Couple with him anyway, because he would make an excellent father to the child she wanted to create. Since Father wouldn't be there to be the dad, somebody else would have to stand in. And because of my genetics, I would make the perfect mother.

"So I had a choice. I could either allow her to artificially inseminate me and keep my mouth shut, letting Nathaniel think he was the father. Or I could refuse and Nathaniel and I would disappear. She'd take what she needed from me and 'gift' some other woman with being the mother to the perfect Enforcer. She gave me twenty-four hours to think about it. I didn't have any choice but to accept. The next day when she came, she brought the doctor with her." She shrugs. "She knew I'd accept. We started treatments and a few months later I was pregnant with you."

"So," I say, anger boiling up in me like a volcano, "I was . . . just a means to an end." I look between Eli and Evangeline. "For Mother I was . . . the beginning of a perfect race of assassins. For you, Evangeline, a way to stay alive, and for you,

Eli? What . . . what was I to you?" My voice gets higher and louder with each word. But I don't let him answer before asking, "I was never wanted? None of you wanted me? Only *Mother*?"

"Oh hell," Asher says.

"It wasn't like that, Evelyn, you have to understand—" Evangeline starts to say.

"I understand perfectly. No one wanted me except Mother, and she only wanted me for my . . . DNA." I swipe my palms together as if to clean them. "I'm just a bunch of spare parts waiting to be assembled into something better. What a terrible inconvenience for you all that I turned out to be a real person!"

"No, no—" she starts to say.

"Evie—" Eli starts to speak but I cut him off with a glare.

"You're the worst of them. You *knew* what she was capable of and you let her do it anyway. To your own *daughter*." My chest aches and my eyes burn miserably. "You didn't even care, did you?"

"Don't answer that," Gavin says to my parents, then turns to me. "It doesn't matter. It doesn't matter the motivation of any of *them*. Look at me." He peers into my eyes when I do. "*I* love you. *I* want you. And no matter what you were created for, that will always be true. Okay?"

His words are like a balm on the open wounds Evangeline just broke open, and I nod, but it doesn't stop me from needing to know the answers. I turn back to Evangeline, who is watching me.

"We loved you, Evie. Me. Nathaniel and—"

"Me," Eli says, and I jerk my head around to look at him. "I loved you, too. We still do."

"But you still sent me to *her*. Sent me to be an Enforcer. Let them"—I search for the word Gavin used—"brainwash me. If you loved me, how could you do that?" I look between the two of them. "How could *any* decent human being do that to *anyone*? *You're despicable*." The burning in my eyes melts into tears, but I refuse to let them fall.

They glance at each other and I can almost see them asking each other how to answer the question. I push myself up to my feet, but stagger when the blood rushes from my head. Both Gavin and Asher rush to catch me before I can fall. My parents exchange another look.

This, of course, makes the volcano of anger boil over and I shout, "Answer me!"

"We didn't have a choice," Evangeline finally says. "Being an Enforcer was . . . is a privilege. Mother's most prestigious designation. We didn't know what would happen."

"Bullshit!" Gavin says.

"Watch your tongue, boy," Eli says. "She wanted answers, she's getting them."

Evangeline looks at Gavin. "We did know about the Conditioning." She turns back to me. "But we *didn't* know that your brain would be able to fight it. If we had, we might have done things differently."

"What?" I demand, crossing my arms over my aching chest. "What would you have done?"

She shakes her head. "I—I don't know. Something. Anything." She meets my eyes and takes my hands in hers, frowning at them. "But you have to know—I loved you. Love you. Very much. It didn't matter to me why you were here, just that you were. You were always *my* daughter, even when she thought of you as hers."

"But you gave me up! You didn't fight for me at all! You let her take me. I *lost* myself before I even knew who I was! How could you do that?" My voice is a whisper. A husk of itself.

"You've seen her," Eli says. "I know you've seen her in those memories. Even if they don't all make sense at the moment. You know what she's like and you also know she's the one who did this to you. And you're not the only one. You're not even the last. But if you want this to stop . . . you know what has to be done."

"What?" I ask, sniffling and running a hand under my running nose.

"You have to eliminate Mother."

Chapter Twenty-eight

Elite Enforcer Testing Requirements

In order to pass training, an Enforcer must:

- *Lift 8 times her own body weight (minimum)*
- *Master all forms of martial art techniques*
- *Be able to name, repair, and correctly use all weapons modern or archaic, while also adapting easily to new technologies*
- *Endure emotional, pain tolerance, and healing tests, while being able to make snap judgments that benefit the whole, even if sacrificing the few*
- *Demonstrate knowledge of all computer skills including but not limited to: extensive knowledge of all operating systems (past and present, and adaptation to new technologies), coding, software for the express purpose of "hacking," forensics, and electronic bypassing*

Evie

I push myself up to my feet. "Absolutely not. I can't kill someone."

Eli keeps his gaze on mine. "You're the only one who can, Evie. You've had Enforcer training—"

"I don't remember it!" A lie. Bits and pieces of those memories crowd my brain, making me dizzy. But it's all jumbled, just like all the rest.

"Your body does, even if you don't."

I flash back to the path in the woods, how I tore the birds' heads from their bodies without even batting an eye. The attack on Asher. And then again when I knocked Gavin out.

The blood rushes from my head, and I have to sit back down. He's right. My body *does* remember what to do. But still . . . "I can't kill her. Then I'm no better than she is."

Gavin squeezes my hand. "Of course you can't kill her." He glares at Eli. "How can you even ask that of her?" He stands, pulling me up with him, and I let him. I don't care that I just found out who my parents are, I just want to get away from these psychotic people.

"You can't leave here," Eli says, stopping Gavin and me in our tracks.

"Yes we can, and we will," Gavin says, his teeth and fists clenching.

"You can. She can't. She'll lose everything again. There's an EMF field around the city. If you leave, the field will cause the bots to hardlock. They'll automatically suppress Evelyn's memories again. It prevents people who've managed to . . . leave—not that it happens very often—from telling our secrets to the Surface Dwellers. But if you help us, I'll figure out a way to bypass that so you can go. Both of you."

I exchange a glance with Gavin. As much as I don't want to believe Eli, there's something that rings true about what he's saying. I think I knew this. Somehow.

I don't say anything, but Asher says, "What if we come up with a compromise?" He glances to me. "We don't have to kill anyone. We could just . . . exile her."

Evangeline's eyes light up. "Yes. To the Surface. For her *that* would be a fate worse than death."

Eli furrows her brow. "How are we going to do that? She's never going to go without a fight. And who's to say she won't find a way to come back in when we're not expecting her? It's too dangerous."

The room becomes quiet again, but I don't care. "I'm not killing anyone," I say. "No matter how horrible she is. Or how I was trained. I'm not taking someone's life. It's wrong. And I refuse to do it again for you or anyone."

Eli holds my gaze for a long minute. "Fine," he says finally. "Exile could work, but we need to remove her from office and find a way to get her out of here and onto the Surface, while figuring out how to keep her from returning. And for that we'll still need you. Your training will still be the best advantage we have, especially if things go wrong."

Gavin shakes his head. "No. This isn't our fight anymore. We appreciate you helping her, but we can't stay. I'm not going to let her get herself hurt again. Mother doesn't know she's here, as far as we know, and I'd rather it stay that way." He looks up at me. "Right, Evie?"

I don't know what to say. My mind is still chaotic. I'm

starting to put together all the information that I've regained access to, but not all of it makes sense. A lot of it doesn't, actually. It's like putting a puzzle together without having the box to tell you what the whole picture is supposed to look like. I can't be certain of anything. I can't even be sure the memories I have are real memories or ones my brain has supplied to fill in the gaps. All I really have is what they've told me. Is that enough for me to risk my life for people I don't even know anymore?

Gavin may be right. This isn't really my fight anymore, and Mother is surely out for my blood. It'd be much better for us—Asher, Gavin, and me—to just leave now.

But that doesn't feel right either.

If what they're saying is right, and there is anything I can do to help, I don't think I'd be able to live with myself if I just left them to fend for themselves. I'd probably end up like Asher's grandmother, trying to get rid of the guilt years later.

They're all still staring at me, but I don't know what to do.

"I don't know," I finally say. "I—I need a few minutes. To think." I press a hand to my pounding head.

Immediately Evangeline jumps up. "Of course you do. You're probably exhausted. After everything you've gone through." She starts leading me down the hall and to the first room on the left.

She pushes open the door to reveal a bedroom decorated in pink. She gestures to the bed. "Please. Rest. You know where to find me if you need me."

I nod and sit on the side of the bed while she stands awkwardly in the doorway. After a minute, she turns and leaves, looking lost.

I know the feeling. I feel lost myself. Engrossed in my thoughts, I don't hear the door open, and when Asher's head pops into my line of view, I have to stifle a scream.

He laughs when I swat at him. "Asher! Don't *do* that!"

"Sorry," he says, still laughing.

I make room for him on the bed and he sits next to me.

We sit in easy silence, until finally he breaks it by saying, "You know that I'm *not* on the side of you dying, right?"

Surprised, I jerk my head up to look at him. "Of course!"

"And that I didn't bring you here to betray you?"

I blink. "Of course you didn't. I've known from the beginning that the only reason you brought me here was to help me. You've been incredibly kind. Thank you."

"Don't thank me," he says. "It wasn't entirely selfless on my part."

"You mean how you're trying to make up to Gavin by helping me?"

"No. At first that was the reason. Then I got to know you and I was doing it for you. You seemed to be able to see right through me and yet . . . you still liked me. I think." He looks up at me and I nod. He smiles; then it falls and he continues. "That doesn't happen to me very often. Even my own father isn't exactly fond of me. I thought I was falling in love with you. I kind of hoped I was because it would have made things so much easier. And I convinced myself that it was mutual." He sighs. "And if it wasn't, that with time, maybe it would be."

My eyes widen as I stare at him. I open my mouth to say something, but I'm so shocked that nothing comes out.

He only laughs. "Yeah. That's what I thought. Don't worry. I've realized that's not gonna happen. And it's okay. Because I do love you. It's just not that kind of love."

"I—I don't understand."

He takes my hand, running a thumb over the back of it. "You didn't realize what Eli was saying back there. Did you?"

"About him being my dad? Yeah, I get it."

He shakes his head. "No. Not exactly. Remember what my grandma said about him? About *them*?" He emphasizes the "them" and stares at me as I frown.

Then slowly I get it. "About them being lovers?"

He looks uncomfortable, squirming a little in his seat, but nods. "What if she was pregnant when she left here?" His eyes bore into mine. "What if my mom is Eli's daughter, too?"

"No. That can't be right." Can it? Do I have family out there I didn't even know about? I stare at Asher. Is *he* part of my family?

He smiles when he sees I understand and his hand grips mine. "You get it now, don't you?"

I slowly nod.

"When Eli said that you were his daughter, it surprised me that it didn't bother me as much as it should have, you know? Because he was my grandma's boyfriend, for God's sake, and that meant you were—well, you could be . . . I realized that it could mean you were family. And it should have been so disgusting, but it's not, because I see you more like my sister than a girl." He laughs. "That didn't come out right. And that's why I get so pissed off at Gavin for the way he treats you sometimes. I'm not jealous—" He bumps my shoulder with his. "—I'm just watching out for my sister."

I stare at him, my heart bursting with happiness. Family. *Real* family. Someone who actually wants to be my family, instead of just tolerating my existence.

I smile at him, then hug him tightly, tears brimming in my eyes. He hugs me back.

"Do you think it's true?" I ask.

"I don't know. It seems possible." He shrugs. "I kind of like the idea of you being my sister."

"You realize I'd actually be your aunt, right?" I ask, grinning.

He rolls his eyes. "Please. You're little-sister material all the way."

Laughing, I feel lighter than air. I can't wait to tell Gavin this new revelation. I've no doubt he'll be happy for me. And maybe this will help him bridge that ridiculous gap between them.

He nudges my shoulder again, before standing and walking to the door. "I know this is probably the hardest decision you'll ever have to make, but I just want you to know that I'm behind you. No matter what you decide." Without saying another word, he steps out of the room.

For a few minutes, I just stare at the open door, trying to

gather my thoughts, until Gavin knocks. He steps in without waiting for an answer and joins me on the bed, linking his fingers with mine.

"You're not seriously thinking of staying, are you?"

"I don't know. If Mother has done half the things they say, I can't just walk away."

He opens his mouth, then shuts it, before sighing. "We can't stay, Evie. You know that. I won't take the chance of you getting hurt again, and Mother is dangerous. There's no way she's just going to let you stroll in and tell her she can't live here anymore."

"But there's no one else to help them. You heard them. I'm the only one."

"So they say. What if you never came back at all? What would they have done then?"

"But I did."

"But what if you didn't?" He pushes off the bed to pace, then stops in front of me. "You are under no obligation to help them. In fact, they have no right"—he balls his hands into fists—"*no right*, to ask this of you. They're your family. Any parent would have saved their daughter's life without asking for *payment*. And they lost the right to ask you for help when they gave you to the psychotic woman and let her *brainwash you*, repeatedly." He goes on, getting louder and more animated by the second.

Finally I cut into his diatribe.

"Gavin?" I ask, looking at him.

He stops, frowning at me. "What?"

"You're not helping."

He stares at me. "You're not just going to make me watch you walk into that black widow's lair. I won't do it, Evie. Not this time. I've already had to endure being back here. I won't let you do this."

At that, anything I would have said flies out of my mind. "You're not going to *let* me?" I push up from the bed.

His eyes widen at my tone and he starts to say something, but I interrupt. "Gavin, I appreciate everything you've done for me. I understand this hasn't been easy. But just because I don't remember much about my life before we met doesn't mean I'm your property. *You* don't let me do anything. If *I* choose to help them, I will do so and there will be nothing you can do to stop me." I turn around so my back is to him, then gesture to the door. "You may leave."

"But, Evie, wait. That's not what I—"

"You may leave," I repeat, swallowing the lump of rage and hurt balling in my throat.

He sighs, but I hear him leave the room, his shoes dragging across the floor. He pauses at the door momentarily, but then he keeps going without saying anything.

An hour later, I've made my decision. I carefully make my way back to the living room to stand at the doorway, being a silent observer for the minute or so before anyone sees me. Evangeline is talking quietly with Eli in a corner of the room. Their backs are to me, and I can't hear what they're saying, but they look nervous. Gavin sits on the couch, curled into himself.

I take a deep breath and instantly feel everyone's eyes on mine. Waiting for an answer I don't want to give because I know what it'll mean and what I'll have to do. When I look up, I meet Asher's gaze first. He nods once and I close my eyes in relief. At least someone is standing by me.

When I open them again, I look all of them in the face, stopping last on Gavin. His eyes narrow, but I don't look away. I want him to know this is something I have to do. I can't just let Mother's tyranny continue. She's already taken everything from me; I can't let her destroy any more lives. Not if I have even the smallest chance of stopping it.

I turn to my parents. "I'll do it. For Elysium." To Asher. "For my family." Then to Gavin. "For us."

A war of words breaks out around me. Gavin is the first up and I expect him to start on me, but he pushes his face into Eli's, screaming as loud as I've ever heard. Eli is screaming right back, gesturing to where I sit. I can't hear anything as everyone is fighting to talk over each other.

The only one not yelling is Asher, who is watching me intently. So intently I wonder if he's trying to tell me something. For a minute, we just sit there watching each other, letting the words crash over us before he breaks it with his signature smile. As if to say, "I've got this."

I smile back. "Thank you," I mouth, and he nods again,

then tips his head toward the door, gesturing for me to exit while everyone is preoccupied.

Then he stands and enters the fight, while I slip quietly to my room to contemplate how to take Mother down.

Chapter Twenty-nine

My daughter has returned to me, as I knew she would. After all, she is my creation. And like anything that requires programming by an outside influence, it is inevitable that she should return to her creator.

Especially when programmed to do so.

—Excerpt from Mother's Journal

Mother

I watch the monitor and smile. They actually believe they got into Elysium without me knowing. I didn't become the Governess by being a fool. I *am* Evelyn's Mother. Everyone's Mother. And nothing escapes me.

I turn to Dr. Friar behind me. "You made sure he got everything he needed?"

"Yes. I made sure the staff was otherwise entertained so all he had to do was 'sneak' in and grab it." He tips his head to the side, that sly smile twinkling in his eyes. "Poor man. Seemed in such a hurry. Didn't even notice it was unusually quiet in the Medical Sector. I do hope nothing is wrong."

I laugh and lean against the back of my chair. "Fantastic." Then a thought occurs to me. "How much of her memory will he be able to recover?"

"Not much, I'm afraid. With the reactivation she may get them all back eventually, but it will be very slow. You'd probably have more success planting new ones."

I nod and lean into my mirror, checking the line of my eyeliner. I press a light finger to the small wrinkles to the side. "Make sure you have everything you need to make that happen." I look at him through the mirror. "She's probably already said yes. They won't wait long. And I'm eager to continue Evelyn's training now that she's passed her test. I must say, I'm pleased that she's brought these fabulous new specimens with her." The side of my mouth lifts. "Such a lovely surprise."

There's a soft knock on the door. "Come," I say.

One of my Maids pokes her head through the opening. "Enforcer Lydia here to see you, ma'am."

I clap my hands. "Wonderful. Send her in."

The Maid quickly disappears to be replaced with the girl Evelyn's age who has taken over as lead Enforcer since Evelyn and that Surface Dweller killed my last leader. She stands just inside the door, staring over my head with her trained gaze. I know she sees everything, even when it looks like she sees nothing.

"The situation is under control," she says, her voice as flat as the floor my chair is sitting on.

"The girl?"

"She's been relocated to Enforcer training."

"And her poor mother?"

"Eliminated."

My smile creeps across my face. "Very good. You may go." I waggle my fingers at the door and spin back around in my seat to look in the mirror again.

"Problems?" Dr. Friar asks.

"None. Everything is going exactly according to plan."

Acknowledgments

As always, turning a manuscript into a novel takes many more people than just the lonely author, writing in her garret. I will never be able to thank everyone who's helped make the mess of words that was originally *Revelations* into the book it is now without making this a novel itself, so I'm not even going to try. *smiles*

A huge thanks to my wonderful agent, Natalie Lakosil, for being in my corner when I needed her the most. And to my editor, Mel, for her awesome insight and for seeing once again the story I was trying to tell and helping me pull it out. And as always, a huge thanks to the cover artist, Eithne, and Tor's art director Seth for yet another beautiful cover.

I definitely couldn't have done this without the support of my family, specifically, my husband, for all those late nights helping me see the simple solutions to the problems I was trying to make more complicated than they needed to be, and for my children for putting up with all the time my imaginary friends took all my attention.

And to my crit partner Liz Czukas for all the brainstorming sessions and for talking me down from all the last-minute freak-outs. Thank you so, so much.

And to my crit partner Larissa Hardesty for making sure my story had heart and soul and wasn't just a mess of words.

A special shout-out and thank-you to Ryan Campbell and his daughter Cordelia for being my first "outside" readers. Your excitement and enthusiasm for my characters and writing gave me the courage to persevere through the dark until I saw the light. You both rock!

And, of course, thank you to God for giving me the talent and perseverance to make my dream a career.

And last but not least, a huge thank-you to all my fabulous readers that loved *Renegade* and loved and rooted for Evie and Gavin. I hope you enjoy the new chapter of their story. I couldn't do this without you. XOXO.

Turn the page for a sneak peek at
the next book in the Elysium Chronicles

Available now from Tor Teen

Chapter One

Sacrifices must be made for the greater good.
—Citizen's Social Code, Volume VI

Evie

My life is just about perfect.

These are the words Mother has permanently etched into my memory, as if it's nothing more than another of the stone plaques placed around the city bearing her Motherisms.

There are times I actually believe it.

But it's not true.

At least not yet.

I've been beaten down. Chased away. Used as a pawn in Mother's sadistic games. My own people see me as a monster and have turned against me. Even my memories have been stolen from me and tampered with or just plain damaged beyond repair.

However, although I'm metaphorically crippled, I've not been broken.

For the past month I've been watching. Waiting. Planning.

Today's the day it's all going to come together. The day we remove Mother from office and put her where she belongs. The Surface.

Luckily, even as messed up as my memories are, the one thing Mother never fiddled with was my knowledge of the city. It's a simple matter to walk through Sector Two from the Residential Sector. I stride right past the Guard at the tunnel to the Palace Wing. My heart skips a beat when he looks up. But like everyone else, he quickly returns his attention to the podium, and I breathe a bit easier.

One step down, and so far everything is going according to plan. That's probably a problem.

From what Father told me and my own warped memories, I know Mother will be holding court during what I'd called Request Day once upon a time. The Enforcer currently in the room will be rotated out in a few minutes, and thanks to Father's interference there will be no one to take her place.

No one but me, that is.

When Father first brought me an Enforcer's uniform, I'd been convinced I wouldn't be able to pull it off. Even with my memories back, it's been so long—I was only ten when I was relieved of duty. The next six years were devoted to being groomed to become the next leader of Elysium. The Daughter of the People. And I'd spent those years being as afraid of the Enforcers as every other Citizen.

But the minute I pulled the cloak around me, everything about me changed. My mind easily adapted. It terrifies me how my brain works now. Gauging everyone and everything and its threat level.

But now, face-to-face with the doors to the Enforcer entrance to the request room, a few doubts slip in. Will Mother see who I really am? Surely she will. Who knows me better than the woman who watched my training personally and then raised me as her own when I "failed" in my Enforcer directive? Even if my mind has changed, my appearance has not.

But that doesn't mean she pays attention to the girls she orders to kill for her. Hopefully, she won't even glance at me.

I push the uncertainty away. I have to make this work. There's no room for failure. I close my eyes and take a deep breath, then blow it out, slow and measured. When I open my eyes again, I've forced all my emotions down. I'm not playing an Enforcer now. I am one.

I push open the doors and step into the large room. A line has already formed inside and extends out the main door. The Citizens step away from me as I pass, avoiding my grazing glance. But then I turn my attention toward the reason I'm here.

I freeze when I see her.

Mother.

A dose of terror makes it impossible to move for a second, and I'm bombarded with a barrage of memories. None of them are nice. I have to clamp down on the emotions they cause.

Mother glances up, and for a second that stretches into eternity I'm sure my cover's blown. But then she turns away again, dismissing me to resume her talks with the couple in front of her.

I force myself to move, slowly making my way around the perimeter of the room, as an Enforcer would. Using the shadows as my cover until I'm standing in the corner—still in the shadows—practically behind Mother.

I survey my surroundings. My position is fairly ideal. It's exactly where an Enforcer would be to make sure Mother is safe from any potentially brave but foolhardy Citizens who think they can take Mother down. I also have a view of all the doors and can see anyone who leaves or enters. The corner is to my back, so no one can sneak up behind me, not even a real Enforcer, should Father be wrong and I'm not alone as an Enforcer in the room today. It's not that I don't have faith in Father, but Mother is far from foolish. She's never trusted anyone but herself, and I can't imagine she'd put enough confidence in Father to tell him the complete truth about anything.

Exactly as I'm thinking that, I look into the corner opposite of where I'm standing and meet the eyes of an Enforcer. A real one. My heart stops as we stare at each other. I'm not sure what to do. She isn't supposed to be here, but she is. And obviously she knows who I am.

One corner of her mouth slides up into a half-smile that chills the blood in my veins. I don't know what that expression means. Enforcers don't show emotion. It's the biggest thing drilled/brainwashed into us. But then something catches my eye and I glance down at the only skin an Enforcer can show—the half circle right under her collarbones. She's wearing a necklace. I reach for my own and worry the pendant between my thumb and first finger. Father told me we had an insider. He wouldn't tell me who it was, just that I'd recognize her when I saw her. He couldn't have meant an Enforcer, could he? If he had an Enforcer on his side, why would he need me?

I meet her eyes again, my mind shouting questions at her from where I stand. She glances at my hand and her smile grows a fraction before she nods and backs into the dark, where I can't see her or where she goes. *If* she goes anywhere.

Warning? Or greeting?

I don't start breathing again until I hear the side door open and then close. That *must* have been our insider. But . . . why? And if she wasn't, what . . . ?

I don't even know where to start with the questions. But I haven't seen anyone else that it could be, and I need my team to know I'm in place.

For the next hour, I stand behind Mother, a pistol held tightly in my hand and hidden in the special pockets of my skirt, waiting impatiently while everything sets up. Or, more accurately, while I hope everything is being set up. This next part has to go flawlessly. One tiny mistake could mean failure.

I stand straighter as the last Citizen vacates the room. It's showtime, as Asher would say.

As if on cue, Asher walks in, dragging a struggling Gavin. Even though I knew this was going to happen, my heart lurches. I want to run to him and drag him out of here, but I can't. So I bide my time, as Father follows directly behind him.

Gavin shouts curses at Asher, who keeps a tight hand on his bound arms. He tosses Gavin to the ground at Mother's feet. I can't tell from my angle what her expression is, but she does lean forward.

"What have we here?" The unmistakable sound of glee in her voice makes me want to hit her, but I stay quiet and slip closer like any good Enforcer would do.

"The Surface Dweller." Asher's voice is deep and sans accent. I have to admit I'm impressed he was able to pull it off. We've worked on it for two weeks, but he never really lost the slight twang. "We caught him skulking around the Medical Sector."

Mother steps down off her throne—I don't really know what else to call it; it's too lavish to be simply a chair. She bends down and then grasps Gavin's chin in her hand. He tries to shake loose, but she holds tight.

"I never thought I'd see you again . . . Gavin, isn't it?"

Gavin only glares at her.

Mother claps her hands twice; my cue that she needs me. I should have already moved closer. A real Enforcer would have, but I'd frozen at the sight of Gavin. I brush off the emotions as best I can and step completely out of the shadows now, my head held high as I slowly walk to her and Gavin.

Making sure my arm doesn't shake, I pull the pistol from

my skirt and aim it level at Gavin's head, as if I'm awaiting orders to shoot him. It gives me the uncomfortable reminder of the time in Sector Three when I did the same thing—when my Conditioned programming took over, and I had every intention of actually killing him. When he glances at me out of the corner of his eye and visibly swallows before turning a glare at Mother again, I wonder if he had the same thought.

"What brings you back here, Surface Dweller? Have you brought my traitorous daughter with you?" There's a slight sound of a laugh in her voice, as if this is just some great joke to her. It sends my instincts humming.

Gavin spits at her.

She jumps back and wrinkles her nose. "Well, I see she hasn't been able to teach you any manners. Pity." She turns to Asher. "How were you able to capture him? Why did you not alert an Enforcer?"

Asher averts his gaze. "He seemed quite desperate. He was muttering something about someone named Evie and infections. It took me only a moment to realize he was the Surface Dweller who kidnapped the Daughter. Forgive me, Mother, but I thought time was of the essence and I did not want him to get away again. I had hoped to find an Enforcer along the way."

Mother jerks her gaze back to Gavin. "Is this true, Surface Dweller?" He doesn't answer, but she nods. "I think it is. Why else would you risk another trip here, knowing what fate awaited you? Did you bring Evelyn with you?" He still doesn't speak and she pushes his head away in disgust. "Just the same as before. But this time, there is no one weak enough to help you escape. You've sealed your own death sentence." She looks to Asher. The way she studies him has me wishing I'd insisted he cut his hair—and the blue streak completely out—instead of just dyeing it. I'm certain she sees a shadow of the blue tint. But then she waves him away. "You may go." She turns to Father. "Escort him from the Palace Wing and then make sure he's fairly compensated for his . . . bravery."

My blood freezes at her tone. She's going to order me to kill Gavin. It's what we've been expecting. It's also the moment I've been dreading. The true test to see if the other side of myself—the Conditioned Enforcer part of me—is wiped out, or at least destroyed enough that I can refuse a direct order.

Father's convinced that this won't even be an issue for me. I've been able to resist her orders before. And the hard reset caused by leaving Elysium in the first place should have erased enough of the old programming.

She glances over at me and I fight the urge to look down. An Enforcer wouldn't. I keep my eyes focused on Gavin.

She stares at me so long, I start to worry she knows who I am. If anyone here knew who I was, it would be her. It's why I've kept my distance and made sure the hood, and its shadow, covered my face. But she's my adoptive mom, and a mother always knows her child.

This was a mistake. I should have listened to Asher and Gavin, not Father. I should have taken more time to hatch a better plan. One that wasn't so bold and risky.

But then she surprises me by saying, "Take him to the

Detainment Center. This time I'm going to get answers from him, whether or not he wants to give them to me." She waves me toward him.

Trying not to show my relief that the plan is working, I pocket the gun, then reach down and yank Gavin to his feet. He fights me as I drag him from the room. I'm slightly worried that I'm hurting him as he struggles against me. But I can't do anything less or Mother will suspect something. We're lucky she hasn't already. But, as expected and hoped for, Mother follows as I drag him across the marble floors of the Palace Wing and then over to the concrete of Sector Two and the Detainment Center.

So far everything has gone as planned, and that worries me. Nothing ever goes as planned. There's always bound to be mistakes. But this is going so smoothly I *know* something's wrong.

It doesn't take long to figure it out. My stomach flips when we step into the Detainment Center.

There's no one here. There's supposed to be members of the Underground waiting to help us subdue Mother and remove her from Elysium. There's supposed to be backup.

For a moment I think something must have changed in the plans, but Gavin stiffens when he sees the empty room. Even from my less than ideal vantage point as I drag him to the cell door, I can see his eyes darting all over the room as if he's expecting the people that are supposed to be here to jump out of some hidden crevice.

I don't know exactly what to do, so I keep walking, then

turn at the glass door of the cell, as if waiting for someone to open it. That's when I notice that Mother has stopped at the door to the Detainment Center. She's smiling at me.

Not Gavin.

Me!

My stomach doesn't just sink; it drops.

She knew the entire time and we fell into her trap like rats.

At least I can be grateful that Asher and Father got away. With only Gavin to protect from Mother, I can do this. I might have to kill her to do it, but if it's a choice between her and Gavin, I don't even have to think about it.

She starts clapping. "Well done, Evelyn. I was beginning to worry that you weren't going to pass."

"What the hell are you talking about?" Gavin demands. His entire posture has changed from the defiant one he'd had before, to angry and protective as he steps a little in front of me. But when his hand takes mine, it trembles a little and I know he's just as afraid as I am.

Mother scoffs. "You didn't think I'd let my daughter just walk out of Elysium, did you?"

"I'm *not* your daughter."

"Of course you are." She sighs. "I raised you. Loved you."

"What you did wasn't love."

"You'll see it my way soon." She purses her lips. "But now we have a problem. You brought *two* Surface Dwellers back with you. That wasn't part of the plan. We only need one."

Mother steps to the side and out of the doorway, revealing

a group of people standing behind her. Two Enforcers rush into the room. One levels a pistol at Gavin, but before I can protect him, my body erupts with a million tiny fires. My screams echo throughout the tiny room as I collapse into a mass of writhing muscles on the hard concrete floor.

I know exactly what's happening; I've felt it before. Every time Dr. Friar brainwashed me with some new memory. Or when Mother wanted to punish me for some wrongdoing— intentional or not. But it had always followed an injection of the nanite serum. I don't understand how it's happening now. My ears ring from my screams and even though my vision tunnels, I can see Gavin struggling to get to me, until an Enforcer hits him over the head with the butt of her gun and he joins me on the floor.

Then, just as my vision almost completely fades, the pain stops as suddenly as it began.

Every single muscle in my body is pulled taut. To even think about moving is a fresh agony, and I'm still whimpering from the memory of the pain, but at least the raging inferno in my body has been doused. Gavin lies on the floor next to me, a trickle of blood seeping from the cut the Enforcer gave him. He seems to be out cold. I try to push myself up to at least crawl to him, but my arms can't even handle that little amount of pressure and I collapse onto the ground again.

The sound of more tussling comes from the doorway and I glance over in horror to see Asher struggling with another Enforcer. The one who saw me in the Palace Wing.

That's why she smiled. Why she let me know she was there. She'd known the whole time. And apparently so did Mother.

Mother crouches down next to me. "I wish you wouldn't have done that, Evelyn. You were doing so well. I hoped not to have to use your nanos like that again, but it's for your own good." She pats my cheek. I have the quick thought that if I could move, I'd rip her arm from her body. She turns to the Enforcer looking down at Gavin. "Pick him up." Once the Enforcer does, Mother smiles at me. "It's too bad he hasn't learned how to control his emotions better. I believe he would have made an acceptable match for you."

I don't really pay attention to what she's saying. I'm starting to get the feeling back in my muscles, but I don't move. I don't want to waste the energy I have. I need it to get to my pistol. I have to get Asher and Gavin out of here.

She turns to Asher. "This one, though." She smiles at him. "He reminds me of Timothy." She looks down at me. "Do you remember him, dear?"

I glare at her. There are no words to describe the amount of hate I feel for her in this instant. "I remember you had him killed so you could Couple me with that *Guard*."

"Ah, yes. A mistake on my part. I should have just let you Couple with Timothy. The Guard was an unfortunate failure and had to be put down after he attacked one of my Enforcers."

"Put down? Like a dog?" Asher asks. The incredulous tone to his voice makes me want to laugh. Of course she killed him, then dismissed him like he was some sick animal she was putting out of its misery.

All of her experiments with the Guards were a failure then. How can someone be so callous? "How can you be like this? How can people be nothing more than toys to you that you just throw away when you break them?" My voice cracks just thinking about how many lives she's destroyed.

"They were broken to begin with. I'm trying to fix them." She shrugs. "You should be grateful."

The feeling is almost completely back in my legs. If I can just move them without her seeing me, I could knock out the Enforcer next to me and then grab Mother. If I held her hostage, she'd *have* to let Asher go. Other people may be disposable, but *she* isn't.

"Bitch," Asher spits at her.

She immediately stands and walks toward Asher, giving me the opportunity to make my move. I jump up and shove the Enforcer leaning over Gavin aside, wincing when she hits the wall and crumples to the floor.

Oops, I think, but wrench the gun from her hand and swing around to grab Mother. She'd make a better hostage anyway. Even though I hold the gun against her temple, Mother laughs.

"You can't do it." Her voice sounds almost like she's singing it. "You can't kill me. I'm Mother."

I merely lift an eyebrow at the other Enforcer and cock the gun. "Wanna try me?" Mother stops laughing. "Let Asher go."

The Enforcer glances at Mother, then at me. Just before she releases him, something crosses her eyes. The look she gives me next is almost an apology as she shoves Asher at me. He knocks into me so hard I fall, losing my grip on Mother. I hear the sound of a gunshot, just milliseconds before I hit the ground. My head bounces off the concrete, and Asher falls on top of me, still as death.